KILLING TIME

"Let me tell you about this guy I knew once . . ."

Soon he had a tale spinning and Molly wide awake, riveted to her seat where she was turned toward him. What a kid. What a great kid. He just couldn't have found a better traveling partner if he'd tried for a month. Too bad that he'd have to kill her in the end. . . .

NIGHT CRUISE

BILLIE SUE MOSIMAN

JOVE BOOKS, NEW YORK

NIGHT CRUISE

A Jove Book / published by arrangement with
the author

PRINTING HISTORY
Jove edition / November 1992

All rights reserved.
Copyright © 1992 by Billie Sue Mosiman.
This book may not be reproduced in whole
or in part, by mimeograph or any other means,
without permission. For information address:
The Berkley Publishing Group,
200 Madison Avenue,
New York, New York 10016.

ISBN: 0-515-10977-0

Jove Books are published by The Berkley Publishing Group,
200 Madison Avenue, New York, New York 10016.
The name "JOVE" and the "J" logo
are trademarks belonging to Jove Publications, Inc.

PRINTED IN THE UNITED STATES OF AMERICA

10 9 8 7 6 5 4 3 2 1

This cautionary tale is for my children,
Suzanne Jane and Stacey Joy,
the best daughters a mother could want.

Death tugs at my ear and says: "Live, I am coming."

—Oliver Wendell Holmes, Sr.

THE FIRST NIGHT

The highways and byways of the great United States belonged to Herod "Cruise" Lavanic. There had been others before him who claimed possession of the roads, notably one Henry Lee Lucas, the lying bastard. Bragged to the Texas cops that he'd murdered hundreds—three hundred, five hundred—the dude could never make up his puny, maladjusted mind. Now look where he was. Sitting on Death Row where the son of a bitch belonged.

Then there was Ted Bundy killing his way from one coast to the other, from Washington State to Florida, with a couple of stops in between, but Bundy was Mickey Mouse. Preened pretty for the press. Had a good face. Showed some cleverness before the cameras. Should have been a movie star. Now the only roads he owned were the roads of hell. He was fried and buried. Cruise and everyone else in the world knew the cowardly cock went down begging and lying just as vain and wild as Henry Lee.

So these days the highways and byways truly belonged to Cruise. No one knew it, of course. If they knew it, they'd stop him. Or try to. There was not yet an inkling of uneasiness about Cruise Lavanic. He knew his qualities, and they were the ones keeping him out of jail. He had been told, and he believed, that he possessed sunny features, a

1

strong, masculine face, an art for sweet talk, and an ability to think on his feet. With his boy-next-door mannerisms and his lack of an arrest record, he was unknown, unsuspected. Except to his victims. They knew him. In their last moments on earth, they knew him better than anyone.

This night, he searched for a hostage. A witness, really. Traveling wasn't any fun without a witness along to see him work. He cruised in a 1979 silver-blue Chrysler Newport, 318 engine with a four barrel. Big square car, looked like an old undercover cop car. Cruise kept a magnetized CB antenna on the trunk to make the car look even more official. He'd taken out the front bench seat and put in a set of blue bucket seats. Never liked the witness to get too near him when he was driving. Between the bucket seats he had installed a small blue Igloo cooler for bottled Cokes. Pepsi was too sweet. Coke, even the rip-off Classic brew the Coca-Cola Company claimed was made from the original recipe though it didn't taste that way to Cruise, had a carbonated kick his stomach lived for.

Cruise crisscrossed the country and lived hand-to-mouth. Sometimes, when he killed, he took money from the victim, but it was never a big take. He didn't kill those too high up the social ladder, people with too much class or influence. Cops would chase him then, put out APBs, write up a profile, start up a task force. Staying free entailed all kinds of precautions and rule number one, as Henry Lee might point out, was to kill the little people nobody'd miss.

He had left New York City the week before, driven down the Eastern Seaboard into the Carolinas, and caught Interstate 10 in Florida to head west. He did all his driving at night, stayed in motels, truck stops, or his car during the day. If Cruise possessed an outstanding eccentricity, it was his love of the dark hours. He had not slept at night since he was a boy. He had not killed during the day for seven years.

In his wallet he carried one hundred ten dollars. Next to him sat the Igloo cooler of Coke. No one was looking for him. He should have been more content, but he was lonesome. Shit, he was singing songs to himself to cheer up, he was so lonesome. "Camptown Races." Do dah. "Little Deuce Coupe." You don't know what I've got.

It was sickening. He was getting on his own nerves.

Outside of Mobile, Alabama, he drove five miles below the speed limit, not slow enough to attract attention, not fast enough to miss something important. Just cruising, eyes watching the cars that passed him, watching the roadside, the pine forests blue-black in the night, the long straight stretch of white pavement rolling ahead. Mind on idle.

Billboards loomed and flashed past. BELLINGRATH GARDENS. MICKEY'S BARBECUE. STUCKEY'S. GENE RAY'S TRUCK STOP.

Cruise took the off ramp, slowed at the stop sign, and turned toward the truck stop where the tall utility poles held up the huge orange GENE RAY'S sign. Eighteen-wheelers rolled slowly around the lot or sat like dull dinosaurs in the diesel slots. Several trucks were parked behind the low brown building. The moon had not risen from behind a pine thicket. Night shadows and the orange sign overhead conspired to turn the red clay ringing the paved area into splotches the color of dried blood. The joint smelled of fuel and grease and exhaust. Just how Cruise liked his fresh air.

With the Newport rolling quietly forward, he checked his gas gauge, remembered he'd filled up in Spanish Fort on the other side of Mobile. Well, gas needs didn't dictate his stops and never had. He was cruising. He didn't have to have a reason for stopping. He could always order a Coke in the truck stop cafe and make them put in plenty of ice. Slurp it through a straw. Get his tongue carbonated all to hell and back.

He angled the Newport into a parking slot facing away from the building. The spots on each side were empty. This didn't look like a place where too many car travelers spent any time. It was strictly Cowboy Trucker City.

As he smoothly maneuvered the bulk of his six-foot-four, two-hundred-seventy-pound frame from the bucket seat, Cruise took his time closing the driver's door. He noticed a couple of Lot Lizards. One working the back area where the truckers took their rigs to rest awhile before hitting the road again. One standing near the front entrance to the cafe.

The one in back didn't fit in. She was a kid, fourteen, fifteen. Too young for truckers. Inexperienced too if he was to judge by the way she slumped her skinny shoulders as if against a gale tearing at her back. Kid looked ashamed. Scared, maybe. Ought to be home with Mommy and Daddy watching *Wheel of Fortune* and munching Fritos.

Cruise kept her in sight as he walked to the cafe door. If she was still there when he came out, she'd make a good witness. Most times he took young boys. Less trouble in the long run, but he had a need for girls, too, on occasion. Runaways of either gender were tender meat, easy to snag, and effortless to dispose of when the journey ended.

Besides. This little no-account redhead looked lost. She needed a guide to help her get by in the cold, cruel, friendless world.

She needed to cruise.

Nothing in all the world belonged to Molly Killany. Or so she thought at the uninformed age of sixteen. Oh, at home with her father she had her own bedroom, but it wasn't really *hers*. She realized by the time she was around nine years old that she was a boarder in the house and nothing she touched belonged to her. Not the stuffed animals or the Panasonic stereo she had received for a Christmas present when she was fifteen, or even the clothes hanging in the closet. Kids were chattel possessed by parents. That was a new word she'd learned in vocabulary lessons. Chattel. In the archaic form it meant "slave." The life of a minor was not his own, so he was a slave to the whims of a parent.

Her father, a retired colonel from the U.S. Marines, often told his only daughter that lives weren't always shaped by self-will, but by circumstance. He used this argument when speaking of her mother's death when Molly was born. "We never planned that you'd grow up motherless, Molly. I never thought I'd raise you alone, that I'd never be able to . . . to love another woman."

When Molly ran away from home it had more than a little to do with feeling owned and possessionless. It also had to do with the high school she attended where everyone was a snob. They thought they owned the world and everything in it. They didn't have a clue about the reality of their situation—how they were owned lock, stock, and Reeboks.

Most of all, it had to do with Mark Killany, her father. Once he retired, after spending twenty years with the Marines, he made too much effort to control her destiny. She became his focus, his darling. His chattel. Not that he ever beat or mistreated her. It could be that he cared too much and that was the real problem. All he did was *lecture* her constantly. Don't do this, don't do that, watch out for the wrong crowd, don't stay out past eleven, don't even *think* about sex. Everything was taboo. Everything potentially threatening. Molly felt so suffocated she nearly stopped eating. Look at her. Skinny as a fence post. Even her breasts, which had been her crowning glory in the physical beauty department (although most people cited her glowing red shoulder-length hair), had squeezed themselves down to little nubs on her washboard-ribbed chest. She'd taken to wearing padded bras to give her any shape at all.

Even now as she walked around in the orange glow of the truck stop, she hunched her shoulders so as not to bring attention to The Nubs, as she thought of them.

Her intention at the truck stop would have given her father a fit. In fact, the idea was giving her a fit too. Though she had made up her mind that no one owned her, that she owned herself and it was herself that she would sell, if she had to, she was finding it impossible not to think about. How was she going to do it? How could she? The thought not only depressed her, but repulsed her more than she had thought it would. The *only* way she was going to face it was to turn her mind off, but so far she'd had no luck. Her head kept rattling thoughts around, some of them silent screams, some of them whispered worries. *You can't have sex with some guy, just any guy!* (If you do, you're garbage, you're scum, you're going to regret it.) *It's going to be awful!* (He will touch you and play with you and you will probably get sick all over him.)

If she'd had jewelry to hock or if someone would have given her an honest job at her age, she wouldn't do it, but she didn't and they hadn't and she was on her own with nothing to her name, not a slim dime, nothing for barter but her bony, nubby, redheaded self. Yet even these realities wouldn't quite kick in and save her from the war going on in her mind. She kept trying to think of another way. She just couldn't find one.

It was amazing that she'd made it all the way from Florida to Alabama hitchhiking without already having to trade on her flesh.

Just outside of Jacksonville, she'd asked if they needed help in the restaurant where her ride stopped for a meal.

"To do what?" The waitress was sincerely befuddled.

"Uh, you know, a job."

"Like being a waitress or something?" More befuddlement.

Molly began to wonder if the woman's brain had taken a hike.

"Sure, like a waitress," Molly said. "Like a dishwasher, like a salad maker, like anything. I need work."

"You need work?" the waitress repeated.

My God Almighty. This woman needed major head surgery. She just couldn't seem to get it together. "Yes," Molly explained clearly and slowly. "I'd like to know if your boss is hiring, please." She added the last word with an emphasis the waitress couldn't miss.

The woman seemed to snap out of it. "Listen, you don't stand a chance. How old are you, kid? Thirteen? You can't work when you're just thirteen. Why, it's against the law!"

Molly stood as tall as she could, never mind the front of her poking out so miserably small. "I'm sixteen years old," she said. "I am not a little kid."

The woman shook her head either in amazement or disbelief, Molly didn't know which. "You'd have to have your parents sign a permission form. And besides, we don't need anybody here. Sorry."

But she hadn't been sorry at all, that was the bad part. She thought Molly was a thirteen-year-old, and she hadn't believed a word Molly said.

Still undefeated, Molly tried getting work again in Pensacola at a service station off the freeway. "Do you need a cashier? I saw your sign." She indicated the HELP WANTED sign in the window.

The paunchy middle-aged man who ran the place looked over his black-framed glasses at her and smiled slowly. "You?"

Damn. No, she felt like saying, *I'm standing here alone asking if you'll hire my invisible rabbit Harvey.* "Yes me. I need a job. And I'm older than I look." She thought she'd better get that in quickly as possible.

"And how old would that be?"

Another skeptic. "Sixteen. I'll be seventeen soon."

He was already shaking his head. "Nope. Can't use you. Need a big strapping boy to help run the station." Then he turned his back and waddled away to sell a quart of oil.

Molly knew then getting work was beyond possibility. They wouldn't believe she was sixteen, or else they'd want parental permission. Either way the job market was a closed world.

So it had come down to sex. Selling it. As bad as it worried her—her stomach wasn't in such good shape just thinking about it—as bad as she didn't want to, she simply couldn't survive any other way. She'd lost her virginity to an awkward, unsmiling boy back in the summer of her fourteenth year on a deserted beach in Dania, Florida. *Don't even think about sex.* Her father's words. How could she not think about it? Every girl she knew had rid herself of virginity just as quickly as she could. Though her father didn't know it, an intact hymen had lost its importance a long time ago. Maybe before she was born. As for selling sex, though, that was something else again. The guys could be old, hairy, heavy, filthy. They were *strangers*. She didn't know how she'd endure the grunting, sweating ten or fifteen minutes to get enough money to move on down the line. She just knew she had to.

She had never tried scoring at truck stops, never tried scoring *anywhere* yet. Before she was even out of the pickup that dropped her at Gene Ray's, a sloe-eyed girl at the corner of the building gave her a long heated look. Right off Molly knew she was hooking. Everyone, Molly guessed, knew that. The girl wore shorts short enough to bare her ass when she stooped over, and a fluorescent green halter top with her breasts swelling out the top and sides like the white coconut goo found in a Mound's bar.

It took some courage for Molly to sidle over and ask advice. She dropped down into what she thought of as her toughest, most adult-sounding voice. "Is there enough action for me to work here with you awhile?"

The girl shifted her weight onto the other leg as if she'd been standing a long time. She smelled like cigarette smoke, damp sex, and spearmint. Molly saw her thoughtfully chewing gum, more like a cow chews a cud, intermittently, and with relish.

"You wanna be a Lot Lizard?"

Molly thought about that. She didn't really, no, that's not what she'd aspire to given any choices, but she hadn't a choice so she supposed that yes, for now, she wanted to be a Lot Lizard. Sounded prehistoric and slimy, but what could you do.

"If that's what it's called, yeah."

"These truckers, honey, they're horny as wild boars. You look a little outta shape to stand the rigor."

What she meant, Molly knew, was that she looked either too young or too skinny. That was plain insulting and, by God, she was getting steamed at how everyone insulted her. Even if she didn't want to hook, even if it scared the living daylights out of her, she still hated being treated like some innocent numbnut. "I'm okay. I can handle it." She squared her shoulders and stared defiantly into the other girl's eyes.

The girl shrugged and chewed her gum. She glanced idly around the parking area and over to the side where the massive trucks pulled up for fueling. "It's your choice, kid. There's plenty of men to service tonight and JoJean ain't showed up yet. You got rubbers?"

Molly nodded, then blushed. Did this dimwit think she'd be selling herself *raw*? She didn't want AIDS, for chrissakes, end up dying before she could get out of her teens. Not to mention the garden variety venereal diseases some people walked around with. She wasn't totally without a brain. In her carryall bag she had a box of lubricated Trojans. She didn't know how she was going to get the guys to use them, but if they didn't, she meant to hightail it, leave them gawking.

The girl had sneaked a look from the corner of her mascara-laden eyes at how Molly nodded to answer the question. "Okay, go on. No skin off'n my ass. Go around back and just bang on the door of a cab till one of 'em opens. I always take the Peterbilts and the Western Stars so stay away from those, but anything else, you go for it big as you can go."

Again Molly nodded, accepting the rules, and left the girl's side. She skirted red muddy puddles behind the building to reach the dozing, idling trucks. She gathered her courage and climbed to the driver's door of the first truck she came to, a moving van company truck, and balling her knuckly fist, she started in. After sixty seconds of steady banging she was about to hop down to try another cab when a face showed in the closed window. He was old. Maybe sixty. Bald. Probably didn't know what an erection was anymore, Molly thought with some despair. She couldn't do this. She'd never be able to give herself to some old grubby man. She bit her lower lip, leaned out of the way so he could open the door.

"Have you been baptized?" he asked.

Molly wondered briefly if he was using another language or if he meant something to do with being clean. The longer she took to answer and the longer she scrutinized his face for clues, the more it came to her that he meant baptized in the regular religious sense. She'd had the awful luck of knocking on the door of a Bible Thumper. Never mind that she was scared to death, that she was about to go against everything she had been brought up to value, she had to face the guilt this stranger meant to heap upon her head.

"I'm going," she said, beginning to clamber down. She didn't need this. Couldn't take it.

"Child, you're living a life of sin. Christ died on the cross for people like you. Won't you be washed in the blood of the lamb?"

"I'm gone," she said, hitting dirt and stalking away. Behind her she heard him above the roar of a dozen rumbling engines.

"Your soul is in high peril! Go immediately to a church and ask them to pray for you!"

Sheez. Mama, if she'd had a mama, would have told her there'd be days like this. The warped hayseed who picked her up in Mobile and dumped her at Gene Ray's had groped her for twenty miles before he got to the point and asked if she'd piss on his back if he could find a place to pull over. She had told him in no unequivocal terms that she wasn't into kinky, and no, she would not piss on his fool back, but she'd knock out his fool teeth if he didn't get her to the next exit before she puked. Now a Bible Thumper laying down God's law to a potential sinner. It was too much.

Sheez.

Molly was so incensed, she forgot all about having nubs for breasts and was stomping across the lot looking for a likely cab to bang on, her shoulders back, hands fisted at her sides. Her small carrying bag of clothes and toiletries swung out behind her as she walked, bumping her hip as she went. A movement at the far corner of the building slowed her walk. She glanced that direction and saw a big guy aimed her way. He threw a monstrous shadow that leapt before him as he moved forward. He was way over six feet and sported massive shoulders, narrow hips, long legs. He wore neat gray tweedy slacks and a pale lemon sport shirt open at the throat, but God, the guy's hair was longer than hers. And *silkier*. But then any hair was silkier than her naturally curly, unruly mop. *His* hair was brown streaked with silver, straight and shiny as a horse's mane. A gray beard, not too bushy, but long enough to touch his chest, covered the lower half of his face. He looked like the Son of the Morning, the fallen angel she had seen portrayed in a picture in a Bible back home. He also looked a little like the guy on the TV show who lived in the wilderness with a bear for a friend. Molly wondered if he was Gene Ray, and if she was about to find her ass in a sling. Maybe in a holding cell in the Mobile jail. That was about what she deserved at this point. Jail and a one-way ticket home.

She stopped in her tracks and hung one arm on her clothes bag. She waited to see what he wanted. She'd try to talk him out of running her in, if that was the problem. She could get a ride out of the truck stop in a hot second if she had to.

He was near enough now for her to tell he was smiling in all that hair covering his face. He couldn't be near as old as his graying hair and beard announced. Maybe it was premature. He was a good-looking guy for someone more than twenty years her senior.

He raised a hand in greeting and she relaxed a little. Maybe he was just a regular guy. Not a guy on the make, but a nice guy. If he turned out to be a customer, her *first* customer, she wasn't sure how she'd handle it. They called them "johns," didn't they? He was too big and too hairy, but he looked clean—woodsy, in some way—and his eyes crinkled as he smiled. She liked that. He looked just like the TV character he reminded her of, what was his name? Oh, yeah, Grizzly Adams! That was wild. Maybe he was the actor, and wouldn't *that* be cool beans?

"What can I do you?" she asked when he was within speaking distance. This shorthand language worked on the road. Men, especially, hated to waste words. There was no extra time when traveling to play the sophisticate and talk about the weather. She had decided early on that she must talk tough no matter how her insides quaked. It was protective coloration; she blended into the background when she talked like older, more experienced women. She wasn't as vulnerable.

He walked right up to her, so close that she felt impelled to move back a step from him. He wasn't the actor, but he looked just as fine. She saw his eyes were beautiful green—almost a mint color. Despite all the hair, he was downright gorgeous, enough to make some girls back in Dania drool like the dweebs they were. She, of course, wouldn't let on she thought he was so fine. After all, he was real old. Old as her father. Ancient.

"Hi there. I saw you on your way back here when I drove in a few minutes ago. Do you need a lift somewhere? I'm heading west."

Sounded nice enough. Like a regular guy. Those green eyes crinkling and glittering like he knew all her secrets and they didn't bother him a bit.

Molly looked around at all the trucks, sniffed the hot, diesely air, and decided in a hasty instant that Lot Lizardry wasn't her specialty. Who wanted to make it in the sleeper of an eighteen-wheeler anyway? Her first time hooking had to be done in a better place than this. It must be cramped in one of those cabs. And smelly. And . . . scary.

She looked carefully at the man, sizing up the possibilities. Virile. Very goddamn big. Maybe she could talk him into something other than straight sex where he'd crush her to death. He had to weigh over two hundred. Maybe he wouldn't want sex at all. But then there was no use living a fantasy, lying to herself. He'd want it. When it came time, she'd have to find a way to steel herself to doing it. There was no other way.

"Sure," she said finally. "I could use a ride on down the road. Seems they're having a camp meeting here." She hooked her thumb back at the Bible Thumper who hadn't given up on her. He was hanging half out of his cab blabbering inanely about Sin and Retribution.

The big fellow spared one glance at the hysterical driver and dismissed him with a shake of his head. "There are too many nuts on the road. You have to be careful."

"You can say that again." Molly hitched the bag higher on her shoulder and started walking beside the big man. "What do you want me to call you? I'm Molly."

"You can call me Cruise, Molly. Because that's what I do. I cruise." And then he laughed.

Molly looked up at him, but couldn't see his face in the new shadows. Several hairs on the nape of her neck stood straight up on end just for a second. She shivered. Too late now. She was taking a ride from the Long Hair and that's all there was to it. She had never welshed on a deal or backed out on a decision once it was made. At least not since she left home.

"Okay, Cruise," she murmured. "Let's eat some miles."

She waited for him to unlock the passenger side of an old blue Chrysler, looked over at the blank plate-glass windows of the cafe, blinked at the Lot Lizard in the halter top, and slid into the bucket seat while Cruise held the door for her.

"Buckle up," he said when he got into the car. He sounded cheerful, happy to have her along.

He started the engine, pulled on the headlights, buckled himself into the seat, shifted into reverse, then drove slowly from the puddle-covered drive onto the entrance road to the freeway.

"So where in the West are you headed?" Molly wanted to be friendly, wanted to forget the cakewalk her hair made at the back of her neck earlier when he laughed.

Cruise gave her a disarming smile. She could see the fleshy part of his lower lip where it hid in the beard. The rosy soft lip in the gray brush made her think of a newborn pup lost in a tangle of barbed wire. It was a lip someone could nibble. She wished he was closer to her age. She could go for him, if he was. But no matter how handsome, he was still too old.

She smiled back, at ease. She had good teeth and liked to smile when she had reason.

"Far as the land will take me," he said. "Right to the shores of the blue Pacific Ocean."

"Job waiting for you out there?"

He eased the Chrysler into traffic on I-10 and held his speed at fifty-five. Most cars overtook him, their headlights swinging out to the left of the car and spearing past into the darkness. "Maybe," he said. "We'll see."

She decided not to press him for details. It was none of her business. "I'm sixteen," she said. "Be seventeen in three months. I'm a runaway and . . . sometimes . . . uh . . . I'm a prostitute. It's, you know, a living."

She knew he suspected as much, but she liked to get it all out in the open from the get-go. She wasn't technically a prostitute yet, but that's what she would have to be in order to survive. She meant to survive no matter what.

"I figured." He spoke with some admiration for her upfront confession. She thought he'd like that. Most of them did.

"I don't need to be saved, redeemed, talked to, lectured at, advised, or otherwise manipulated. I do what I do strictly to take care of myself and I'm not ashamed of it. I'm not looking for a Sugar Daddy or a pimp. I'm my own person." She said all this in one long breath, then sucked in air and turned her face to the window to keep the blush that rose in her cheeks from his view.

"I figured that too."

"Good. Now we're all straight," she said to the night outside the window.

"Want a Coke?" He lifted the lid of the Igloo cooler between the seats and gestured she take one. She screwed off the lid on a sixteen-ouncer and drank thirstily. Coke for supper was her diet when she didn't have Waffle House money. She preferred it over Pepsi. It put hair on her tongue and fire in her belly. He would probably buy her food somewhere later on. Before the night was over he'd no doubt expect repayment, and that was life, this adult life she'd chosen, tit for tat. She'd find a way to turn off her mind while she did it. She had a lot of things to get used to. Sex with strangers was one of them. She couldn't fault herself since she'd tried to find decent work before turning to it. It was as hard on the road as she thought it might be. She'd just have to be tough enough.

She was scheming how to explain to him in some politic fashion that frontal, missionary-position sex was going to be a problem for them when they passed a green road sign for the Pascagoula, Mississippi, exit. Molly never noticed the moment they left the state of Alabama in the wings. She'd crossed two state lines now and wasn't going to be bothered about it. That was the least of her worries. It was money and getting by that she had to do all her worrying about.

"You don't look sixteen," he said, never taking his eyes from the road.

Molly sighed. It was a damn shame she couldn't do something about that. She hunched her shoulders in the seat to shield her breasts. "I need to gain weight," she admitted. She weighed a hundred pounds on her good days. "How old do I look?"

"Thirteen. Fourteen."

Molly took a sip of Coke and nursed her silence. She wished to God she had her boobs back. It was bad enough being young. It was worse to look even younger. What kind of hooker was she going to make if she looked like a kid?

"You're cute. Beautiful hair."

She smiled a little, her lips curving around the bottle top. She lowered the Coke to her lap. "That's what people say. Personally I don't like red hair. I might bleach it."

"That would be a shame. It certainly makes you stand out from a crowd."

"Irish ancestry kicking in. My dad's hair . . ." She bit her tongue. She hadn't meant to bring up her father. She didn't want to talk about him. Now she really sounded like a homesick, silly-ass little kid. *Damn.*

"Red too?" he asked.

"Yeah. Redder. Mine's got a little blond in it to tone it down. His, though, is fiery red."

Cruise whistled low in appreciation.

"Are you one of those old hippies?" Molly wanted to make him feel as uncomfortable as she had just felt when she slipped up and mentioned her father. Tit for tat.

Cruise laughed and this time she didn't get any shivery premonitory hair tricks at the back of her neck. It was a pleased, cheerful kind of laugh.

"I never was a hippie," he said. "Never cared for them."

"You wear your hair like a hippie. Some of the kids do that, stuff with the headbands and peace signs on their jackets and hair to their butts, things like that. I don't know *what* they think they're doing, reliving the sixties or what. I think it's real dumb."

"I just don't like barbers. It has nothing to do with any group."

Molly waited for further illumination but when he didn't continue, she shrugged her bony shoulders. "Doesn't matter to me. Your hair, I mean. Why you wear it like that. I don't really care. In fact, it makes you look a little bit Christ-like. Like the *pictures* of Christ, you know." Actually she meant he looked like the Son of the Morning angel—Great Lucifer himself—but she didn't know how to explain that without sounding rude so she settled for Christ.

He gave her a winning smile and she settled into the bucket seat with the bottle of Coke. He was an all-right guy. Very sweet. Not pushy. Not grabby. A real gentleman and regular guy.

She was cruising with Cruise, going where she had never been before, and that's what mattered.

That's all that mattered.

Cruise worked at being open, appealing, friendly. It was a knack he had. People warmed to him, always had, and it was an advantage. Little Molly would find out soon enough about him. About the dying. If he played it right, she'd be so caught up in him before he made his next kill, she'd find a way to accept it. Some of them did. It was strange how the kids could adjust to nearly any way of life. Already Molly called herself a prostitute to earn her way. He knew that she was almost certainly from a good middle-class home where morals had been instilled in her. Yet she'd found a way to dump them as soon as she got on her own. Her manner of speech and vocabulary told him she wasn't raised to the life.

She was insecure about her looks and that was why she hunched her shoulders, but she liked compliments. She was no one's dummy. He hoped she wasn't *too* smart or he'd have to get rid of her in a roadside ditch or leave her remains in a restaurant dumpster. Be a fucking shame.

Sum total, he thought he'd made the perfect choice for companion. His witness. Little Irish Molly. He thought he could train her. There was time to find out.

He must gain her confidence, learn more about that father she mentioned. Kid might stay in touch with home and that could bollix up plans. She needed to be cut free before he could trust her to any extent. She started thinking about what her father would want her to do or be, she might not bend to his will on the trip west. That would never do.

Pretending to stretch, Cruise leaned back in his seat and reached his left arm over and behind his head. He yawned and grunted, meanwhile lightly touching, checking the back of his head with the pads of his fingers. Underneath the long hair, he kept a small area shaved. He had glued a Velcro patch there and the matching patch to the tiny, four-and-one-half-inch, hooked-end knife he carried. It was too dangerous to drive across country with a weapon the cops might find on casual inspection during a traffic violation. (Bundy had been found with handcuffs in his trunk. *Handcuffs.* That little oversight put him behind bars in Colorado, the stupid bastard.)

Cruise had grown his hair long and kept the knife concealed there for more than three years now. It was stainless steel and razor-sharp. The handle was slightly curved so that it fit in a good grip around his index finger when he used it. On the side of the handle was a silver skull and crossbones.

The hook on the business end of the blade caught and ripped flesh. He had found the odd little lethal knife in a pawnshop in Chicago. The idea of strapping it to his head and beneath his hair was a stroke of pure genius. His victims never expected a man to pull Death from his hair and wield it with such lightning-quick movement. Cruise could rip open a man's throat with his special little knife in three seconds flat. In the first second they saw it. The eyes reflected deep, paralyzing fear. In the second instant they felt the cool metal against their warm throats. In the third second Cruise had them; they belonged to him.

Feeling the knife securely in place, he lowered his arm and asked the girl if she wanted something to eat when they reached Hammond, Louisiana.

"Sure. Wake me when we get there, okay?"

He assured her that he would.

He tried to keep his mind occupied by listing the rivers they crossed. Outside of Mobile he began the river name game. He crossed Singing River. Beautiful name for a river. The next was the Biloxi. Then Wolf. The names rolled through his thoughts until he lost their order. There was the Jourdan, Pearl, Amite, Mississippi River, Whiskey Bay, Atchafalaya, Lake Pelba, Lake Bigbeaux.

His thoughts gradually wandered over to his passenger. Little Molly. Then for the next hundred miles while oncoming lights streamed past on the freeway, and she slept slumped against the car window, he stole lustful glances at her slight body. All the while he admonished himself to take it easy, go slow, work the girl around until she loved him.

Until she worshiped him as a god.

Mark Killany knew his daughter was moving away from him on Interstate 10 West.

After frantic questioning of her friends, he discovered she was headed to California. Since their home was in Dania, Florida, the most direct route to the opposite coast was by I-10. She had but a few hours start on him. He had left to do some grocery shopping and on his return found her note.

I'm sorry, Daddy, but I have to leave. I can't be perfect the way you want me to. We're driving one another crazy. I'm not going to the counselors anymore. Don't come after me because you won't find me.

Molly

It took him some time to withdraw money from the bank, pack a few clothes, question her friends and acquaintances. As far as he could tell from investigating her room, she had taken few clothes and no personal articles. She didn't have money except for the ten-dollar allowance he had given her the day before so she had to be traveling as a hitchhiker.

God. Molly on the roads hitching. She could get raped or killed before she left the state. Her chance of making it all the way to California by hitching rides was impossible. That was just one of the illusions she was working under. She was a kid. Just a shavetail kid. She didn't know what she was doing. Even now she might be on the roadside in the rain or stranded at some gas station or off ramp.

He hurried as fast as he could to finish preparations, then he started out. He didn't care that the statistics said thousands of kids run away from home every year and just disappear, never to be heard from again. He didn't care, even, that he was probably the responsible party in this debacle. All he cared about was his little girl. He'd get her back safely or spend the rest of his life trying. She was all he had. If he had botched her raising, he'd fix it.

A nagging voice said, *You should have fixed it before you lost her.* He shut off the voice. First he must find her and bring her home. No matter what effort or how long it took. Then he'd repair whatever had caused her to run away.

He thought she might have taken Interstate 95 north to the top of the state since it went right through Dania. That's the route he followed. At every station where he bought gas or stopped to grab food to go, he asked if anyone had seen her, and he showed the latest picture he had, her junior-year school photo. With that red hair and slate-gray eyes, she was memorable. At least he had one thing in his favor. Yet no one had seen her so he doggedly drove north, worrying, scrubbing down his crew-cut red hair, watching the roadside and on ramps for hitchhikers.

"Molly, Molly, Molly . . ." He said her name aloud repetitively as he drove.

How could his daughter desert him? He must have appeared an ogre to her, a strict disciplinarian who left her no way out but to run. There had been arguments, but he never suspected she was so unhappy she'd leave him.

Maybe he should have remarried, found a woman to help love and raise her. Maybe he should have been more permissive, made fewer restraints on her freedom. Maybe he hadn't listened during the times he should. Maybe the counselor he paid exorbitant fees was right, though he had failed to admit it; he was as much at fault for the conflicts with his teenage daughter as she was. Maybe he should have put her into a private girls' school where she would have been carefully watched.

To hell with it. He had to stop this train of thought. Recriminations wouldn't get Molly back. It produced zero profit. He'd never know what to do right for her until he could find and bring her home. *Then* he could go over the reasons she felt she must escape her home. Let's face it.

Escape *him*. Until then, he had to keep his mind on the road and watch the entrance ramps.

It was not until he hit I-10 west out of Jacksonville that he found someone who had seen her. He had driven like a maniac, flat out, foot to the pedal, the radar detector signaling with high beeps when a patrol car lurked nearby. He drove all day and was so tired his back ached, his head throbbed.

At a Conoco station where he filled up, he took the picture around to the employees, asking each one the same question. "Have you seen this girl?"

A boy not yet out of his teens recognized Molly. "Yeah, she was here," he said, grinning to show a god-awful over-bite.

"Well?"

"Well, what? I saw her. What about it?"

Mark drew on his bank account of patience. If need be, he'd also draw out his wallet and offer a bribe. When his money ran out, he had a bank card good for withdrawals all over the country. He'd get more. He had savings, credit cards, gas cards, his retirement income from the Marines going into direct deposit. Money wasn't the problem.

Mark said, his voice only slightly impatient, "She's my daughter and she's run away from home. Who was she with? What color and kind of car did she leave in?"

The boy hiked the bill of his Conoco cap back on his head and stared out at the pumps. They stood in the service bay where a mechanic was changing a flat tire. The noise from the hydraulic machines clanged in Mark's ears. He waited. Patience running out by the millisecond. He hated slow thinkers. Hated them when he trained them in boot camp. Hated them in the Congress. Hated them at checkout counters in grocery stores. Lost his patience and his temper a dozen times a day with them in one way or the other. His

C.O. once told him he was a Class A personality type, ripe for a heart attack, quick to anger, volatile when frustrated by the most mundane everyday obstacles. He kicked things out of his way rather than bend over, pick them up, and move them. Then he'd be angry at the dumbfuck who left the mess in his way in the first place.

"Uh . . ." The boy was still thinking if his wrinkled brow meant anything. "She . . . uh . . . was riding with a young couple . . ."

"All right."

"Yuppies in a gray BMW. Nice car. New."

"Good." Mark reached for his wallet, opened it slowly. The boy's eyes flicked over, saw the money, peered out again at the pumps pretending indifference.

"Which way did the BMW head?" Mark had the twenty out hovering in midair.

"Back on the on ramp." His hand snaked out and slipped the twenty into his pocket. His eyes were still front forward.

"West?"

"Yeah."

"Remember anything else? Did my daughter look all right? What was she wearing?"

"She looked fine." He shrugged, reached up, pulled the bill of the cap back down over his eyes. He acted like a kid who didn't know what to say to a girl's father.

The boy licked his lips before continuing. "Her hair was tied back with a white ribbon, I remember that. Her red hair, that's why I remember her. She had on stone-washed jeans and a white blouse. The couple filled up and left. That's it."

"When did you see them?"

"About four hours ago. I'd just come on shift."

Mark thanked him and walked to his car. He would have paid two hundred, two thousand to find out he was on the right track.

Four hours ahead of him. His hope soared.

His hope died during the long desperate night when stopping along the way, he found no one else who had seen Molly. He drove straight through, stopping at a rest area to sleep little more than two hours before driving again. He lost time getting off the freeway and showing Molly's picture at little cafes and service stations between Jacksonville and Tallahassee. No one had seen her. What did he expect, he wondered, a trail of bread crumbs? It was going to be nearly impossible to find her, though that impossibility wasn't something he could think about for too long. He had to feed his hope.

At noon his stomach cramped and he had to stop again to buy a roll of Tums. His eyes burned from straining to see a gray BMW in every small compact car he drove past. His back continued to ache and he was growing hungry.

"Molly, Molly, Molly . . ."

It was the second night on the road when he left Mobile. When he saw the cluster of signs, one of which was for Gene Ray's Truck Stop, he decided to stop again, show the picture, and get something to eat.

Before entering the cafe, he pulled Molly's picture from his khaki shirt pocket to show it to a girl wearing shorts and a green halter top. She stood around like she was waiting to be picked up and Mark took her for a hooker. The signal code was the same in Hong Kong, the Philippines, or Mobile, Alabama. A look in the eyes. A nod of the head, sway of the hip. A smile, tempting, and sometimes expensive.

"I'm looking for my daughter," he began. As soon as the girl had the snapshot in her hand, he saw how her expression changed. She recognized Molly. "You've seen her." He was thrilled and completely surprised to have picked up the trail again. "Look, let me give you a twenty spot. I need help and I don't mind paying for it."

The girl looked sly as she said, "I get more than twenty bucks, don't you worry about it."

"I'm not trying to buy that," he said. "I just want to know about my daughter. She's only sixteen and . . ."

"She's old enough."

Now his patience played out. What right did she have telling him anything about his own child? Old enough for what? Rolling around in the sack with truckers at fifty a pop? Jesus Christ. He wished he could throttle someone.

"I'll take forty since you're not interested in fun and games." The girl reached over to where he had his wallet spread to extract two twenties with deft fingers. She folded and put them into a black patent leather purse hanging from a gold chain off her shoulder. She snapped the purse shut, then shifted her weight to the other foot.

"Now tell me," he said. "When was she here?"

"Let's see, it's about ten o'clock? She was here around six-thirty, seven."

His heart stepped up in rhythm. "What did she leave in?"

"Guy picked her up."

"And . . . ?"

"He was driving a blue Chrysler, light blue. Old."

"How old?"

"How the shit do I know, man? Just old. Square. Boxy. It looked like . . ."

"What?"

"An old cop car. You know. Without the lights on top and all. The kind they used in the seventies, you know?"

"Undercover cop car, you mean?"

"Yeah. But old, like they used to have. Nowadays they got these fast Mustangs and shit."

"Good. Now did you talk to her, did she say anything about where she was going?"

"Yes and no."

Mark wanted to paw the ground like a bull. Why were people so deliberately obtuse? Once he paid them, they should open like clams, but no, they had to give him grief. "Yes, you did talk to her, and no, she didn't say where she was going. Do I have that correct?"

"Yes."

"What did she say then?"

"She was going to try her luck out back."

Mark knew exactly what that meant. His baby. Prostituting. It squeezed his heart so hard he thought he would die right there. He would crumple to his knees and sink through the ground and lie in the earth until the worms came to do their just work.

"But I don't think she had any luck," the girl said when she saw him pale.

Mark felt himself rise again, from earth to sky. "Why—why do you say that?"

"She left real quick after she went back there."

Mark expelled his breath. "What did the guy look like?"

"Big guy, real tall."

"Taller than me?" Mark stood an inch over six feet.

The girl glanced at him, then nodded. "Yeah. Bigger too. Heavier, you know? But not fat. Shoulders like a wrestler."

"Did you see his face? What did he look like?"

"He had long hair, straight, past his shoulders. Brown with some gray in it. And a beard. He was pretty fine, looked kinda like that guy played on TV, in that wilderness show where he had a bear for a friend and he lived in a cabin in the woods . . . ?"

"I never watch television. Was he a biker?" He was thinking of the long hair and beard. After all this wasn't the sixties anymore. Who wore long hair except a few dingbats in rock videos?

The girl hesitated, biting her lower lip. She shook her head finally. "I don't think so. He was too clean. Wore slacks and a nice shirt. Great smile. He smiled at me when he came outta the cafe." She arched her back a little and gave him one of her knowing looks.

Mark thought the stranger who picked up his daughter must be some charmer. He'd bowled over this girl. That might not be a good sign.

"Which way did they drive when they left?"

The girl pointed west.

"You're sure? You watched them leave?"

"I said so, didn't I?" She sounded offended, and her lower lip went into a pout. It wasn't a pretty sight. Not sexy or sultry as he was sure she meant it to be.

"All right. Was there anything else you can tell me?"

The girl shook her head. She opened her pocketbook and took out a pack of Wrigley's spearmint gum, offered it to him, and, when he refused, shook out a piece to unwrap. She contentedly chewed the slice as he walked to his car.

He was hungry. He had wanted to get a burger and fries to go, but Molly and an old hippie had a three-hour jump on him. At least. He'd grab something to eat later. Later when he could afford to waste the time.

Cruise stopped at a Jack in the Box. He ordered bacon cheeseburgers, onion rings, and large Cokes. He noticed Molly ate as if she had gone without food all day. Probably had. She ate just like a kid, sloppily, mayonnaise and tomato dripping onto napkins spread in her lap. He smiled at her, offered to buy her something else when she finished, but she burped quietly behind her hand, and said she was full, thanks.

Once on the freeway and driving steadily, she fell asleep again, head against the window. Cruise tooled on down the road, thinking about the pure animal bliss of certain functions. Eating, sleeping, fucking, waking. The perfect cycle of it. He had not indulged in the fucking part in a long time. He wouldn't, not until the girl really wanted him to. He'd make sure she wanted him. If she did it because she felt she owed him, that would ruin the whole performance. He had never in his life forced a woman. It was a matter of pride. There was no *bliss* in it. It was like forcing yourself to eat on a full stomach or sleeping when you weren't tired or waking up before you were ready.

Besides, his major joy in life had nothing to do with the perfect cycle of life. He could go without food, drink, sleep, and sex when he had to. The thing that really made him tick loud as a time bomb had to do with death dealing.

The working up to it. The building of the pressure. The quiet approach, the jovial front he presented, the harmless exterior that wooed his victim. And then the moment of total abandonment when the cold rage swarmed from the top of his head where he imagined it slept like a hibernating beast, crept forward first into his eyes where he couldn't deflect it, and then it was upon him, swooping down over him like the shadow of a hawk. He always concentrated on the look in his victims' eyes when they recognized, in their final moments, how they'd been sorely tricked, how they had mislaid their trust, how they had but seconds before the razored steel began to tear and rip them from stem to stern.

It was always so bloody. The air itself spun with blood when he whipped out his knife and began to dispatch a victim. His height prevented the blood from getting on his face in most instances, but from his chest down the red rain soaked him. He didn't know how many clothes he'd had to bury or burn because of that. He didn't like the scent of blood when it dried, when it was old. It never smelled right unless it was fresh. Warm. Once it thickened into clots and strings on his clothes or where it splashed his arms, he went into a frenzy to get it off him.

For emergencies, when he could not find a place to wash, he carried a case of bottled water in the trunk. Nothing felt better than to strip off the killing clothes, step out of his shoes, and stand with the water pouring down from his head, sluicing over his chest, flat belly, draining down his groin and buttocks.

Thinking about his ablutions, he could feel again the cold shock of the water, and he shivered where he sat driving.

"Are you cold?" Molly asked. She straightened from where she'd been leaning against the window. She blinked sleepily. Cool late summer night air wove a stream from the open windows through the car. It ruffled her curly red hair from behind, lifting ends of it to trail toward the roof of the car like the tatters of a shroud on a floating ghost.

Cruise looked at her. He must have been unable to make his mouth work right because he knew he'd tried to smile, but she frowned in return. That meant his facial muscles were frozen; he'd lost control of them momentarily while indulging in the memory of blood. He faced the road again, tried to repress his wandering thoughts of death.

"No," he said. "I'm not cold. The air's just fine."

"Oh."

"Are you cold? We can roll the windows up."

"I'm okay." She leaned her head against the partially rolled window again. "Tired. Do you drive all night?"

"I make better time. I don't like driving during the day. I sleep then."

"In the car or what?"

"Sometimes. Sometimes I get a room, pull all the curtains."

"Oh."

This time she sounded a little worried. He wanted to reassure her that she wouldn't have to have sex with him until she wanted to, or *never* if it came to that, but he couldn't think of a way to say it without making her suspicious, without sounding like a liar. He opted to say nothing instead.

"Where are we?" she asked.

"Still in Louisiana."

"Where do you think you'll stop?"

"It should be getting daylight when we get somewhere in Texas."

Hours later while Molly dozed on and off, waking only long enough to ask where they were now, Cruise noticed the lightening of the sky. It looked as if the heavens were a bowl of pewter turned down over the land. Stars winked out. The moon disappeared. Strips of fleecy clouds formed on the low horizon.

He had crossed Henderson Swamp, the Sabine River, and the Neches. He took the Walden Road exit in Beaumont, Texas, passed a monster-size Metro Truck Stop that he gave a wistful glance. He continued past it, crossed a railroad track, and drove down a road called Terrell Park Drive where there was a golf course and older suburban homes. He turned into a paved area by a park where swings and jungle gyms hunkered in wisps of early morning eddies of fog. He killed the engine.

Molly woke abruptly. Looked around. She stretched like a cat limbering up for the day ahead. He envied those who could stand the light. They were normal in that respect where he was not, he understood that implicitly.

"Texas?" she asked.

"Yeah. I'm going to sleep now. Do what you want to do. There's a little store back there if you want anything. Here's five bucks." He handed her the bill.

"Do you want me to wake you in a little while?"

"No. I'll wake on my own."

He reached beside the seat and depressed the lever. The back folded down until it hit the back bench seat. He felt on the rear floorboard for the folded kitchen towel he kept there, draped it over his eyes.

He heard Molly unbuckle her seat belt and leave the car.

He fell to sleep almost immediately, bird song and the squeak of swing chains in his ears.

In his dreams he relived the high and low points of his life. His past trailed him into sleep and always had. When he had been a boy, he dreamed of babyhood. When a teen, he dreamed of boyhood. Now he dreamed of the entire fabric of life he'd lived to the present.

Always in trouble with authority, mainly his father, he had taken on a decidedly secretive nature. He came from a big brawling family of children who were mercilessly beaten by their heavy-handed father. So bad were those days that when he dreamed of them, he wept in his sleep and woke to find his face wet with tears. His father did not drink. He did not curse. He did not whore or fail to bring home a paycheck. Nevertheless, he was cruelly warped in some essential way, part of his humanity driven so deep underground that it would never come to the fore. He suffered no breach of his ironclad rule, but his rule was too strict for even a hardened soldier, much less a child, so they all failed him; they all, his five brothers, his four sisters, courted and promptly received daily punishment.

There was the time they were lined up before their brutal father to recite the alphabet. They ranged in age from three years old to fourteen. Cruise had been six. When one of them failed to speak loudly enough or faltered in the sing-song recitation of letters, his father struck out fiercely with a wide belt across their faces.

Then there was the time Cruise, growing ever more rebellious and volatile, tried to run away. He was twelve. His father brought him back and chained him to the metal kitchen table leg for a week. It was forbidden for the others to speak to him, and he was fed scraps like a dog, like a mongrel dog begging favor.

When Cruise reached adulthood he wandered the country like a vagabond, working just long enough to provide funds to keep on the move. It was as if he stayed in one spot long enough, his past would catch up with him and swallow him whole, make him mad, destroy the only peace of mind he could ever find.

When at first the idea came to him that he could kill rather than work or steal, that killing *was* a living, a way of life, he wasn't at all shocked by the thought. He had committed murder early on and the lesser crime of robbery without being caught, so the thought of punishment held no sway. *His father* knew how to punish. The law swatted, it stung, it didn't punish.

He came to the conclusion, after long years thinking about it, that he could not lay the blame for his ways on his upbringing, on his father. As far as he knew none of his nine brothers or sisters displayed a violent streak. The same childhood that molded them, and allowed a sort of normalcy, also shaped him. No, he couldn't, like Henry Lee Lucas, go around currying forgiveness because of his horrid past. He couldn't ask the psychologists, who were so eager to find reason, to blame murder on background.

It wasn't Daddy's fault. It wasn't Mommy's fault. Though for some time he might have liked to claim that convenient excuse. He knew deep down it was a lie, a damned lie if he bought it.

The truth, as far as he'd been able to deduce it, was that he hadn't the ambition or the patience to be "normal." It did not suit his taste. It made him want to cringe to think of living with a wife, begetting children, working a steady job, paying for a mortgage. An abnormal life-style suited him. Like his father before him, he could not live according to the edicts of others. Not that abnormality was a proven fact in his mind. Maybe the rest of the world had adopted rites and rituals they merely thought normal. They had all accepted a cultural image and agreed upon it. Majority rule. That did not mean he had to.

As far as that goes, there were plenty who didn't fit the ordinary pattern. They might not kill, as he did, in order to live, but how normal was it to spend a life as a politician, for example? Conning people, making concessions, playing a strange power game. Or how normal was it to be an artist, to spend a life committed to paint or music or dance or words? And what about geniuses? Did the scientist who stared into the universe and expound on reaching the edge of space lead a normal existence? His thoughts had to be so far removed from the mundane world that he might even be considered another species of human. Or was the pious monk chanting in his solitary retreat on a mountain slope different from others? The monk, the artist, so many people who didn't fit the pattern, who couldn't get with the program, but no one called them insane or abnormal. He decided they were just as deformed as he. *Or*. They were just as normal.

Cruise finally shook down the idea until he thought he belonged to an elite worldwide group of people who did not fit, who were oddities for one reason or another. There were no monsters or saints in the world he understood. There were no laws he recognized, being above and beyond all law and lawgivers. There were no morals in any book, religious or otherwise, that could make him place guilt upon his shoulders.

Cruise Lavanic would not grovel in the mud and blame the past or any of the people who made it the hell it was.

There was no blame.

It was, all aspects taken under consideration, simply easier to kill than to rob, to kill than to settle in and work and let the world grind him down.

Once he'd come to this conclusion, he went on his way satisfied he was not a madman, insane, or clinically verifiable. If anything, he was superior to the rest of mankind for he'd been able to throw off the shackles of a binding, suffocating, deadening culture that said his bread must come from labor, that he should live in a house and keep a woman, that he should own property and buy more obsolete merchandise than he could use. He *would not* watch television six hours a day, pay his heavy unfair burden of taxes, and shop at the discount stores on weekends.

He wouldn't. He didn't. And when he dreamed of murders he had committed they came to him without a layer of guilt, stripped of moral object lessons, and nothing if not thrilling.

He woke once, the towel having slipped from his eyes. Sun blinded him with shafts like fire and his eyes watered instantly. The girl Molly was nowhere around. So what? He didn't care. She'd be back.

He turned onto his side in the lowered seat, draped the towel again, and drifted off.

He had been dreaming of the Lot Lizard he did in Charlotte, North Carolina. She was his last kill, still fresh in his mind. He now reached for her and for the pleasantness of the dream. Entering the dreamscape, he saw himself walking toward a picnic table set on gravel behind a trailer. It was a truck stop just north of Charlotte. A weekend when the truck drivers generally were laid over with their loads until Monday deliveries. The lots were packed, trucks lined up side by side, row by row, deep, thick, growling machines that rumbled day and night.

The trailer was a makeshift trucker's lounge with a color TV, ratty living-room furniture boasting scarred pine armrests, and a few video arcade games. The picnic table sat behind it, crooked, leaning in the gray gravel. To each side of the table the trucks purred like fat, hungry predator cats. Cruise had been parked at this truck stop listening on his CB to the truckers talk in their peculiar lingo.

They called plaintively, as the sun set and their loneliness deepened, for "Baby Dolls," the polite euphemism for Lot Lizards. Cruise recognized the voice of one trucker who called himself Dirty Old Man. He, more than all the others, persistently made a plea for female companionship.

"C'mon, Baby Dolls, where y'all at tonight? I'm looking for some commercial company. C'mon and talk to your Dirty Old Man."

Every few minutes Dirty Old Man made his call. When it was full dark a feminine voice answered back.

"Hello there, boys. This here Baby Doll is on the prowl. Are there any interested parties out there?"

Dirty Old Man immediately piped up. His voice was low and grizzled as he said, "Oh, Baby Doll, I've been waiting just about forever to meet you, honey. Where you at, Sugar? What's your ten-twenty?"

The sultry voice returned. Now all the truckers were listening, having abandoned their rambling complaints about layovers and long hours and not getting home when promised. "I'm over here near Jack's," she said. "Where you at, baby?"

Cruise squirmed in his seat. He loved listening in on these assignations. It had a voyeuristic flavor that kept a smile glued to his lips. He turned up the volume control on the CB. She was right here near Jack's Truck Stop somewhere.

He could get to her first if she would say where she'd meet her trick.

"Darnit, Baby Doll," Dirty Old Man crooned. He chuckled, almost went into a coughing spree in his eagerness. "I'm over here at the 76 Truck Stop and you're over there under the sign with the big blue star. What you look like, Doll?"

"I got the bluest eyes and I'm pretty as a picture. Why don't you come on over here to Jack's and see for yourself? I'll wait for you at the picnic table behind the lounge."

A barrage of male voices all came on at once to vie for her attention.

"Mind if I come too, Baby Doll?"

"Hooo doggie, commercial company!"

"You got any friends?"

"You gonna be busy later, Baby Doll of the blue eyes?"

Cruise heard her key the mike and laugh a sensual laugh that must have set the boys slobbering over their knees. "There's just me, sweeties, but we got all night. Y'all come on out, you hear? Let's do us some partying down."

Cruise, having parked at a strategic point that gave him a wide view of Jack's, watched from his Chrysler as the girl walked out of nowhere toward the picnic table. She was about five feet three, short blond hair chopped in a boyish cut, wearing jeans and a prim light pink blouse with embroidery on the collar. She wasn't young. Middle thirties, he guessed.

He got to her before Dirty Old Man or any of the others, just as he supposed he would.

"Hi, Hon," she said, putting her arm familiarly around his waist as he walked up. "I'm Minde. M-i-n-d-e. Now I don't do this sort of thing for a living, you know. Trucker dumped me here in Charlotte with no way home. I never been in that predickerment before. I'm from St. Louis and

I don't have no way back there unless I get a little help from a friend."

Cruise had heard all the stories whores told and this one was terribly uncreative, but no matter, he didn't want her for her brain. She looked relatively clean, and at least she wasn't fat. She might have weighed slightly over a hundred, but not much. And from having rested his hand on her rump, he knew she had stashed some money. Not smart of her, but her profession wasn't known for having smarts.

"Come on with me," he said, giving her the smile they loved. "I'll get you to St. Louis."

As they started walking away, a dusty, bug-splattered Mack rolled across the gravel drive. The driver braked on seeing them. The roar of the engine drowned their ears with a rumble that shook the ground beneath them. Churned gravel dust hung in the air. The man climbed down from the cab to block their way. "I'm Dirty Old Man. Are you my Baby Doll?"

Minde looked up at Cruise. She looked back at the bedraggled old fellow with his gut hanging out and his day-old unshaven gray chin. "Sorry, Dirty Old Man. I might see you later. Never can tell. You keep listening for me, you hear?"

Cruise swept her past him without saying a word. There were going to be some horny drivers tonight when Minde didn't come back. But then it was early. There might be more Lot Lizards prowling the lots before the night was out. If there weren't, let all the poor suckers jack off.

Minde didn't make it to St. Louis. She didn't make it out of the state of North Carolina, the redbird state. She died south of Charlotte in a patch of forest off a dirt road that wouldn't see a bulldozer for years. Cruise made love to her first. That's the way he thought of it. *Lovemaking*.

He crooned into her ear and made her happy to be alive before he slipped the knife from his hair in the moonlight. She gasped upon seeing its glint, then fought him with a fierceness bred of desperation. "You bastard!" she screamed. Fighting him. Wrestling. Kicking and gouging. "You crazy motherfucking son of a bitch!"

It was a fight worth remembering, but she succumbed in the end, her throat pumping blood against Cruise's arm where it rested beneath the crook of her neck.

Cruise found three hundred dollars folded neatly in her back pocket. "You could have taken a plane," he whispered to her as he wrapped her in the blanket, leaves sticking to it in the wet places. He moved her body to the waiting hole he had dug earlier in the day in preparation for a victim.

As the dream ended with the burial and the cold water cleansing afterward, Cruise smiled in his sleep. He felt again the cold slap of water, the shock and breathtaking thrill of it. He felt the roughness of towel-drying his body, the warmth of his clothes, the bracing scent of green forest dew-deep and washed with night breeze. The best of all, though, was the *satisfaction* he felt of having earned his way in the world without taking any chances, without giving up anything of himself for it.

Dirty Old Man never got a good look at his face in the thick shadows of the truck stop. No one knew who he was. They'd be looking for a trucker who offed a whore. They wouldn't even look too long or too hard. Lot Lizards were officially barred from all the truck stops across America now. The ones who worked the trade took their chances. Minde happened to lose.

The sun dipped west. Afternoon brought a damp chill with it. Shadows lengthened. Golfers came off the course. Parents corralled their children from the playground.

Molly sat in a swing watching the car. She wound a length of hair around one finger and put it between her small white teeth to chew. It had the texture of tin foil.

She waited for Cruise to wake and drive her across Texas. It had been a long, boring day, but now with the night coming on, they'd be on the move.

Any minute now. Any minute she'd see his large chest rise up in the seat and he'd beckon to her.

The seconds slipped by as the area continued to empty. A cooling breeze pressed at her shoulders. Molly could smell the water from the goldfish pond a few feet away from the swings. It smelled stagnant and unwholesome. Her stomach rolled from the two Mars bars she had eaten for lunch. She wanted to brush her teeth. She'd like a bath. She had washed in the ladies' room in a service station, but that wasn't a bath. She didn't feel any cleaner once she had done balling the brown hand towels and throwing them in the trash.

She blinked with surprise when Cruise sat upright in the Chrysler. Her mind had been on hot showers and white, fragrantly scented, fluffy towels. She stood, her bottom numb from the wooden swing seat. She saw there was little light left. Shadows marched across the ground and obscured the path.

Cruise started the car. Switched on the headlights. Molly ran to the parking area and grabbed the door handle.

"Hi," she said breathlessly. She hoped he hadn't forgotten her, that he still wanted her along. "Here I am."

"Yes," he said. "There you are. It's time to travel."

The automatic street lamps came on just as Cruise put the car into reverse.

Molly thought she'd never be happier to see the last of a place. It seemed she had spent weeks waiting for him to get enough sleep to drive through the night.

"Buckle up," he said. "Have a Coke. We'll eat later."

Molly grinned and did as she was told. She could get used to funny old Cruise with his long hair and strange sleeping habits. She *could*. What an adventure running away from home was turning out to be!

Wouldn't her daddy just die.

THE SECOND NIGHT

Molly was wired, all her senses jouncing to an internal beat. She hadn't slept much the night before, and during the day she had wandered around the park waiting for Cruise to wake. Now fatigue had taken over, but it left her mind strung out like an addict looking for a fix. This happened when she went too long without sleep. She chattered like a monkey until her mind closed shop and faded to black.

"Sure was boring hanging around all day while you were sleeping." She bit the inside of her cheek. Real smart. Cruise was taking her to California, and so far it was a free ride. She must try not to complain.

"I'm sorry about that." He sounded genuinely upset. "I just can't drive in the day. The light hurts my eyes."

She peered at him in the gloom of the car. Dusk was thick and the sky was devoid of stars. "You have a problem seeing?"

"Only in sunlight. It's been that way since I was a kid. I'm a night person. You heard of the lark and the owl? I'm the owl. The night is cooler, cleaner in some ways. I like the shadows of trees and hills, the houses and closed shops sleeping in the towns. I like neon. Ever notice how neon lights sizzle? You walk beneath them on a sidewalk and you can hear them. It's like bacon frying."

42

"How'd you go to school if you stayed up all night?"

"I missed it as much as I could." He smiled, remembering. She saw that. She understood that. Wasn't she missing school? Wasn't school for idiots anyway? All that regimentation. All those dumb authority games. Principals and teachers playing like they were army sergeants. Students kissing ass or acting up, one or the other. Just about everyone on drugs. There was more LSD in the schools than there had ever been at the Woodstock concert. Straight kids were on the make or trying to outdo everyone else. A dumb exercise in futility for goobheads.

"I even like truck stops," Cruise was saying.

"Truck stops? Really?"

"It's the meeting place for the underworld."

"Truckers, you mean?"

"Yeah, truckers. Their girls. Travelers. Night workers. They live like I do. On the road driving, living in a machine with wheels on it, meeting strangers . . ." He looked at her. She smiled, his stranger.

"I never knew anyone who liked truck stops." She had never heard anyone even *mention* truck stops.

"Most people don't know about them. It's where everything's happening while the rest of the world sleeps. Men are in there showering, doing their laundry, shopping, eating breakfast at three in the morning. People are awake in truck stops even in the middle of the darkest hours."

"I see you have a CB. You talk to truckers too?"

He glanced at the mike hanging from its slot below the radio. "I talk to them sometimes."

"They're all cowboys, right? Jeans and boots and big bellies."

Cruise shook his head. "Not all of 'em. That's what people think. Maybe that's the way it was years ago. Today these guys are the independents. They're the men who won't work regular jobs, who don't fit in. And they're not ignorant. You don't drive forty tons of steel at seventy miles an hour and live to tell about it if you're stupid."

Molly brought her right thumb to her lips and chewed softly on the fleshy part. "That's cool beans." Though she wasn't sure she believed it.

"Cool beans." He laughed. "Yeah."

"You ever drive trucks?"

He smiled. "No, not me. I do my cruising in four-wheelers."

"That's why you're called Cruise, right?"

"Sure. I told you."

"Like they called you Cruise when you were a kid, huh?" She knew teasing him might be a mistake, but she couldn't stop her mouth from running. Nervous energy twanged through her until she was drops of water dancing on hot coals.

"When I was a kid," he said slowly, "I had an awful name."

"What was it?"

"Herod."

"Hmmm." She sucked her thumb to keep from busting out with a derisive laugh.

"Herod. The king who ordered the murder of all male babies in Jerusalem. He was trying to do away with Christ, remember?"

She didn't, but she believed him. "Why did your mom name you that then? You Jewish or something?"

"No. She just had a bad sense of humor, I guess. Or she didn't know her Bible. Probably the latter. She gave us all formal-sounding names. Orson. Edward. No one called him Eddie. Evelander. We call her Lannie, but my mother didn't approve. Georgine. It goes on. I had a big family."

"Well, I like Cruise better. Herod doesn't fit you, you know?"

"I didn't think so either."

Molly fell silent, her mind finally slowing a bit, enough for her to seize control of it. The fatigue had made its sluggish way through her body, up her neck, and was now beginning to circle the wagons in her skull. She blinked sleepily.

"I knew a guy once," Cruise began slowly.

Molly stretched in her seat. She wondered if it had a lever that let the seat back the way his seat reclined.

"This guy," Cruise continued, "went to Hollywood to write scripts for the movies."

Molly's ears perked up. "Did he? Write for the movies?" She loved movies and movie stars. Debra Winger. Rutger Hauer. Richard Gere. Cory Haime. Now there was a guy you could sink your teeth into. When he acted he always had his mouth open, even when he was a kid in the movies. Like he was a fly-catcher, unofficially, of course.

"He wanted to real bad," Cruise said. "He'd gone to one of those fancy colleges out east and he'd studied and he wanted more than anything to write screenplays. I met him in Hollywood. He was sitting in an all-night cafe drinking coffee. We started talking."

"Yeah? I bet they do that a lot, sit in cafes, those writers."

"This one did. See, he had a problem."

"He couldn't sell any of his scripts."

"That's right. He was up against the best. And this guy had money. He came from a family with money so it wasn't like he had to make it in Hollywood. But in another way he did. He had stopped taking money from his mother. But she came over to his little apartment all the time, bitching him out, asking him what he thought he was doing wasting himself. He had graduated from Princeton or Harvard or some shit like that. She wanted him to do something else. Be useful, make a real living, have an office and a desk. On top of her nagging, she was always sending over her maid to clean his place. Wouldn't even ask him if he wanted that. She just did it."

"What an asshole. She was on his case bad, huh?"

"Every chance she got. And this guy, he was losing it. He was living like a pig and his mind was going. Failure does that to some people. Not getting the dream they think they deserve."

Molly said thoughtfully, "I can feature that."

"So this guy starts freaking out. He imagines things."

"Like what? Winning an academy award?"

"Nothing that wholesome. He started thinking he had worms and rats in his stomach. He thought they were always coming out. He thought he vomited them."

"Oh, ga-ross. You mean he *told* you this? Over coffee?"

"Yeah, we talked all night. He said he was sure people were going to know soon. About the things in his stomach. He said they moved around, beneath his shirt, and someone was going to see it. Or he'd vomit and they'd know. His mother came over so much, she was going to discover it. He thought maybe someone had given him something, some kind of new biological germ or something."

"Weirded out."

"That's what I figured."

"So what happened to him?"

"About a month later I came back through Hollywood and I dropped by his apartment to see him. When he let me in it smelled in there. Rancid, nasty. Like vomit. He was carrying around a knife."

"What for?"

"For protection, I guess. By then he was suspicious of everybody. I think he was getting ready to kill the rats and worms he thought were coming out of his mouth. I tried to talk him down, but . . ."

"Why didn't his mom do something?"

"She was a bitch. She didn't know he was a guy dying like that. She thought he was just being stubborn or something. She thought she could nag him out of it. Turn him into a contributing member of society. Make him into a top executive."

"Could you help him?"

"You don't help someone who's carrying around a butcher knife. You don't even try."

"That's too bad." Molly felt terrible. Rats in the stomach. God.

"The next time I came through Hollywood, his apartment was empty. He was gone. He had given me his mother's phone number. I called her and she said he'd slit his throat. Over the sink. She didn't know why and she was bawling so hard I hung up. But I know why he did it."

"Over the sink?"

"Yeah. When I was there before he told me he always threw up in the kitchen sink so he could flush those things down the disposal. It was the only way he knew to get rid of them. Grind 'em up."

"Christ."

Cruise was silent. Molly swallowed hard, the idea of a slit throat squeezing her neck muscles tight.

"I've met some strange folk," Cruise said finally.

"I bet. Rats and worms. Ugh."

"If he'd just sold one script," Cruise said.

"He might not have gone crazy," Molly supplied.

"Maybe," Cruise agreed. "Maybe not."

Molly was no longer sleepy. In fact she might not sleep for a year. She stared wide-eyed out the windshield imagining the desperation it took to make someone commit suicide over the top of a disposal.

He saw Molly nodding now. She was tired, poor baby. Her waking and sleeping cycles did not yet fit his own. She was still a day person. If he woke her every couple of hours and kept her awake, he'd gradually change the cycles until she too would sleep during the day. He'd let her snooze just a little. Wake her again later.

He concentrated on the bright lights he approached. The city of Houston. Interstate 10 took him through the heart of the city. He could see it off to his right on the loop, the tall skyline of multiple dark rectangles against the night sky. Two of the buildings were identically wedge-shaped, butted close against each other. Dallas, he knew, was a more spectacular scene at night with buildings outlined in multicolored neon, but Houston wasn't bad. One building had a square of lime green around its roof, a few had white outlines. Streetlights twinkled in straight lines down the canyons. Cars streamed past on the freeway, all of them going ten or twenty miles faster than the speed limit. It was at least seventy miles across the city from one side to the other. It spread from the NASA complex south of the city all the way to Humble, Texas, a suburb town to the north.

Texas was a frightening place. Cruise didn't kill in Texas. The cops were hardasses. Smart. Tough. They were alert. What he did not need was a Texas lawman sticking one of those nickel-plated big goddamn .357 Magnums in his face. Some of the highway patrolmen would blow you away as easy as look at you. Uh-uh. Driving across Texas always gave him the creeps. He kept to the speed limit, stayed in his lane, and drove on autopilot until he hit the New Mexico line.

It was a long haul from Houston to the western border. Maybe he'd go down into Juárez, Mexico, outside of El Paso for a spot of relief.

He sneaked a glance at his passenger. She was snoring lightly, little mouth open. He thought about her breath smelling of milk, like a baby, although he knew it wouldn't, if anything it would smell like Coca-Cola. He thought about her angular, pubescent body. Tiny breasts budding on her chest. Hips so small he could hold them in the palms of his big hands like slabs of rich steak.

Oh, boy, did he need relief. He was thinking of her in terms of *food*, for chrissakes.

He wondered if she'd dream of the scriptwriter with rats and worms in his stomach. The one with the rich mama and the failed dreams. Even now, somewhere in Hollywood there was another guy just like that. They were out there, all those suicides and hucksters and nagging mothers. All those nightmares and paranoiacs.

Cruise knew them and their stories.

He lived one of the stories himself, the most bizarre of all. He was able to live out the fantasy, live out his dreams others called warped and depraved only because they didn't understand, because they weren't members of the outlaw elite.

Houston's lights melted into the background as he moved across the huge state of Texas going west. He raced the sun threatening to rise at his back. Every night he raced against the sun. Already his eyes came down into slits against the peril of dawn.

He'd wake Molly and tell her another story. That always helped to keep the night with him, the sunrise at bay.

"Molly," he called. "C'mon, wake up, baby."

"Huh . . . ? What?"

"We'll stop pretty soon and you can sleep then. Keep me company, okay?"

He heard her clear her throat, saw her straighten from the slump of sleep, trying to come awake and please him. "Almost morning?"

He squinted into the darkness. "Soon."

"I'm really beat . . ."

"Talk to me a little bit. I got a long stretch here to drive across Texas. Let me tell you about this guy I knew once . . ."

Soon he had a tale spinning and Molly wide awake, riveted to her seat where she was turned toward him. What a kid. What a great kid. He just couldn't have found a better traveling partner if he'd tried for a month. Too bad that he'd have to kill her in the end. He was as fond of her as he had been of any of his former witnesses.

The edge of the sun slipped up behind him as he talked. The landscape changed from gray to pink to molten orange. The land looked wild and desolate painted in the vivid Van Gogh colors. They were in the dry plains where nothing but mesquite trees and cacti dared to try to make a go of it. It was too open, the sky too big, a maw opening to swallow him. He hated fucking Texas.

Cruise saw an exit for a truck stop and slowed to take the ramp. He was somewhere between San Antonio and El Paso. He had to drive this goddamn state in chunks. No other way to get across the bastard.

"You can hang out in the store or the restaurant while I sleep," he said, hooking a thumb at the one-story building. "Just don't talk much to the truckers. They'll think you're . . ."

"Hooking. I know."

"Sure. You'll be okay."

As he parked he heard her yawn. "Sleepy?" he asked.

"Yeah, I think I'll snooze out if you don't mind. I'm still beat."

"Pull the lever beside your seat and the back will recline."

Cruise made his own seat into a half bed, covered his eyes with the towel from the floorboard, and sighed with satisfaction.

Molly was coming around nicely. What a great little kid.

Car and truck lights washed over the blue Chrysler as vehicles from the interstate pulled into the truck stop for a rest or food or fuel. From the back lot the rhythmic thump and drone of the idling truck engines soothed Cruise's ears. It sounded to him like one giant heartbeat. The sound raised and lowered with the pulse in his wrists and in his temples. Through the cracked window the scent of smoke came to his nostrils. In the smoke he could distinguish the aroma of fried foods, diesel exhaust, and a faint hint of tar and rubber. Road smells. The scent of freedom.

It didn't surprise him to hear, after a bit, Molly's light snore. That soothed him too. He wanted her happy to be with him, feeling easy, unafraid. They had been together two nights. He was closer to enjoying her confidence. He hadn't made a move toward her, nothing threatening. Had said nothing to alarm her. Had made her identify with his way of life, at least a little. At least a *part* of his life. If she slept until nearly noon, she'd be awake more come night again. She'd be better company to him. She'd get closer to revealing her real self.

Then he'd take her to Mexico. He had made up his mind. Texas always made him want to run away, run completely out of the country. It'd just be a foray, a stopover. They wouldn't have to stay long, though they could really stay as long as they wanted once he talked Molly into it.

He knew a town across the border just east of glitzy, westernized Juárez, one owned entirely by Mexican drug lords. They knew him there from his frequent visits. There he was treated kingly. As long as he performed a few chores for the boss. The money from it wasn't bad, either.

Shit. Always that. He had forgotten his money was running out.

He would have to do something to get more, preferably something for Ramirez. With or without Molly knowing about it, though he preferred that she witness whatever he must do to get the cash.

He yawned big and had to redrape the towel over his face.

No use worrying about it. Never had before. If he wanted a Mexican whore, and if he wanted to show Molly the extent of his traveling experience, then he would simply do what he must do, what came naturally.

Besides, it was time. It had been days, maybe a week, maybe more, since he did the girl in Charlotte, North Carolina. His fingers itched to touch the knife hidden under his hair. Touch and fondle it, renew himself with its power.

He heard a truck's air horn blast and twitched. It came from the back lot, though, nothing he must get up and see about. Beyond his closed eyelids and the folded towel he could still see the bright wash of car lights swing past the car window though it was almost daylight.

The world was alive, teeming with night people, many of them winding down now as the dawn slipped catlike over the land. He must be asleep by then. Before the sunrise. Before the world was burning fire and the land revealed its seams and cracks, its underlying ugliness and squalor.

He replayed the life and death of the doomed Hollywood scriptwriter, and drifted softly into a comforting dream.

• • •

Mark Killany unlocked the door to room 202 at the Holiday Inn just west of Beaumont, Texas. At his back and below him stretched the lobby with the waterfall in its center. Rising high above him on three sides were balconies dripping long green vines. The air was misty and green. A few people in the lobby sat in club chairs watching a big-screen television. It looked like a situation comedy was playing. Two patrons were belly-up to the bar, neither of them giving attention to the other.

Mark ignored the activity behind him and slipped quickly into his room. He dropped his suitcase near the bed and went into the bath, turned on the shower full force, waited for the temperature to get to the proper degree while he undressed.

It was turning into a long, lonesome trip. He wasn't used to the melancholy mood that was upon him. It cramped his style, made him lapse into periods of self-pity. All his life he'd been in control of his own destiny. He knew what he wanted out of the military and worked hard to get it: authority, security, respect. He had met Molly's mother after he made lieutenant and knew he wanted her in his life. She never complained about compound housing, official politics, or his dedication to his job. She gave him what he needed. Unconditional love, loyalty, and a beautiful, intelligent daughter. She had given her life, he realized in regret, to bring a child into the world. And he had always *thought* Molly intelligent, that is, until she'd pulled this stunt of running away from home.

Now his destiny was uncertain, his life in a chaos not of his making, and evidently beyond his control. Molly had usurped his authority, left him to worry himself sick over her. While he drove sometimes he felt the anger coming like a runaway train. Molly was a spoiled, selfish creature unfit to be called his daughter. She'd learned nothing from his examples, rejected those values and beliefs he felt she needed most.

Other times sadness invaded him, that quality of melancholy that filled him like pie in a pastry shell, and he moaned aloud, wishing to be anywhere, in any situation except this one. Dealing with a teenager was turning out to be like defusing a bomb. It took iron will, steady hands, unswerving patience, and skill. All those characteristics he lacked except for the will. And that had been too muscular, not limber enough for the job at hand.

He stepped into the shower's spray and let it cascade over his bowed head. He closed his eyes and breathed through his mouth.

He was neither angry nor sad right now. Just beaten. No telling how far ahead she was. She might have changed cars, hitched with another driver. She might have decided not to go to the West Coast, and at this moment was on her way back east or north or even to the Midwest. The United States was a big country, all spread out., thousands of places to hide or get lost in. She might have stopped off in one of the towns along the route he traveled, and was now melting into New Orleans or Lake Charles, vanishing like a wisp of fog.

It was sheer misery that drove him to continue. He needed rest. A few hours in a bed. But then he'd be on his way again, heading west, asking his questions, showing Molly's picture. He knew no other way to live with himself. Even if he hired private investigators, they might take months and come up with nothing. The agencies looking for runaways were swamped with calls from frantic parents looking for kids. He knew there was little hope in that direction. Hell, look at the pictures of missing kids on the sides of milk cartons. It was an epidemic; no one knew what to do. He must go forward and hope Molly headed for California the way she'd told her Florida friends. If she'd lied, if she'd changed her mind, he was shit out of luck. It might be years before he found her. *Dammit.*

He washed, shampooed his short, crew-cut hair, rinsed, and stepped from the shower stall. After drying off, shaving, brushing his teeth, donning the bottoms of a pair of plain white pajamas, he threw back the covers on one of the two double beds and flopped onto his back. He had a wake-up call at five-thirty. He should do a few sit-ups—it was harder to stay in shape since his retirement—but sleep pulled him into its silky depths.

He slept with the table lamp on, his mouth open, his hands straight at his sides. He never moved a limb all night. And if he dreamed, the dreams fell over the precipice of his subconscious and were lost the way the waterfall in the lobby fell from its great height and disappeared in the foaming aquamarine pond at its sculpted base.

THE THIRD NIGHT

Molly floated in a flushing pink dream of sex. *Hormone typhoon*, she thought at the edge of waking. *Stop it*, she thought, *dream something else*. But the dream was too exciting and blessedly real for her to stop it. She felt every inch of her body ripe and full to the bursting point with lustful feelings. Her muscles clenched and unclenched creating a wave of yearning that washed down through to her core. She fantasized a lover with long, silky hair that swung on each side of his face as he moved above her, his weight familiar, his warmth increasing her own. The hair of his legs slid along her own bare calves and inner thighs and she sighed in her sleep, twisting a little to better position herself to open and receive him.

Then a car door banged shut nearby and Molly came up from the reclining seat of the Chrysler like a shot. She was trembling, the heat that had been spreading outward from her thighs now creeping into her cheeks. She looked over quickly to where Cruise lay peacefully sleeping. She sucked in a breath and rubbed her eyes against the afternoon sun beating through the windshield. It felt like midsummer here in Texas. Hot as a griddle.

Her heart beat fast and strong in her chest. She felt as if

she'd used up as much energy as she might have running laps around a football field.

She'd been dreaming of making it with Cruise. A whole truckload of shame suffused her. Guilt at the betrayal of her body. She sometimes had these disturbing sexual dreams. She'd never had the nerve to ask other girls if they too sometimes woke from naps or in the night after experiencing vividly detailed romps with men. She was afraid they'd tell her no, and then she'd know for sure she was abnormal, her sexual appetite too large for so young a girl, so inexperienced a girl. Before losing her virginity—or rather, before giving it away—she had these same dreams, but they were what she called "baby" sex dreams once she knew better. She fantasized being touched, kissing, fondling in the dark. She would wake to find herself rocking belly down, massaging herself against the mattress. She didn't know what it felt like to make love.

After having sex the dreams changed completely. They had little to do with foreplay, with kissing or snuggling or touching. They got right down to the crux of the matter where she dreamed of penetration, of the slick thrust and pump of the act itself. She dreamed of being filled. Of reaching for orgasm and nearly missing each time she woke dripping sweat, her small breasts tingling, nipples swollen, a fire burning down below. Sometimes when she was too excited to forestall it, she masturbated, gently with her finger, probingly, then furiously until she came, her breath caught in her throat, her hand lodged between her legs, back arched.

She wished fervently to be rid of these kinds of fantasies that plagued her, that brought along with them guilt and sometimes shame at a runaway subconscious. Yet about once a month or so they returned like bold demons sharing her bed, driving her crazy with unfulfilled longing.

She'd die if Cruise knew she'd dreamed of him that

way. She peeked a look at his body. Let her gaze travel from heavy black lashes lying on his cheeks, down to his lips hiding beneath mustache and beard, over his muscular chest stretching at the material of his shirt, down to the belt in his slacks, the bulge in his crotch. Lingered there before traveling on down his legs to his feet. A trembling thrill rolled down her. Again she sucked in a breath and held it.

Crazy. She had to get out of the car before she did something incredibly stupid like reaching for him. She could already feel his big hands on her. She began to burn again, to squirm uncomfortably in the seat. She grabbed the door handle and jerked open the door, scrambled out into the fresh air. She shut the door quietly, just until it clicked, leaning down to stare through the window at Cruise's sleeping face to be sure he hadn't wakened. She smoothed her hair as well as she could. She composed herself, trying to quiet the hidden hunger. She would go into the truck stop and wash in the ladies' room. She'd drink some coffee and get over this mad rush of maniacal lust.

What was wrong with her? Is this what it was to be an adult, to feel this uncontrollable, aching fire take you even as you slept innocent and pure?

She noticed most of the day was gone. The sun was falling down the sky, sinking fast to the flat horizon. It was a shock to think she'd slept most of the daylight hours away. Getting just like Cruise. But what could she expect with him telling her stories all through the night, keeping her captive with his melodic voice. She suspected that's what he wanted—to rearrange her sleeping rhythms. Well, he was the boss on this particular joyride.

She looked up at the sign perched on the edge of the roof of the restaurant and read the name. The White Elephant Café. A fat dirty white elephant sat back on his haunches and trumpeted at the sky. Hah. Out here in the middle of God knew where, that's all they could think to call it, she guessed. It was a low-slung job in mud-red brick. The trim was painted brown and white. It could be torn down and no one would lose money.

She went through a glass door and found herself in a small store. Refrigerated cases of beer and soft drinks, milk, cheeses, luncheon meats. Aisles of trucker stuff. CB mikes and connections, logbooks, envelopes, every over-the-counter medicine ever put on the market.

A dull, wrung-out rag of a woman manned the cash register. She filed her nails, not bothering to look up as Molly entered.

To the left was a hallway with rest rooms. Molly headed for the ladies and held open the door for a big woman dressed in tight jeans and a blue workman's jacket. She must be a trucker, Molly assumed. Looked the part anyway. Didn't look like anybody's momma.

After relieving herself, washing her face, hands, neck, and upper arms with soap and water, she tried to get a brush through her red frowsy hair. Giving up trying to get it to lie down and behave, she scooped water into her hands and smoothed it over her head. The natural curl coiled into even tighter ringlets that fell around her pale face like corkscrewed ribbons. She patted them into place with a brown paper towel. Satisfied she was presentable, she left the rest room to find the cafe.

It was at the end of the hallway past four video games lined on one wall. A trucker in greasy jeans played Tetris, the Russian game of falling shapes one had to fit together into lines. Molly noted in passing he wasn't too damn good at it either. She could beat him with one hand tied and her eyes blindfolded.

She wandered into the jumbo room of the cafe. She took

a trucker's booth where a black phone hung on the wall at table level. She sat staring at it a full minute. Nah. She couldn't call him, her dad. He'd want to know where she was, why'd she leave, would she come back? She couldn't stand the pain of it. To be truthful she missed him already, but she'd get over it, she knew. She had to. She could not live with him, could not, could not.

She watched the young waitress. Her hair was short and lacquered stiffly. She wore a teddy bear sweatshirt and faded jeans that fit her all too well. While she waited to be served, Molly cataloged the stuff this joint had on the puke-pink Formica table. The jumble sat on every table.

McIlhenny Co. Tabasco sauce, Cajun Chef hot sauce, ketchup, sugar shaker, salt and pepper shakers, napkin holder, margarine and jelly tubs (apple and mixed fruit), low-cal sugar packets, creamer packets, and a generic black plastic ashtray. Good God. Did they provide for the customers or what?

The little waitress wore a short red change apron with black stitching across the front. Molly read it when she approached. "My name is Stinky." Molly suppressed a giggle threatening to get up and out.

"Stinky?" she asked when the girl stood over her.

The waitress looked down at the apron. "Uh, no, this ain't my apron. My name's Lynette."

Molly thought that was pretty fortunate for the girl. "Just coffee right now. I'll look at a menu."

Lynette bounced away and came back with a tan plastic mug of steamy java and a plastic-encased menu. There were black thumbprints on the front edges.

Molly decided on the huevos rancheros. Two eggs served on a corn tortilla with beans, rice, and their own special sauce. $2.95. Sounded like a regular bargain if the heartburn didn't kill her.

While she waited for the meal, Molly kept looking the place over. She didn't know what it was about truck stops that Cruise might like. The floor was black and white tiles. None too clean. The tables out in the center of the room had chairs with vinyl backs and seats of sick mustard-yellow. Bad color to have around food, she'd think. On white vinyl-covered walls hung wooden pictures of sunsets and Indians, a picture-frame clock of a semi-trailer truck parked in autumn leaves.

In the booth facing Molly she saw the back of a driver's head. Leaning slightly to the left or right she could see around him to get a view of his partner's billed cap. It was black with a red-and-white eagle on the front. Beneath the eagle was the legend RIDE TO LIVE, LIVE TO RIDE. At least it didn't say BORN TO LOSE.

There was a salad and ice cream bar. Another waitress took care of the trade at the center tables. She was fiftyish, gray hair, blue pants uniform, and a light gray fleece-lined sweater jacket. She looked tired. Compared to the bouncy Lynette of the red apron, she looked dead.

The huevos rancheros arrived and looked every bit as inviting as a roadkill. Molly's stomach did a flip-flop looking at how the fragile eggs were buried under the heaps of beans and rice.

Lynette said, "There's Tabasco sauce there if you want it."

Molly nodded dumbly. She'd have to drink her coffee before she'd ever get up the courage to tackle this thing.

While she sipped the black brew, two truckers entered trailed by a woman, dressed as they were, in jeans and sweatshirts and jackets. They passed Molly's booth. The woman had long blond hair. Bleached, but pretty. On the back of her black jacket was an American flag. Below the flag it read STONE MOUNTAIN. Molly knew where that was. In Georgia. A big ring of keys jingled and clanked on the woman's sturdy hips as she moved past. Molly thought she smelled the scorched scent of a hot radiator as they wove through tables to the back.

Travelers. Just like her. Driving those big rigs and eating in dumps like this one.

And Cruise liked them. She'd have to get him to confide in her just exactly what it was about bad art, scrubby jeans, and greasy food that he found intriguing.

Then again, come to think of it, it was really highly amusing. She never saw Tabasco sauce on the cafe tables in South Florida. She'd never in her life seen a female truck driver. And thank God, she'd never known a girl named Stinky—and wouldn't, she guessed.

The eggs were quite good despite their caked and drowned appearance. The beans were hot, the rice spicy. Molly ate every bite and burped politely behind a napkin. Damn gas bothered her like crazy when she ate spicy foods.

Lynette didn't say anything to her about sitting at a table reserved for truckers. Probably because the place wasn't exactly packed to the rafters. Molly let her cup be refilled four times before she made any move to leave. She lingered, savoring the place, the sounds, the way the truckers moved beneath their thick jackets and their cowboy and gimmee hats. One fellow at the counter had great buns—tight and small and cute as the cheeks of a panda bear—and just about the longest legs Molly had ever seen. Dwight Yoakum, the country singer who sang songs through his nose, had legs like that. Went on forever. The trucker wore gray lizard-skin cowboy boots, the pointy-toed ones, and his shirt had pearl snaps instead of buttons. He sat drinking coffee and kidding pretty Lynette about her silly apron.

All of a sudden Molly felt loneliness descend, a black curtain settling just behind her eyes. She wished the cowboy would talk to her, kid her about something. She wished the damn sun would set, goddammit, so Cruise would wake up and keep her company. She might as well be invisible, sitting nursing a cup of coffee, trailing a finger through a puddle of water condensed off her yellow plastic glass of iced water.

Just how was she going to make it in this world? When she got to California, that golden West, that Pacific paradise, just how was she going to keep herself off the street? She expected she was going to get hungry, learn all about how it felt to have your stomach shrink and your clothes fall off your hips. Learn all about staying out of the way of drug addicts, pimps, pushers, and muggers. Learn how to sleep standing up, leaning on a wall, arms folded. She'd seen people do that in downtown Miami. Stand there like a leaning pole, propped against the side of a wall, chin on chest, arms crossed, asleep. She guessed they locked their knees to keep from falling on their faces.

It had to be hard.

Life. It was a tough deal.

Tears swarmed in her eyes and she angrily brushed them away by pretending to wipe her face with a napkin.

Shit. Self-pitying asshole. She lurched up from the table and turned her back on the cute cowboy and his doll of a waitress. She paid at the cashier's counter and hurried out the door. The coolness of evening braced and refreshed her. She eyed the sky, measuring how far the sun had to go to hit sundown. An hour. Forty-five minutes.

She glanced around the parking lot for a place to wait it out. She picked the parking curb near the Chrysler. She lay her head on crossed arms against her knees, face turned so she could see the western sky. She could count the colors of sunset, gift the layers with all new names. Clam white. Pussy pink. Well. She had to have some fun. Then there was larva lavender. Jazz blue. Bruise purple. Scalding red. Tabby-cat orange. Bone ivory. Summer squash yellow.

Daydream. She could daydream about sex with Cruise. Or the cowboy with the lizard boots and pearl snap buttons. He was younger, though not quite as attractive. It was all right when she was awake and could control the images, not let it get too out of hand where her body started feeling all hot and achy and thrumming for a touch, any touch.

Slowly a masculine hand pulled down the zipper of her jeans. Another hand, unattached to body, to face, slipped up under her blouse and tugged the padded bra aside. Tweaked one tiny pink-brown nipple. Covered her breast softly. Moved gently down over her abdomen past the elastic waist of her bikini panties . . .

Hell and damnation.

That wasn't all that much fun either. Made her start panting like a bitch in heat so anybody'd know what she was thinking if they walked by her.

Raging fucking hormones.

And they said only guys got horny. Boy, were they wrong! If she didn't get this stuff out of her brain, she'd wind up trying to throw herself all over poor Cruise, and what would that look like, huh?

He probably didn't even like her. She was too young. Looked thirteen, fourteen, he said. Probably too skinny. No boobs. Hardly any hips. She was just a hitchhiker he was taking along to keep him awake while he drove nights. He wouldn't touch her if she begged for it.

The sun dipped through low-lying clouds. The colors over the land smeared unevenly and darkened.

Molly watched the car door on the Chrysler for Cruise. *Wake up.*

The cowboy of the long legs sauntered out the cafe door chewing a toothpick. He never even glanced her way. Molly watched his tight little butt as he circled the building to the back lot where his rig was parked. She sighed to see him go. He'd had thick black curly hair and dark eyes. She would have to dream of him tonight. It was as close as she was going to get to heaven this century.

Mark Killany thought he'd lost Molly's trail for good. He had overslept in Beaumont, cradling the phone receiver on his chest after the wake-up call. Cursing himself upon waking, he hurried from the Holiday Inn to his car, his shirt trailing out the back of his pants. He had needed to shave again, but there hadn't been time. He ran a hand over his grizzled chin now, frowning at how he was slowly losing all control over events in his life. He wasn't exercising, he wasn't shaving enough, his clothes needed an iron run over them.

He crossed the Old and Lost Rivers and thought how apt the name was to his state of mind. If his mind wasn't old and lost, he didn't know what was.

He stopped along the way between Beaumont and Houston, showing Molly's picture. No one had seen her. He kept losing time exiting, parking, walking around to question service-station employees. He had known he was handicapped from the outset, that she'd be ahead of him and gaining ground west each time he chose to stop. But he'd optimistically thought he could find a clearer trail. Trail! He had a wisp. A promise. Not a trail.

Now it was late afternoon, the sun setting in a blaze at his back. He was somewhere between San Antonio and El Paso on Interstate 10, out in the center of the tumbleweed desert, and he hadn't once found a person who had seen his daughter.

A vibration in the rear of his car that he'd noticed earlier, but didn't want to stop to check, now turned to a walloping sound. A flat. Of all the damned luck . . .

He pulled over into the emergency lane and stopped just as the tire went so flat he could hear the car running on the metal rim. Big eighteen-wheelers whooshed past, their wind hot and full of stink. The displaced air from them rocked his car on its wheels.

Mark carefully exited the car, eyes squinted against the ball of fire to the west. He circled to the rear right tire and stooped to inspect it. Shredded. Metal strands showing through the flaps. When was the last time he'd bought tires? he wondered. Sloppy. Not at all like him.

He must hurry.

He popped the trunk, took out the spare and the tools required to change the tire. He sweated during the time-consuming ordeal, threw the ripped tire into the trunk, and wiped his hands on a red rag he kept there.

Now it was nearly dark. Telephone poles marched down his side of the freeway leading straight through the desert. On the other side of the rusted barbed-wire fence he could see nothing but sand and mesquite trees and cacti. He supposed the wire fence was meant to confine cattle, but where were they? West Texas made him feel exposed and insignificant. The sooner he got out of here, the better.

God, he was tired. He was used to hard work, but not to the toll stationary driving took on his muscles. The strain showed in his face shadowed with the day-old beard. His blue eyes were dim as swamp water, his mouth set between twin age lines cut deep into the flesh. Haggard wouldn't even get near to describing the way he was beginning to look.

Once on the road again, he sped toward the steel-gray horizon. How in hell did he think he could find her? The blue Chrysler could easily be in New Mexico by now. For all he knew her ride, the guy with the long hair and beard, could have taken her another route and done anything to her, anything. He could have murdered her and left her body for the buzzards and the sandstorms.

This thought so frightened him he edged the speed-ometer needle past seventy to eighty, eighty-five, racing toward nowhere, lost in West Texas, sure he was now on a mission doomed to failure. First he'd overslept, then lost time on the exits, and now the flat made him lose more precious time.

"Molly, God, Molly, where are you?" he mumbled into the thickening clot of darkness overtaking the car's interi-or.

Got to find her, he thought, a fierceness entering into his attitude that hadn't been there before. Clamping his hands tight on the steering wheel, he drove furiously, bypassing even the speeding truckers who had less reason to reach a destination than he. A line of traffic trailed him and eventually disappeared into the murk of night as headlights began to sprinkle the oncoming lanes.

It was crazy, what he was doing, he admitted that much earlier in the trip. He was always so obsessed with results, and this time he might not have any. He could drive straight into the far Pacific Ocean and still never reach his goal.

But that wouldn't stop him.

Nothing could stop him short of finding his girl.

Cruise drove at a steady fifty-five miles an hour west across the Texas desert. He periodically dipped a big hand into a bag of Cheetos, munching them as he told Molly a story. He had eaten the huevos rancheros in the White Elephant, but still felt hungry as a bear cub fed on berries for a month.

"I had a buddy in Vietnam once," he said, "we called Boots. He had these big goddamned feet, size sixteen or something. He said he'd been called that ever since he was

a kid and he got lost in North Michigan, up in the thumb—
that's a spit of land that heads up toward the Canadian
border—anyway, he was up there with his old man ice
fishing one winter."

"Yeah? Bet that was cold. I've never been up north."

Cruise, a good storyteller who added facial expressions,
sounds, and gestures, shivered and shook himself all over.
"Cold wasn't the word for it, Boots said. He was sent to
look for firewood and a blizzard came up. He was lost,
couldn't find the camp, and he was trying to follow his
footprints—had big feet even back then. But the snow blew
so hard, it was wiping out the trail. He was just lucky to
stumble back in his old man's arms to miss freezing to
death. From then on his family called him Boots.

"So me and Boots, we get caught in the middle of an
enemy attack in 'Nam. Our whole platoon gets scattered.
Guys were falling all around us. We took off together in
one direction and we outsmart the Cong, but we lose our
platoon leader."

"Geez."

Cruise paused to eat a handful of Cheetos. The sound of
the crunching coming through his jaws to his ears reminded
him of walking on little sticks, trying to be quiet. "It was
real bad. All we had were our rifles and side arms. We
didn't have any food or a radio, not even a map or a
compass. But we knew there was going to be a chopper
rescue lift forty miles to the west in four days. We started
heading that way. It was the only choice we had. No
way could we ever find the base, far as we'd been out
on maneuvers."

"Did you have to go four days without food?"

"More or less. We ate roots and shit, but we threw up
most of it, just couldn't keep it down. We had to drink
from stagnant ponds, rice paddies, muddy little streams,

anywhere we could find water. I was a kid then, eighteen, and Boots was older than me. I was tired, pessimistic about our chances of making it. I kept complaining and wanting to stop to rest. But there were Cong everyfuckingwhere. Boots kept telling me I could make it, *we* could make it, we just had to have heart, we had to have faith.

"Then to keep me going, he'd tell me stories . . ."

"Kind of like you tell me, huh?" Molly asked.

"Well, sort of except the stories Boots told were all about how he made it out of the blizzard just because he kept going. Then about being a Boy Scout and wandering off from the troop when camping and falling off a mountain path. Broke his leg. He was lying there on the edge of a cliff, just a kid, and he told me how he had to last out until they found him. I knew these were true stories because Boots was that kind of guy. A regular, gold-plated hero. The best soldier I'd ever known.

"So I kept going, slogging through the jungle like a dazed bull, just putting one foot in front of the other. You couldn't let a guy like Boots down."

"Looks like you made it to the airlift."

Cruise glanced over at her and smiled as if to say, *That's quite evident.* He continued, "On the third day of the trek I was hanging back again and Boots danced off a little way in front of me trying to get me to change my attitude, cheer me up, trying to keep me entertained so I wouldn't think about being hungry, thirsty, scared to death we'd be hit by sniper fire."

Cruise thoughtfully chewed a couple of Cheetos. Crunching sounds. Little sticks underfoot. When he didn't pick up the thread of his story right away, Molly asked, "He was ahead of you and . . . ?"

"Hit a trip mine. Blew him backward through the air."

"Damn."

"Well, we knew we were in dangerous territory. It could have happened to me or to both of us. I ran to him and his legs were gone."

Molly turned her head to the side window, grimacing.

"I held on to him and the last words he said were, 'The cocksuckers got me, didn't they? But you can make it, Cruise. Don't give up now.' I buried him there in the jungle the best I could. Had to dig a spot with my knife and my hands. I remember crying the whole time like a baby. Without Boots I didn't really believe I had any chance of reaching the landing site. I think I was doing most of my crying for myself. He'd pulled me through three days of absolute hell, the hours pure terror, and without him I lost much of my purpose. I just staggered out of there, heading toward where the sun set, not much hope left."

"That was an awful war, wasn't it?" Molly asked.

"Piece of shit war. A war where men were used for cannon fodder and rifle practice. That's what all wars are. I guarantee you I'd never have volunteered—we had a draft then, you know. Anyway, I stopped to drink water once and when I looked in the pool I thought I saw Boots behind me, laughing. He was saying, 'Keep going, Cruise! Don't stop yet.'

"I jumped and turned around, but he wasn't there, of course. I guess I was getting punch drunk from fatigue and no food. I was seeing things. But later in the day I saw him again. Just ahead of me, clowning, smiling, telling me I could make it if I'd keep trying.

"By that time I knew I had to be hallucinating, but I was talking to him, cursing him for dying on me, telling him to get the fuck out of my way."

Cruise folded the top of the Cheetos bag and handed it to Molly. Couldn't stand the sound anymore. She took it as if in a trance and held it in her lap careful not to crinkle the bag or make any noise.

"Well, I walked all night because every time I'd fall down and try to sleep, there was Boots's ghost urging me to get up, to keep walking. It was terrifying. He just wouldn't stop coming around. By the next morning I was totally out of my head, talking to Boots just like he was at my side. I came to a grassy field and fell down. I must have passed out. Then the next thing I hear are chopper blades churning the air and making the ground shake, and Boots right next to me coming to his feet, yelling for me to hurry, we're gonna be rescued. 'RESCUE,' he screamed. 'We made it, Cruise, we made it!'

"I don't know how I got to my feet, but next thing I knew I was running and out of this field comes a dozen other guys, all of us heading for that chopper fluttering down out of the morning sun like a huge green glittering butterfly. I see Boots ahead of me, climbing up with the other men, and I get on board with him. But when I turn around, he's not there, he's nowhere to be seen. I started hauling on the rescue team, asking them what happened to Boots, and they can see, I guess, I'm outta my head. They lift off and I look out the open side door."

"Boots is on the ground, you see him?"

"Yeah. Waving good-bye. Like his mission was to get me rescued and he was ready to really lie down and stay dead now."

"Wow. That's some ghost story," Molly said.

Cruise turned to her and this time he wasn't smiling. "It wasn't a ghost story." His voice was ominous in its warning. "It's the truth. Boots got me home. I owe him my life."

"Well, sure . . ."

"He was the best guy I ever knew. He didn't deserve to die that way and end up in a nameless grave."

"Well, of course not . . ."

"You don't understand. You weren't even born yet. It was a stinking, sadistic war and we didn't even win it, even with guys like Boots on our side. We fucking gave up. Something Boots never did. Even after death."

Molly felt a wave of intensity in the dark car that came off Cruise like invisible heat. She had never heard him cuss so much before. He scared her into silence.

"Open me a Coke, will you?"

Molly lifted the Igloo cooler's top and took out a bottle. She uncapped it and handed it to him. It was lukewarm. "My dad was in Vietnam," she said carefully. "But he never talked about it."

"I shouldn't have either." He upended the Coke and drank several swallows. "Talking about Boots gets me depressed." He glanced at Molly and saw she looked nerved up, on standby for any sort of emergency action. "It's all right," he said, changing his tone of voice so that it wasn't so hard and unrelenting. "That's one story I shouldn't have told you. I hate thinking about Boots over there in Vietnam. I never could tell them where he was buried. I handed over his dog tags and tried to forget about him. I don't think I'll ever forget, though."

Molly watched the road ahead without comment.

Cruise tried to turn his attention to his driving. They were passing through land where uniformly flat-topped mountains stood off to the right and left of the freeway. They were a hundred seventy miles east of El Paso and he had not mentioned going down into Mexico to Molly. If she didn't want to, he'd make her, so it didn't make any difference to tell her his plans.

They passed a small hill where a diorama was set up. Cruise pointed to it. "Out here in the middle of nowhere," he said.

"What is it?"

"A diorama. That's what the sign says. I guess it means some kind of stationary play. See the crosses and the figures? Supposed to represent the crucifixion."

"Oh. I don't know much about religion. Dad never made me go to church or anything."

"More's the pity. Everyone needs to start off with a little religion. Especially if you're going to give it up."

"Have you given it up?"

"Long time ago." He had an image of his father beating his brothers and sisters. Crucifixion in the home. Diorama come to life. All the bleeding Jesuses. Where was God when anyone needed Him? Nowhere. That was the point.

The highway began to cut through the Apache Mountains. The sides of the cut-throughs were pale, sparkling in the starlight. The mountains were made of shell or limestone, Cruise decided, although he knew he didn't know shit about geology. For all he knew they were made of diamond dust and Kryptonite. Up the mountainsides were black dots of shrubs that hugged the dry land like scabs on a dog. The earth was brown and rust. As a wind came up, Cruise saw tumbleweeds rolling side by side in the roadside ditch. Outside of Stanton, Texas, a welcome sign read HOME OF 3000 FRIENDLY PEOPLE AND A FEW OLD SOREHEADS.

Molly had read it too. She chuckled and mumbled, "Soreheads. Cool beans."

Cruise thought about the Apaches who roamed this land on horseback, following buffalo herds. Now semis prowled the roads going east and west. Some of the mountains in view had sheared-off tops, some few were pointed skyward like huge thrusting breasts of earth awaiting a touch from the hand of a giant. Cruise wondered if a glacier had come through and lopped off some of the mountaintops and bypassed others. There seemed no other explanation for the two distinct shapes. If they were made from volcanic action, then it meant some volcanoes erupted, others didn't. He wished sometimes he knew more about things, about the *world*. There were great chunks of information lost to him because of his lack of formal schooling. To hell with it. He knew all he needed to know.

The freeway began to rise up through the mountains. Plains stretched out behind them. Long lazy clouds streaked the night sky blowing to the south, strobe-lit when the moonlight hit them, moving fast. As he drove off the prairie into the Apaches, the four lanes were bounded on one side by telephone poles, sentinels of civilization that cut through West Texas carrying thousands of voices.

Cruise noticed the names of the exits for the few cities that tried to survive out here in the blistering southwest: Van Horn, Kent, Boracho Station, Plateau, Michigan Flat, Allamore, Hot Wells. Before they reached El Paso they'd pass Sierra Blanca.

"There's a couple of pumpkin trucks," Cruise said, pointing to the oncoming lanes.

"Pumpkin trucks?"

"Truckers' lingo for those orange trucks owned by Schneider. If you see a semi that hauls cars stacked on two levels, they're called parking lots. If one truck is hauling two trailers, that's piggy-backing."

"Truckers have their own language, don't they?"

Cruise said, "Rest areas—they're called pickle parks because that's where four-wheelers stop for picnics. You hear a trucker saying he's looking for a pickle park, now you know what he means. He wants to pull over and rest awhile."

"What's some of the other stuff they say?"

"They call prostitutes Lot Lizards. That other girl at the truck stop in Mobile, remember her?" Molly nodded her head. "She was a Lot Lizard. Truckers call them that behind their backs, of course. I suppose it comes from Lounge Lizards. Some guys have a sticker on their side windows that shows a lizard inside a circle with a line drawn through it. That means they're not in the market. When they want sex, they talk to them nice, and call them baby dolls. Or commercial company. The girls don't seem to mind that."

Molly laughed. "That's good," she said. "That's what they are, all right."

"We'll stop at the next truck stop for a few minutes, stretch our legs. I'll turn on the CB, let you hear them talk."

"Okay."

"You're having a good time?" He glanced at her.

"Better than I ever had in school," she said.

"Good, that's good. I want you to enjoy yourself."

He passed by two truck stops that were deserted, dark, windblown. Cracked windows, broken doors, rusting fuel pumps. "Guess they couldn't make it out here in the desert and hills."

When he saw a billboard for Love's Truck Stop, he took the exit. "Appropriate name, isn't it? You'd think it was, but most of the Love stops are just convenience stores with a little fast-food eating area. Never much going on at them. Not much love happening."

"I could stand to walk around a little anyway."

"I've got to get a fill-up too." He pulled into the brightly lit truck stop with the big yellow Love's sign. He filled the tank while Molly waited inside the car. "Go ahead, I'll catch up with you in a minute," he said, switching on the CB to static. "Here's a twenty for the gas. Pay them for me, will you?"

He circled to the back and parked a little ways from five trucks lined up on the tarmac. He watched Molly cross to the convenience store while he adjusted the radio. He listened for the sound of a Lot Lizard offering her wares on the CB. No such luck. The truckers were alone, beefing about California runs and the need to get loads there on time. Cruise flicked off the CB and got out of the car. He breathed deeply of cool, dry air that cleared his sinuses and dried his mucus membranes. Ever since they'd left San Antonio, his nose had been drying up like laundry hung in the hot sun. It made it almost painful to breathe through his nostrils.

He thought about Boots, then put his ghost away. He thought about Indians on ponies whipping up dust storms across the valley floor. As much as he hated Texas and Texas lawmen, he never failed to relish the past he imagined lingering just at the edge of modern society out in the desert regions. There were worlds beneath worlds, even if they couldn't be seen.

Despite what he told Molly, he liked the idea of ghosts, did not think them macabre or frightening. If the ghost of an Apache warrior strode up to him right this second, he wouldn't be all that surprised.

It was Indian land, stolen from them, drenched in their blood and tears. He felt them all around him and was comforted in thinking they watched the white man's progress through the sacred mountains. At least the travelers weren't alone with just the desolate landscape and the dome of the night sky pressing down overhead.

He took another deep dry aching breath before moving toward where Molly waited in the building surrounded by reflected yellow Love light. He strained to hear the hissing from the neon tubes but could hear nothing beyond the throaty idle of semi-truck engines.

He spied Molly coming out the ladies' room door and waved her over. "How about an apple?" He led her to a refrigerated counter and gestured for the clerk to give him two red delicious apples.

Molly took the fruit and bit into it as they strolled over to the coffee machine. Cruise poured a big cup, asked if she wanted any.

"No, thanks." She worked at demolishing the apple.

Outside again, Cruise sipped at the coffee. He frowned at the taste. Burned. Old. Pissed him off when the fuckers didn't keep the coffee fresh. "No Lot Lizards here tonight," he said. "They'll be all over El Paso. It's a wide-open city because it's so close to the border. Cops can't control the place."

"Are we far from there?"

"Another hundred miles or so. You ever been to Mexico?"

"New Mexico?"

"No, *old* Mexico."

"I haven't been anywhere much. You're not going to Mexico, are you?" She sounded suddenly worried.

"I was thinking of crossing the border at El Paso. Just for one night." When Molly didn't say anything as she climbed into the passenger seat he said, "You're not on a tight schedule or anything, are you? I'll get you to California."

"I don't care. It's your car."

Cruise set the coffee cup into the holder on the floorboard between the seats. It was horse piss coffee, hardly worth drinking. He'd like to take it back inside and pour it all over someone's head. Instead, he pulled back onto the freeway. "You'll like it," he said. "Me-hi-co. You ever see Richard Gere in *Breathless*? He was driving the stolen Porsche and beating the steering wheel in time to a Jerry Lee Lewis song? Well, he said Mexico like that. *Me-hi-co. Me and Monica in Me-hi-co*. There's a little town over the border I'd like you to see."

He could tell she was in a silent stew over his pronounce-
ment. She might even want to leave him and catch another
ride out of El Paso. He'd never let her, of course, but she
might *want* to. He wouldn't know until they got there. He
wasn't sure yet how much of a hold he had over the girl.
He certainly didn't want to kill her so soon. Wasn't time
yet. He wasn't finished with her.

He contentedly munched on the juicy apple, drank the
bad coffee, and thought about Mexican whores. Skinny
ones, fat ones, dark brown skin or light cream, raven-haired,
but, most of all, willing.

And he still needed money.

Soon he would kill to get it.

Molly slept as Cruise drove toward the huddled lights
spread at the feet of a mountain range. Van Horn. Not
far to El Paso.

A night breeze blew through his partially lowered window. It swept aside his long hair and caressed his neck. The
metal of the knife he kept hidden there cooled into a thin
strip of chilled flesh at the base of his scalp. Sometimes
the glue of the Velcro patch made him itch. Sometimes
it abraded his skin and caused a red, bumpy irritation.
And sometimes the glue came loose after he shampooed
his hair. He carried extra Velcro pads in his travel bag.
Every so often he had to take a Bic shaver to scrape off
the bristly hair that tried to grow back, then replace the old
Velcro patch with a new one.

He reached behind his head now and checked how well
the knife was holding. Two edges of the Velcro were loose
and the little knife sagged. Tonight in El Paso when he
bathed, he would shave his hair there and replace the patch.

During the next hours on the road Cruise indulged in
fantasies and memories of his kills. The miles disappeared.

Time ceased to exist. As he approached El Paso, his mind wrenched itself into the present. First there was a string of lights on the horizon, a sparkling necklace of pearls strewn all in a row. Nearer the city the lights were scattered across the foot of the mountains like multifaceted jewels. The mountains to the rear of the city blocked out the stars and moon. As Cruise drove, he watched the skyline and saw a pure white sickle moon emerge, suspended low over the city. If the Comanches, Kiowas, Apaches, and Lipan Indians who roamed West Texas living on buffalo before the mid-1800s were to ride into El Paso today, the brilliance of the lights would stun them into either reverent silence or a mad fury to destroy the invading infidels.

Interstate 10's twin lanes going west soon expanded to four lanes and filled with heavier traffic. Minutes before he saw the huge green Metro Truck Stop sign, Cruise woke Molly. "We're here," he said. "Now I'll show you a *real* truck stop. You're gonna love it."

Molly readjusted the reclining seat so that she was sitting up. She rubbed her face and spoke in a groggy voice. "Big, isn't it?"

"Largest city between Houston and Albuquerque. By the time you get to El Paso you're starved for a city and after you leave it, you starve a long while more until you reach another of any size. It's the last outpost. On trail drives back in the heyday of the Old West, El Paso must have seemed like paradise to the cowboys. The last stop for hundreds of miles in any direction. It still is."

Cruise took an exit. Molly grew more interested in her surroundings, craning her head to look out the window. Cruise turned left on an overpass. Not far from the freeway he pointed to the Metro sign. "That's it," he said.

"Jesus. It looks like a shopping mall."

Cruise grinned. "That's kind of what it is. Wait till you see." He knew he sounded like a carnival barker trying to get the unsuspecting to come into the geek house, talk the innocents into watching a boy with strong teeth bite off the head of a chicken. And that was exactly what he was doing too. Luring Molly into his world where the lights burned all night, bartering for sex rampant and quite evident, liaisons being made everywhere you turned. Beneath the lights and the clean rest rooms and the aisles of polished glass cases, there was a lurid, steamy world where you could buy anything your heart desired—women, boys, radio and CB equipment, hot merchandise off the trucks, drugs, or a combination of any sort of entertainment you might want. Or need. This outpost town with its Old West flavor offered the unwary danger, the innocent an education, and the jaded new thrills.

Cruise loved it. He reveled in it. Where anything goes, Cruise felt unbound. Life here came with a promise of an eternal playground, and the advertisement wasn't a lie. If you couldn't find satisfaction in El Paso, it wasn't to be had.

Cruise parked to the side of the restaurant area, not far from where the big rigs lined up ten deep and twenty long. Trucks pulled in and out, behemoths lumbering slowly and making exquisitely precise turns or backing-up maneuvers. That was just one parking lot. The entire complex had three more. Across a fence west of the restaurant he saw a couple of small sleazy trailer houses and billboards announcing ADULT VIDEOS, MAGAZINES, BOOKS.

"Come on inside, I want you to see this place." Although he didn't tell her, he also wanted to find a Lot Lizard who went by the name of Chloe. He really needed a couple of hours with a woman other than his young witness.

He waited in front of the grille of the car for Molly. She bounced along beside him like a young athlete limbering up for a race. He could feel her energy like an aura that touched his skin and made it hum in tune to her high-pitched current. He grinned all the way inside the glass doors of the Metro.

Once inside what appeared to be a busy lobby, Cruise guided Molly to the right toward the restaurant. Though it was three o'clock in the morning, the tables and booths were full of truckers and travelers. Sounds rang from the busy kitchen to mingle with dozens of conversations, phone calls going on at the booths, waitresses taking orders, bus-boys clearing tables. Cruise looked around the room for Chloe, but she wasn't there.

Cruise ordered two coffees at the counter, swirled on his seat to grin at Molly. "What do you think so far?"

"Does no one sleep around here?"

"Oh, they sleep, out in their cabs, but these are the men who just got into town or they're getting ready to leave it. You can walk in here anytime of day or night and find it this way." He gazed around at the commotion, drinking it in, letting it revive him after his own long haul of driving. It was like getting an electrical charge. His weariness receded, his brain woke to the various sounds, sights, and smells. There was the scent of cinnamon rolls, coffee brewed fresh, the early morning smell of bacon and fried eggs. Now if he could just spend a short time doing the Big Nasty with Chloe everything would be perfect.

"I think I'm going to need this." Molly used both hands to steady the cup of coffee at her lips. "This place is hopping."

"Drink up and we'll go explore the rest of it."

Outside the restaurant after paying their bill, Cruise took Molly across the lobby to the travel store. They saw Indian blankets and headdresses, pottery, Navajo turquoise jewelry, tapes, video movies, books, souvenirs. Cruise bought a hair comb made of an abalone shell. He waited as Molly thanked him and used it to hold one side of her red hair from her face.

"Now let's see what else they have," he said, hustling her into the open lobby area once more.

With a proprietary air he pointed out the ice cream shop, the barber, the shoe shine stand, the full-size theater, the TV room, the knife shop, rest rooms, showers, a game room, and a laundry. One area was unlike any he had found in other truck stops across the Southwest. There was a glass-enclosed room with a sign on the door that said simply, THE QUIET ROOM. Inside were pastel flowered sofas and comfortable chairs, a long polished table with more chairs pushed around it, plants, bare walls, magazines scattered around. In there a trucker could relax and pretend he was in his own living room at home, all sounds from outside masked, dampened, set at a distance. There was no TV there, nothing to infringe on the feeling of womblike isolation.

In each shop and room he and Molly looked, Cruise watched for the short black cap of hair that made Chloe stand out from other women. She was like a shadow, sometimes here, sometimes there, always on the move. He doubted he could find her, but he wished he could; he hoped desperately to see her in every female face he saw. His testicles tightened at the thought of her paper-white skin, her shiny black hair and eyes. She was one girl he never felt the urge to kill. He saw her as seldom as once a year on his travels, but their coming together stayed with him for months afterward. She knew tricks no one else had even thought of yet.

Behind a jewelry counter selling silver necklaces, he

showed Molly the four clocks on the wall that gave all standard U.S. time zones.

There were people milling everywhere. Men getting their boots shined, buying jewelry trinkets, doing laundry, watching television, playing games, eating ice cream cones. Some of them just sat on the benches placed throughout the lobby, watching the traffic ebb and flow. Some stood talking in an open line of phone booths to their dispatchers or their wives at home. But nowhere did he see the woman he really needed. She was probably in some dark sleeper in a rumbling cab, showing a trucker the time of his life.

"Seen enough?" The tour had taken them half an hour. He was tired of playing the guide.

"This is incredible," Molly said, staring openmouthed as she tried to assimilate all the strange goings-on happening simultaneously within the truck stop complex. "This sure isn't like the White Elephant Café," she added. "This isn't like *anything* I've ever seen before."

Cruise was as pleased as he would have been had he created the place from scratch for her amusement. At the double entrance doors leading outside again, they passed two young couples talking together in an animated fashion. Cruise touched Molly's arm lightly and nodded toward them.

"What?" Molly asked.

Once outside Cruise said, "Lot Lizards and their dates."

"Really?" She turned entirely around and gazed back. "But those girls look like college students or something. How do you know?"

"I overheard them discussing price. El Paso, I told you, is a wide-open kind of town. It has equal parts of rawness and sophistication. Not all Lizards look like your regular street hookers. Those girls probably do go to college. But they can make enough out here at the truck stop on one weekend to pay their tuitions." *And you should see Chloe*, he thought. *She looks like a senator's wife on vacation.*

"Well, they fooled the hell out of me."

Cruise laughed. "If you had any hell in you you'd have recognized what they were."

Molly frowned, sore at being caught out. "I know enough," she said. "I'm not a total dweeb."

"No one said you were, kid. But the world is wider and stranger than you would ever believe. There's more goes on in it than you can possibly imagine."

"I'll agree with you on that. I mean that one girl wore glasses and preppy clothes. And she's a Lot Lizard. I'd never've guessed that in a million years."

"Come on, and let's listen to the CB. The girls are all over the channels." Since there was no chance of finding Chloe, he might as well continue being Molly's host into the underworld of the night.

Installed inside the car, Molly adjusted her seat to a half recline, her gray eyes closed to slits. She watched Cruise. He turned up the volume on channel nineteen, the trucker's channel. The voice traffic was a horrendous mishmash. Cruise turned down the squelch control. They listened.

"What about a guy with twenty-five in his pocket? Anybody else for commercial company?" The voice was a woman's, slightly accented. "Mexican," Cruise said.

"Where you at, Baby Doll? Come on over here to the 76."

"Can't do it. 76 has security. Meet me in the bar parking lot next to the Metro."

"You pretty clean?"

There was a pause as if the woman was trying to decide

how to answer that. "Yeah," she said finally. "I just got here."

"You ain't gonna give me anything to take home to my ole lady she wouldn't want to have, are you?"

"That's a negatory. What's your handle?" the woman asked.

"Call me Sugar."

"Back?"

"They call me Sugar."

Another male voice overrode Sugar's. He said, "Spend the night with me?"

The same woman replied, "Come over here, we'll talk about it, okay?"

"Let's talk it over now."

"Come on down to ten, one-oh. This is Melody. If you want a good massage, get all your muscles relieved, come down to ten, we'll talk."

Cruise reached out and clicked the channel tuner to ten. Melody's voice came on immediately. "That all-nighter, are you there? Come back."

"Hey, baby, what you want for all night with Big Hooch here?"

"Back?"

"I want you all night. I want you to sleep with me."

"That'll be a hundred twenty-five."

"Does that include everything?"

"Whole body massage. It's well worth it. You'll be relaxed, not tired."

"I'll see you in a few minutes then. I gotta fix my radio first."

"Call me back on ten when you're ready."

The channel went silent. Cruise flicked back to channel nineteen. Melody and another girl calling herself Candy put out their calls. "Anybody else for commercial company, come on."

One man said, "Any ladies out there want to go to Shakey's?"

Someone answered, "Who the hell, male or female, wants to go to Shakey's?" He sounded incredulous.

Another man remarked, "Sounds like a goddamned parched monkey to me."

A third man said, "Best soap opera I heard all week."

Another voice cut in, "Anybody need any electronic work done on their radio, come back to the Electronic Man."

While Cruise and Molly listened in, they heard handles like Hannibal, Top Dollar, Shaker, Yankee Doodle, and of course, Sugar and Big Hooch, the fellow who wanted Melody for the night and the full body massage.

"They're everywhere," Molly said, sitting up in the seat to peer out the windshield as if she'd find truckers and the Lot Lizards strolling the paved parking area. Except for diners going to and from the restaurant, she was disappointed.

"You won't see them out there. All the action's here on the CB. You heard Melody. They have to go to a specific place to meet her. These guys are in their cabs setting up the times, the prices, what they want to get."

"There must have been a hundred guys talking on there."

"At least," Cruise said.

"How many of them do you think one of those girls takes, uh, care of?"

"Who knows? Ten, twenty a night. No telling." Cruise turned down the CB volume and reclined his seat back. He lay like that a full minute before speaking again. "Did you see that sign inside the truck stop for the guided tours?"

"No."

"For ten bucks they'll pick you up here and take you over the border shopping in Juárez, then bring you back. Quite a bargain."

"I didn't see it," she repeated.

"Not that we'd want to go on a guided tour. I know more about life south of the border than they do, probably. Want to go with me down there when it gets night again?"

"Uh . . . I don't know . . ."

"Just for one night. I'll take you to a place I know. The natives are friendly. You can eat real Mexican food, see the sights. You liked this truck stop, wait till you see Mexico." He thought that might convince her.

"You don't really need company down in Mexico," she said carefully. "Maybe I should see about another ride . . ."

Cruise nearly lost his temper and said something unforgivable. Like what a snot-nosed kid she was. Like hadn't he taken care of her this far? Hadn't made a pass, hadn't asked anything from her, hadn't tried to scare her. Like who did she think she was trying to ruin his plans? She was his witness. She was *his*. And until he cut her goddamned throat she'd stay his.

But he said none of this. He just lay quietly waiting for her to come around. Because if she didn't, she'd be going to Mexico anyway, but she'd be bound hand and foot, lying on the floorboard with a rag stuck in her mouth.

After a short pause he heard her draw a deep breath and twist in her seat until she faced him. "Well, I guess it wouldn't matter, really. We'll be back on the road for California in a day or so, you said. And you were right, I'm not on a schedule or anything. I don't actually have any pressing plans or people waiting for me."

Cruise rose up in the seat and leaning over, patted her folded hands that lay like cold rocks in her lap. "That's great. I knew you'd want to come. Now how's 'bout we get a little shut eye? It's going to be dawn soon. Too soon."

He switched off the CB and silence intruded on them like the boom of an ocean wave until their ears adjusted to the lack of squeal and crackle. Cruise draped the towel over his eyes. "Tomorrow we'll get a shower," he said.

"A real shower?"

"Absolutely. With soap and water, the whole shooting match. Even real towels."

"God, that'd be good."

He heard her seat reclining. His smile stretched grotesquely behind the cover of the kitchen towel. He amused himself with an image of her naked, wet, slick hair plastered to her head. He would like to stand her out in the desert beneath that sickle moon poised over El Paso's corruption, stand her naked there and dump a few gallons of purified water over her head until she shivered and trembled with newfound fear at what he might do to her. He'd like to see her turn and run, like to chase her like a jackrabbit across the desert floor, see her fall helpless, begging mercy.

Sleep came to muffle the edge of his imagination. It turned his dream into nightmare where the naked girl was armed with an Indian's spear tipped with flint, feathers dangling from a leather throng attached to the end. She menaced him, laughed at how small his knife was, how it disappeared in the thickness of his great hand. She threw the spear. It sliced through the air, singing *tum, tum, tum*, a death song, narrowly missed him, stuck quivering in the hard-packed ground. When he turned back to her, she had a bow, an arrow tautly strung, and meant to end his days. His nights! The arrow released even as he screamed for her not to kill him, and it sang on the wind, *tum, tum, tum, tum*, a death song that meant to end his days . . . his nights . . .

• • •

Molly lay in the reclining car seat with her eyes closed, heart bumping heavy and slow. She experienced the mental equivalent of gnawing at a pesky hangnail. *Mexico.* She had acquiesced to Cruise's wishes, but even now her thoughts turned over a fiery pit of protest. Somewhere deep inside, she *knew* she should not go. Going with Cruise—still a virtual stranger to her despite the stories he had told about his life—gave over to him her freedom. She would have no one to turn to in a foreign country if for some reason she wished to escape his company. She could not speak Spanish. She didn't know the customs or what was expected of her in Mexico. Did she need a passport, a visa? God, she was still so stupid, but at least she knew it. And she might be dumber yet to put herself into Cruise's hands, dependent upon him to protect her. She was not yet convinced she should.

In the States she could always walk away from Cruise, get another ride in a truck stop or service station. Or she could appeal to someone for help if something went wrong between them. But in Mexico, helpless, disadvantaged, she must rely on his good intentions. The worry stemmed from that. For she didn't know for sure what his intentions were. Oh, he had not made any untoward move and he had not said a word to intentionally frighten her—just the opposite—yet . . . yet . . . It was risky, wasn't it, to give herself into his total care? She liked him. She was attracted to him, who wouldn't be? But still . . .

It was all academic now. She had agreed to go. She must go. To refuse at this point would create a fracas, and she didn't want to alienate him. She *did* like him, found him intriguing and strange. He exerted a pull on her she couldn't deny. It wasn't sexual, not exactly, not *all* the time, although that worked into the equation. It was more as if she had fallen under a spell, charmed as a cobra in a basket lured into the sunlight by the notes from a haunting flute.

Cruise was teaching her about a world she had never known existed. It was an underground night world where people behaved impulsively, and in ways they might not behave during the day. Truckers and Lot Lizards and travelers who crisscrossed the country, they were all bound together in a neon-lit world that hummed while the rest of humanity slept unaware in their beds. They had different agendas. They lived so unconventionally.

She liked it. This new world opened doors and led down dark passages she didn't know were there. She wanted to see it, to walk with the night people and be one of them. The things she had witnessed in the Metro Truck Stop ignited her curiosity even further. The voices clamoring on the CB sparked her prurient interest. It was like a voyage through a science fiction movie filmed in sepia tones. These were humans engaged in activities normally done during the day, except for the sex, activities like eating, laundry, bathing, driving. It was an upside-down world, an Alice in Wonderland place where the unexpected experience waited around the next corner.

If she wished to prolong her contact with that world, she must accompany Cruise across the border. It might be a harmless trip, full of exciting characters and revelations, but it also involved chance; there might be danger there.

She squirmed in the seat, her spine aching, her shoulders pinched in the confines of the seat back. So tired. Sleepy. Wished she had a bed to rest in.

Oh, well, it was pointless to wish for what she didn't have. Pointless to indulge in self-recrimination now. She had said she would go. She had sealed her fate. She must continue trusting Cruise, and rid herself of the nagging warning voice that argued against risk. Hadn't she already broken ties with normal society by leaving home? She'd dropped out of school, turned her back on her father and his rules, accepted the idea, however much it scared her, that she would sell herself in order to survive. Could a side trip into Mexico be such a bad thing?

It was just that . . . just that she didn't know what to expect. How to behave. What might happen to her.

Or why it was important to Cruise to leave the country right at this time. As if pursued by something invisible, something threatening at his back. She didn't know why she felt this way, but it was her impression that Cruise identified with the night world for more reason than that the light hurt his eyes, as he claimed. There *had* to be more to it than that.

To calm herself, Molly imagined a lovely time shopping for sombreros and serapes, eating exotic foods, watching the sun set over a foreign horizon while sipping a cold, imported bottle of Coca-Cola on a veranda surrounded by flowering plants.

It would be all right. She would have a glorious time. She was about to become a world traveler, thanks to Cruise. He wouldn't let anything bad happen to her.

Anything bad. Happen to her.

THE FOURTH NIGHT

The evening crept over El Paso with chill stealth. Cruise stirred in the car seat, eyelids fluttering. Like a predator that does its hunting at night, his consciousness returned as the sun left bloodred streaks west behind the mountains. He came fully awake and rubbed down his bare arms. He and Molly had left the windows partially open for fresh air that now had turned cool without the sun's rays to heat it.

Cruise needed a sweater. He looked at Molly where she slept scrunched up into an uncomfortable fetal position, knees pulled to her chest. She was cold too. Tonight he would rent rooms so they could get the kink out of their abused bodies. At least a room would protect them from tomorrow's nippy-aired dusk. A mattress to sleep on would feel like a cloud.

"Molly?"

Her knees slid to the floorboard and she stretched, eyes still closed tightly. He could see the outline of her bra through her white blouse. Small. Sweet.

"Molly, wake up. It's time for breakfast and a shower."

That woke her completely. She blinked at him and licked her lips. She cleared her throat, wrapped her arms around herself. "Cold." More a statement of fact than a complaint.

"Do you have a jacket or a sweater?"

Molly shook her head. "Forgot. It's never very cold in Florida. I just forgot. California's supposed to be warm too."

"I'll buy you one in Mexico. Ready to go inside?"

She sat and depressed the lever so her seat was upright. "I need my blue bag if I'm going to take a shower."

Cruise was already out of the car. He reached around the doorpost to unlock the back door of the Chrysler. He drew out the carrying bag, locked, and slammed shut the door. He walked to the front of the car and handed it to her. "Wait for me inside at the restaurant. I've got to get my gear."

Molly took her bag and walked off slowly toward the truck stop complex. Cruise waited until she was a good distance away before inserting the trunk key and giving it a twist. He didn't want her to see the case of bottled water, the stack of towels. There was no way he could explain it to her.

He took out a brown leather-and-cloth satchel and closed the trunk. Inside the Metro he found Molly at one of the booths near the restaurant entrance. She sat hunched like a derelict over a cup of coffee. Her hair was wild and needed combing. Her clothes were rumpled from having been slept in. There were pale blue circles marring the skin beneath her fine gray eyes. The trip was taking its toll. As used as he was to travel and living on the road, he sometimes looked as bad or worse than she did now. He felt a camaraderie, a closeness born of shared circumstance. He always identified with the kids when they grew weary and beaten. They needed him more than they knew. They were after all just kids. Gullible, trusting, thinking themselves worldly wise, but lacking nearly all the proper survival instincts. He kept them up nights disrupting their sleep patterns until finally they were vulnerable, fully under his power, easily persuaded, effortlessly *duped*. But he shared their fatigue, an old friend he knew well.

Cruise ordered big breakfasts for them. Eggs, hash browns, bacon, sausage, biscuits. The food wasn't as great as it should have been for the price, but it filled and warmed them. Molly was incommunicado until after she'd eaten. Once the blood flowed back into the lightly freckled skin of her face, she was able to smile, to talk to him.

"We're still going to Mexico?" she asked.

He knew she'd already committed herself and probably would not back out now. He said. "You're going to like it, I promise. I'll get a hotel tonight so you can rest up."

He saw a look of concern cross her face before she was able to mask it. "Don't worry," he said, giving the impression that he had read her mind. "You'll have your own room. Alone."

She ducked her head and stared down at her hands. "Thanks. I don't know how I can repay you for all these meals and a room and all . . ."

"No problem. You don't owe me." *You* do, he thought, *but I'm not supposed to say it.*

"C'mon, let's go hit the showers. I've got half a week's worth of dirt to wash off." He swung his bag from where he had dropped it on the seat beside him. Molly followed to the cash register, stood idly looking around while he paid. At another desk he anted up a twenty-dollar deposit for the keys to two shower rooms. They each carried a bundle of towels, washcloths, small wrapped bars of soap. He showed Molly to her cubicle, handed over the key, and left her. "Meet you in the lobby later."

Once locked inside the small bathroom, Cruise shed his clothes quickly. Nakedness felt delicious. He had worn his clothes so long, riding in them, sleeping in them, that it was like shedding a hard shell to find new skin beneath. He carefully detached the knife from the Velcro and placed it on the counter. For some seconds he gazed down at the glittering stainless-steel blade. It felt odd to have this extension of him separated from his flesh. If he touched it now he'd feel the warmth of body temperature. Once the metal cooled it stopped being a part of him and returned to its real state as a deadly weapon. He wrenched his gaze from it, feeling time passing too swiftly.

He squinted in anticipation as he ripped off the patch painfully from the short hair growing back on his scalp. He stood leaning on his hands at the sink, staring into green eyes the color of spring grass.

"You need money," he told his reflection. "Do it here or do it in Mexico, but do it."

He nodded at himself, confirming his resolve. He'd do it. When he had first started this life, he had sometimes waited too long, waited until all his money was gone and he was destitute. That narrowed his choices. He had to hit anyone at hand just to make sure he could survive. These days he did not wait so long unless there was a witness like Molly along, someone he had in training and could not afford to frighten too early in the game. He knew now how much money was left. He'd noticed when he paid the breakfast bill. Thirty-five dollars. That was enough for gas and Cokes, nothing more.

Tonight, late tonight, in Mexico, he would find someone with money. He had decided against an out-and-out murder in front of Molly. She wasn't ready for that just yet. But he did have a plan that involved her. She would misinterpret the scene just as he wanted her to. She'd be even more in his debt after tonight.

He turned on the shower and stepped in before the temperature was adjusted. He liked the cold shock of water anyway. Then he let it run hot, so hot his skin pinked and he was breathing steam as he lathered his body and washed it down.

By the time he was dried, the patch on his scalp newly shaven and Velcroed, freshly dressed, all his things put away, he had been in the white-tiled shower room for over an hour. He stared once more into his own eyes searching for something he had never yet found—that remorse they all said he should feel. *They*, of course, were fools and sons of fools and sons of bitches too. But that did not keep him from looking, when there was a mirror and privacy available, for the pitying heart the world told him he walked without. In a curious way he thought perhaps *they*, those experts on man's troubles, were wrong. He *knew* he had a heart, though full of pity, he sincerely doubted. It didn't occur often, not enough obviously to convince him, but sometimes when he looked down into those luminous green depths of soul he thought he saw a tiny man staring back at him, a miniature Cruise, if you will, older, stooped, *changed*, but Cruise all the same. He was locked behind the wide orbs, and that small man waved at him to signal the start of something, a beginning of warmth, of compassion, of *humaneness*.

Today the reflection was not there. The eyes went on unblinkingly staring back from heartless, remorseless, unfeeling voids. This meant he was all right. He was sane and safe from guilt, that bag of snakes he had discarded so many years in the past. There was no little man in there smiling like the Devil himself, smug bastard, waving him to enter the dark passageway that led to the place where he must shoulder responsibility.

Good. Most excellent, dude, as the kids said. He didn't need to encounter anything inside himself that so far he'd been able to live without.

He found Molly hanging over a video game watching a grown man trying to beat a rigged machine. "Boo," Cruise said softly, coming close behind her. She smelled of Safeguard soap and baby powder. Maybe the baby powder was her underarm deodorant. It was faint but lovely. He inhaled as she flinched and turned to him.

"Oh, hi!"

"Been waiting long? Ready to shake this place?"

"No, uh, yeah."

Cruise smiled and, taking her arm, led her from the Metro Truck Stop into the settling gloom of another clear starry night meant for the road.

Over the border into Mexico Cruise moved away in his mind from the raucous hilarity that was Juárez. He knew Molly was excited by the strange tongue spoken by the people in Juárez, by the filled dilapidated buses hobbling through the potholed streets, by the many lights, and the hordes of people tumbling into storefronts and clubs. He had been here too many times to find a scintilla of excitement about the Mexicans anymore. He thought of them as a subspecies if he thought of them at all. The bright ones headed across the border despite the risks, and it was the poor and stupid ones left behind to scratch a living from the tourists. He despised Juárez as he despised all the border towns. They were traps for Americans, full of laughing brown liars and cheaters who spent all their waking hours trying to part a man from his money in one way or another, while not so secretly envying him his freedom, country, and income.

Cruise spent as little time as he could getting through Juárez and onto the road outside town that led back east along the border. When he failed to answer some of Molly's questions, she stopped asking. He didn't want to talk. He wasn't a goddamn tourist guide. He just wanted to

get out of Juárez without mishap and find the town that
welcomed him.

There, in that nameless place unrecorded on any maps,
the hotel and bars and whorehouses were run by Adolpho
Ramirez, the mightiest drug lord in all of northern Mexico.
The people who lived in that town were owned and in
the employ of Ramirez. Locals didn't frequent his place.
Federales did not dare invade it. Americans, except those
who came to buy the illegal goods in large quantities, were
not permitted. Cruise had been rudely routed away when
first he wandered close to Ramirez's territory. But the second time he came, he brought a young boy as an offering,
a shy, gangly kid from Oklahoma who hadn't turned out to
be a good witness. The boy's brain was sizzled from drug
abuse, at age fourteen, and Cruise hadn't any use for him.
But Ramirez admired young, pale-skinned American males,
and once accepting the gift, he praised Cruise for his taste
and generosity. From then on Cruise was given free run of
the town, a trusted visitor. Ramirez even used him, when
he came into town, as an assassin to dispatch men known to
have filched money or a personal stash of drugs. He didn't
like to use his own men as assassins for he claimed it stirred
a blood lust that might one day be turned his direction. As
long as Cruise handled the thieves, that danger was averted.

Cruise was given free rooms at the hotel for as long as he
wished, food, women, and any money the thief was carrying
at the moment of his death. Sometimes that amounted to
quite a lot for Ramirez's men were not the poverty-stricken
peons that inhabited other Mexican towns. Most of them
carried enough dinero on their persons to feed a normal
family for a year. They were the richest men in all of
the northern districts. It was just that some of them were
greedier than others, and these were the ones Cruise murdered without compunction.

"Where are we going?"

Cruise blinked, startled from reverie. Lost in his thoughts, he'd forgotten about Molly and her gee-whiz chatter. "A town I know. It's better than Juárez."

"Is it far?" Molly peered out the open window at the dark desert reaches that bounded the rutted highway.

"Another thirty miles or so. Not far."

She must have picked up on his mood. She sat quietly without asking more questions while the night wind blew through the car and the headlights pierced the ultimate darkness ahead. Vehicles did not travel this road from Juárez. It was too dangerous to enter Ramirez's territory without a standing invitation. Molly wouldn't have seen them, but Cruise knew they had passed a patrol point a couple of miles back. Just at a turn in the road there was a bank of land hiding men with binoculars. They scanned passing traffic. Armed with rifles fitted with night-scopes, had they not recognized Cruise's looks—the long hair, beard, and mustache—and his signal—a blink of his headlights to dim and then back to high—he wouldn't have been allowed passage.

This lonely dark stretch of highway reminded Cruise of Arkansas country roads in his youth. No streetlights or houses, just vast black walls bounding either side of the roadway. You might be lost on the dark side of the moon and never find your way home again. He didn't drive those roads, though, when he was a boy. By the time he owned a car, they had been paved, and there were houses and mobile homes to relieve the monotony of night. When he was small he plodded down those roads alone, the chill air buffeting him. There were all sorts of monsters that lurked beyond the safe roadbed, and he imagined they snarled and fought to get to him.

His father made him walk six miles, at night, always a night when it was most frightening for young minds, to his aunt's house on errands. Cruise, after a time, realized these enforced marches were meant for other than to fetch a cup of sugar for his mother or a screwdriver for his father. They were *punishments* of the sort only his father could devise. Sometimes he let Cruise's sister, Lannie, walk with him. But more often than not he was forced to go alone and battle the fear without help.

When Lannie accompanied him, Cruise used her for a sounding board in order to puzzle out the reasons his family did as they did. "We don't really need vanilla extract tonight, do we?" he'd ask, trying to find out if Lannie understood what was happening. "I mean, Mama's not baking a cake or anything. She's not even cooking tonight."

"We have to get the vanilla," Lannie said. "Daddy said so."

"Well, I *know*, we have to get it, but we don't *need* it, do we?"

"We do if we don't want a whipping."

"So we have to walk twelve miles round-trip in the dark, in the cold, just so we won't be whipped." He couldn't make it any more crystal-clear to her than that.

"Shut up and let's just walk faster."

"Lannie, do you love them?"

"Who?"

She sounded like an owl. Whooo. Whooo. "You know who."

"I don't care," she said. She strode ahead of him and he had to rush to catch up before she was lost in the dark.

"But do you love them?" he persisted.

"They're nuts."

"I *know* that, but . . ."

"Shut up and walk faster. I have homework to finish when we get back."

"Lannie, why does he hate us so much?"

"I don't know."

"Why don't we run away?"

She stopped in the roadbed and grabbed him by the arms to shake him. She was taller than he, though he was a year older. In another two years he would experience a growth spurt and be as tall as his father. "Don't say that again! He'd kill you if you ran away. Don't even say it." She let him go and he could hear her sniffling back tears. "Besides, where would we go? We don't have nowhere to go."

Well, that was true if nothing else.

His aunt, whose house they were sent to on errands, was much older than his father, so old she smelled like the handkerchiefs pressed for years between the pages of a Bible. She lived alone, an old widow, and she wasn't quite right in the head, either. She thought Lannie was Mama and he was Daddy; she never got their names right. *Senile*, his mother told him once, but he didn't know what that was. To him she was just wrong-headed and lost and lonely. It always took her the longest time to find whatever it was they had come to borrow. "A flashlight? I think there's one beneath the bed. No? Then let's look in the attic. No? My land, it must be in the kitchen, look under the sink, it's probably there."

He hadn't any other relatives that he knew about, none he could run to. They didn't have friends, not *his* family, and they didn't go to church or social functions so he knew no one to help or advise him. If he told the teachers at school that his father beat them mercilessly over the smallest infraction, they would have taken him away, but he had heard where children went who were torn from the bosom of their families. They went to *institutions* and they were made *orphans*. Terrible, terrible words. What choice was that, and how could he run from one hellhole to another if he had any sense?

The night breeze rustled the leaves of the trees that pressed up to the ditches lining the roadbed. Cruise shivered, thinking the leaves were voices of demons lying in wait for two children hurrying and stumbling through the darkness. He knew what they must look like, those demons, with their monster teeth and claws and tails that whipped behind them like snakes. He had never glimpsed them as much as he stared into the dark to see the evidence of his fear, but he knew they were scary, they were truly the stuff of nightmares. Despite the fact his family were not churchgoers, he had read parts of the Bible. He knew about these things.

"Lannie? What are you going to be when you grow up?" If she'd only talk to him, he wouldn't have to think about the monsters in the trees.

She rushed ahead again and he had to run to catch her. "Lannie?"

"I'm going to be a country singer," she said. "Like Tammy Wynette. I'm gonna have a big house in Memphis and drive a fancy convertible car."

"But you can't sing."

"Yes, I can. You just never heard me, that's all. I sing by myself."

"Sing for me, Lannie. Go ahead, I'd like to hear you sing, please?"

She sang then, and her voice stopped Cruise in his tracks. She halted, feeling with her hands in the dark for him. She held onto his arms and he couldn't even see her face, but he heard her soft, melodic voice, and it filled him with a longing he could not name. It was a church hymn, "Amazing Grace," and it was sung by an angel on her knees before the throne of God. It made him ache. It made him cry. " . . . how sweet the sound, that saved a wretch like me . . ." It made him lift his hands and grip her elbows to keep her from ascending to heaven. *Oh, Lannie*, he thought, hoping her voice would never stop. *Oh, Lannie you do sing, you do*!

When she finished and let him go, she turned and hurried away. When he could get hold of his emotions, he ran as fast as he could. He reached for the back of her shirt to stop her. "That was . . ." He was out of breath. "That was . . . was . . . great."

"Stupid," she said.

"No, it was wonderful. You can be Tammy Wynette when you grow up, I know you can."

"I can be nothing. I *am* nothing. And if you tell that I sang a song, I'll kill you. I'll tell Daddy to kill you, then I'll help him bury you in a deep grave where the worms will eat off your face. Now c'mon. We're almost there. I've got homework to do when we get home."

Dreams that die. Cruise knew all about those. That's why he knew what was going to happen to the screenwriter in Hollywood who cut his own throat. Lannie might as well have cut hers, same difference. She left home at sixteen with a boy who had joined the Army. After six years and five babies, he left her to raise them on her own. She worked in a sewing factory in Arizona making curtains until her hands were scarred, her back bent, her eyes dim and bespectacled. She never sang. She never bought a house in Memphis. The angelic voice that made him soar died with her childhood and couldn't be reborn. It was interred in the country roads and woods and black nights where they grew up.

Lannie had been the single child of nine children who had any sort of artistic talent at all. That she put it away and let it die made him hate her more than any of the others. If *he* had had a voice like that, he'd have been a different man. Lannie could have been a different woman, yet she threw it away, hid it until it shriveled from lack of light, and she got exactly what she deserved. A non-life. A dull, dishwater death-in-life just like the one she had left behind. Though now she took care of their elderly father, he could not forgive her for having lacked the courage to pursue another path. *He* had courage. He had embraced the nomad life and lived by the death of others, the way Lannie might have lived had she not killed her own dream. Let his sisters and brothers think their "normal" lives more honorable than his. They were as deluded as his senile old aunt had been, stuck in memories of the past.

He was the only one to escape. The rest of them simply took up the threads of the same lives they had led in childhood. Beaten. Degraded. Deadening.

"Cockroaches," he whispered.

"What?" Molly asked. "Did you say something?"

He shook his head, cleared his throat of the tightness that had come there from thinking about Lannie. "Nothing," he said. "Look." He pointed ahead. "There's where we're going."

"It looks like an oasis out in the middle of nowhere." Colored lights shimmered in the near distance against a black background.

"It is. You'll like it."

He slowed as he drove down the main street. Here the people were not so frantic as they were in Juárez, although the streets were full of pedestrians, people on bicycles, and the clubs were packed. But the lights were dimmer, the neon less, the shadows thicker. Men strolled the wide sidewalks arm in arm with their women. From open-air cantinas drifted happy music. The smell of enchiladas, beans, corn tortillas, and roasting meats came through the car windows and made Cruise's mouth water. He had eaten truck-stop food for so long, he couldn't remember what real food tasted like.

"It looks nice," Molly said. "Smells good too."

"After we take our stuff up to our rooms at the El Presidente, I'll take you exploring and we'll get something to eat."

Some men waved and called, "Hey, amigo!" to Cruise as he drove past them. Others, knowing and fearing his lethal purpose, turned their eyes away and scurried deeper into the shadows.

Cruise waved back and wondered which ones would find their deaths at his hands tonight. He hadn't been here in over six months. Ramirez would surely need his services right away.

"This looks much better than Juárez," Molly said.

He knew she'd like it.

The El Presidente Hotel would not have been out of place among the high-priced accommodations strewn along the aqua coast of Acapulco or Cozumel. Wide marble steps led up to shining glass doors with brass handles. A doorman in braided uniform and crisp tulip red cap nodded deferentially. He ushered them inside the sumptuous lobby. Gold-leaf-decorated moldings ran along the eighteen-foot ceilings. A gargantuan chandelier that might have graced a palace hung ablaze over the center of the carpeted area. Gleaming wood adorned the service desk, and a brass rail ran along its foot. Deep red leather club chairs and sofas were arranged tastefully, though they stood empty.

Unlike other beautiful hotels in Mexico, this one was not meant for the entertainment of touristas. The El Presidente was owned by Adolpho Ramirez, and it was where he lived in the penthouse suite. His men, guests, and buyers occupied the lower floors.

Cruise saw how impressed Molly looked as he led her to the desk to secure a room key. Had she ever been in nice hotels? He thought not. "You'll tell Adolpho I'm here?" Cruise asked as he took possession of the key to his usual luxury suite.

"*Sí*, senor."

"Good. And I'd like another room for my friend."

The desk man wore a black suit, white shirt, and his teeth shone brilliantly from his dark face when he smiled, rather like a shark sensing prey. "Surely," he said, handing over a second passkey with a flourish.

Cruise installed Molly in her room. "Relax for a while. I have some business to attend to, and then we'll go out."

"This is some hotel," she said, slinging her carryall bag into a white satin chair. "I guess the owner's your friend, huh?"

"Yeah, I know him. I come through here when I cross the country sometimes. It beats sleeping in the car in truck stops," he said. "I'll be back soon to check on you."

He was back in twenty minutes having gotten the name and whereabouts of the one traitor Ramirez felt he must be rid of. Molly was still in the bath. Her second one in a few hours. She was not used to going without bathing as he was after years of living on the road. He heard the water being turned off. The water pipes gurgled and thumped. He took a seat on the bed to wait. With his foot he pushed around Molly's jeans where she'd left them in a pile on the floor. When she emerged, dressed, hair in a towel, she started at seeing him. "Back already! I'm almost through."

"No hurry. Take your time."

Ignoring that, she hurried to the dressing table and whipped the turbaned towel from her head. She fluffed out the crinkly ringlets with her fingers as he watched. *Nervous*, he thought. *I'm on her bed, invading her space. She thinks I'll make a pass.*

He stood and took the chair, crossing his legs while he watched her.

"You saw your friend?" she asked.

"I saw him."

"He must run this town."

"What makes you think that?"

"I don't know. It's not a tourist town, I can see that. And your friend owns this big hotel . . ." She swept her arm around at her surroundings for emphasis. She glanced at him in the mirror while applying lipstick.

Cruise didn't answer her. She wasn't going to know everything, not about this place, no matter how many questions she asked.

"Okay." She turned to him and gave a tentative smile. "I'm ready to go out again. That was my second shower tonight. Making up for those days without one. My hair might get clean yet."

"You're not sleepy?" It was close to midnight.

She shook her head. "I'm getting used to the night. With so much going on, how could I sleep now?"

He went to the door and let her follow behind. In the empty elevator to the lobby he said, "You smell like baby powder."

She stared at the elevator doors. "My deodorant. Secret."

"It's a secret?"

"No, that's what kind it is. Baby powder scent."

"It's nice. Better than perfume."

The doors opened and they stepped into the deserted lobby. Even the desk attendant was missing. Only the doorman stood watch, opening the door for them before they were close enough to touch the door handles. He bowed deeply as they went past.

"Let's walk," Cruise said, going down the steps.

The hotel was the center architectural triumph of the

small town. It dwarfed other buildings, most of which were one-story native affairs made of stucco and thick tarry timbers. Cruise headed for the cantina where his target was supposed to be carousing, unaware he had been marked for assassination. It was but two blocks away.

Overhead the sky spun with stars, and the sickle moon rode high over the world. Women dressed in revealing clothing and wearing plenty of eye makeup suggestively jostled against Cruise as he and Molly maneuvered the busy sidewalks to the cantina. Men catcalled and reached out toward Molly's red hair as she passed them. She shrunk closer to Cruise. He put an arm around her shoulders and she gave a little shudder.

"They won't bother you," he said. "It's your red hair they find interesting."

He thought he heard Molly humming below her breath, perhaps just to calm herself. He bypassed the cantina where the man he searched for was supposed to be, and stopped at the next cafe where small round wrought-iron tables were set out on the sidewalk. He gestured Molly toward the nearest empty table. "Wait here a minute. I'll be right back. Order a Coke. Here." He took out his wallet and gave her a ten-dollar bill. He'd have more soon. "Buy whatever you want."

"Where are you going?" She looked around at the couples at the other tables, and at the men swarming around the cafe as they moved in waves up and down the street. Two of them kissed the air in her direction and said something in Spanish.

"Stay here," he admonished, leaving her. "You'll be okay."

He backtracked to the cantina and once inside, stood rock still to survey the assemblage. Four men played a game of billiards at the pool table. Others sat in shadowed booths, speaking in soft voices to their women. He grabbed the arm of a woman waiting tables. The beer bottles trembled on the brown serving tray she carried in the other hand. "Senor Cruise!"

He spoke to her in Spanish. "Which one is Riaro?"

"At the back, the one standing next to the jukebox."

A gorgeously colored antique Rockola stood at the back, loudly playing Mexican records. Lime-green and popsicle-orange tubes pumped color up and down the front of the machine. Cruise moved to it. He singled out Riaro, edging another man aside, and said, "You know me?"

Jesus Riaro cringed from the man who was a gringo legend in Ramirez's town. Avenging Angel, they called him when he wasn't around to hear. "*Sí*," Riaro said cautiously. He looked around, wondering why he was so favored with the gringo's attention. He noticed everyone else moving slowly away. He broke out in an immediate sweat. He wiped down his face with a blue bandanna he carried in his back pocket.

"I brought a girl here. Little *gringa*, red hair. Young. You want her?"

"Oh!" So that was it. He wasn't in any trouble, no one knew about the coke he was now addicted to and forced to pilfer from his boss. Cruise sometimes sold his little friends he brought along on his visits.

"Red hair? Pretty?"

"And young," Cruise repeated. "She's waiting for you. At the cafe next door. You can pay me later."

Riaro let out a great whoosh of air, relieved and now happy to have been offered first dibs on Cruise's girl. "No problem from her?" he asked, switching to broken English.

"None. She knows you're coming."

Riaro grinned. A gold incisor slick with saliva gleamed

in the rainbow light from the Rockola. He gave Cruise a
handshake and moved through the crowd for the door.

Cruise waited five beats, the harsh loud tones of the
mariachi music bombarding his ears, then followed Riaro.
By the time he reached the outdoor cafe, Riaro and Molly
were embroiled in a tangle of arms and legs and flying hair.
Molly, panicked, yelled for someone to help her. Riaro kept
grinning and trying to drag her into the street.

Molly saw Cruise. She turned pleading eyes on him, and
cried, "What's he want? He says I'm supposed to go with
him to the hotel."

Riaro turned then. He stood off the curb, in the street,
hauling on Molly's thin arm. He paused, but did not let go
of his prize. "This is her? Red hair? I am not mistaken?"

"Worst mistake of your life, friend." Cruise jerked Riaro's
hand from Molly's arm. She reeled back until she bumped
into a woman sitting at a table behind her. The woman
stood and fled with her companion.

Riaro's grin died, but did not disappear. It hung on his
face frozen in place, an unpleasant rictus. "But . . . but . . .
you told me . . . you said . . ."

"I hope you saw your priest, Riaro."

Understanding dawned in the Mexican's eyes. His right
hand whipped a switchblade from his back pocket. It flicked
open. He waved it in front of his belly, low and menacing.
Molly screamed. Customers at the tables stood and pressed
back into the cantina.

"Ramirez sent you for me." Riaro spoke Spanish now.
"It was all a lie about the girl."

Cruise stood quietly, hands held out from his sides. He
also switched to Spanish. "You cheated your employer. You
stole from him, he says."

Riaro waved the knife, looked behind him at the rapidly
emptying sidewalk and street. "I didn't," he claimed in a

whispery, fear-laden voice. "I know better than to do that. I'm not a stupid man."

"Yes, you are. You're the dumbest fuck in town." Cruise waited for the rage to build. Riaro wouldn't rush him yet. He had time. He concentrated on the other man's face, the gleam of the gold tooth, the movements of the knife, his unsteady, shifting stance. Most of his victims weren't able to fight back. He must handle the situation with great care and skill. This was all for Molly's benefit. He was about to save her honor, wasn't he? She would never know Riaro's death was preordained. She would think he had kept her from being molested.

She'd adore him for it. He accomplished two ends at once: Molly's loyalty, Riaro's death, and enough money, if he was lucky, to see him through another week or more.

Riaro was talking, his words rapid-fire, unintelligible to Cruise whose Spanish was not strong enough to allow him to follow the emotional outburst from his victim. The cafe tables were abandoned. Chairs lay on their backs, beer bottles overturned and dripping their contents onto the rough concrete. Molly hung back with her hands over her mouth, little whimpering sounds coming from her.

He felt it now. That icy cold aura that settled from his head over his shoulders, gripping his mighty chest with a vise, invading his loins, tightening the muscles of his legs. He reached behind his head and felt beneath his hair for the knife. Riaro knew about that. They all knew about Cruise's knife and where he kept it. The Mexican reacted instantly, dancing away down the street as if on a bed of blue-white coals, babbling something in Spanish about another chance, didn't mean it, would repay Ramirez if given reprieve from the Avenging Angel tonight. But there would be no reprieve and Riaro knew the rules on that. Once you betrayed Ramirez you paid the ultimate price.

Cruise had the small weapon in the open. The handle was hidden in the palm of his hand. Just the short, razor-sharp blade protruded from his fist. He heard Molly gasp, but the sound was on the periphery of his senses. It was over-whelmed and drowned, her frightened sound, by Riaro's retreating dance steps ringing on the street, and by his heavy breathing, and his useless patter seeking mercy.

"Come to me," Cruise said more to himself than to Riaro. "Come. To. Me."

Riaro made a break for it, running for all he was worth away and down the suddenly deserted street. Cruise easily caught up with him, his legs being longer, his strides more powerful. Riaro turned to the assault just as Cruise closed on him, not many yards from the cafe. Cruise's knife hand shot out and cut Riaro from his shoulder blade to his gut. His shirt flapped open in the melee, and blood flowed over his belt. Cruise knocked the switchblade from his hand with a blow to that arm, and the knife clattered onto the street. A car came toward them, speared them in its headlights. It halted, idling in the center of the street, outlining the fight as on an eerie stage.

Riaro swung with his fists and Cruise's knife went up and under his flailing arms, in close, an embrace of enemies. Cruise sank the small weapon into soft stomach, lifted upward with force, pierced a lung, and drove toward the heart. Riaro came off his feet with the lunge, fell back from the invading steel. Cruise stepped back, his fist sucked from Riaro's gut with a sickening slurping sound that hung in his ears long after it had ended.

Riaro fell onto his back, eyes already glazed. A hole gaped in his midsection pumping blood and intestines. The lights from the car held steady on the scene, making the blood look black as oil as it coursed from the dead man onto the street.

Cruise stood with the knife in his bloody fist. He looked at it, shivered, and sighed.

All he could think about was getting to a place where he could have water run over his body to cleanse him of this filth. But there was something yet he must do. He waved in agitation at the stopped car. It backed up and made a U-turn in the center of the street, the driver gunning the engine and squealing the tires to gain traction as it roared away.

In the resultant darkness, stars pirouetted before Cruise's eyes. He moved forward until he could make out Riaro's sprawled body. He stooped and felt in his pockets. Withdrew his wallet. Took a thick wad of American money, threw the few pesos on the still body. When Cruise stood again and glanced at Molly, he saw she had slumped into one of the cafe chairs, her face in her hands. A few of the earlier patrons of the cafe wandered out, but didn't linger. They scurried down the sidewalks in both directions, anywhere away from the gringo, Cruise Lavanic, the hired killer Ramirez visited upon the wicked.

Molly probably hadn't seen him rob the dead man, Cruise decided. If she did, he didn't care. He had a story and a reason for that too, if she demanded it. But why would she question him when he'd just saved her from a scumbag ready to ravage her?

He stuffed the money into his front pocket. He stepped over the curb. He stood a moment looking down at Molly's bowed head. He resisted an urge to pat her with his bloody hand, reassure her the way a parent would reassure a mourning child. "I'll be back out in a minute," he told her instead.

She was crying, great hiccuping cries, as if her heart were broken.

Cruise pushed inside the cantina and went behind the

bar to the sink. There he washed his hands, his knife, and lifting his hair, replaced it on the Velcro patch. A few idlers watched darkly from corners, but looked elsewhere when Cruise glanced their direction. "Don't fuck with Ramirez. When are you jerks gonna learn?" he asked.

Outside again, he took Molly's arm and lifted her to her feet. He guided her to the hotel, said nothing in the elevator to the fourth floor where their rooms were. In her room, he placed her on the bed. He moved to the bathroom and closed the door, stripped from the bloody clothes, and stepped beneath cold water. Cleansed, he slipped on his slacks, left his blood-soaked shirt on the floor, and went barefoot to where Molly lay on the bed. He sat in the chair nearby.

The sliver of moon rode past the top of the hotel window and he waited. While Molly cried, he waited. While his heart slowed to a gentle and contented rhythm . . .

He waited.

Cruise let the moon move past the top of the window before he approached Molly. She had stopped crying. Silence hung like a heavy veil between them. He leaned over the bed. Touched her shoulder. Slowly she lifted her head from where she had it cradled in her arms against the coverlet.

"I want to go back to Texas," she said in a small voice.

"We're going. We'll leave tomorrow."

"Good." She began to turn her face away.

"I want you to come with me somewhere, it won't take long."

"Now?"

"Please."

Molly raised herself wearily to the side of the bed. Cruise moved back. "I'll go to my room for a clean shirt. Wait for me at the elevator."

He gathered his shoes and socks, his bloodied shirt, and left the room. Minutes later he joined Molly. She stood looking at the carpet, avoiding his eyes.

"Where are we going?" she asked. "I don't feel well. I'm tired." She sounded grouchy the way a weary child began acting out of sorts when it has not had enough rest. The pretenses between them were falling away. All the walls disappearing.

"I know, but this won't take long, I promise." In the lobby he guided her out the door, down the steps of the hotel, and along the sidewalk. Most inhabitants had gone to bed, few cantinas were open, many of the lights doused in the shops and houses. It was the deepest part of the night, the time when even the cats had ceased their caterwauling and the ravenous dogs their garbage poaching.

"Cruise . . . ?"

"Go ahead," he said. "Get it off your chest. You'll feel better."

That small encouragement was all she needed. "Didn't it bother you at all? How could you just . . . ?"

"Kill someone?"

"Yes."

"He would have taken you off to some filthy place and done unspeakable things to you." He paused, let that thought sink in. "He pulled a knife first."

"What was he saying to you in Spanish?"

"I don't remember now."

He was leading her away from the town's center past storage buildings and loading docks toward the edge of the dry desert. He saw the familiar black spindly trees dying of thirst, their skeletal arms thrust into the sky. They threw long moon shadows into the arroyos. Humped anthills dotted the sandy earth as if the land had erupted with an infectious disease. Low clumps of cacti spread their flat, spiked limbs along the ground like clawed alien sea creatures crawling along the floor of an ocean.

Cruise knew his way. He often visited this desolate spot he intended to show her.

"Where are we? Why are we leaving town? Cruise?"

"Take it easy. It's just a place I want to show you."

"What *kind* of place?"

"A cemetery."

Molly halted so abruptly that Cruise was a yard past her before he also stopped. He looked back, let out an exasperated breath. She was so much trouble. The damn kids were always so much trouble. "What's the matter?" As if he didn't know. Everyone got spooked around graves.

"A *cemetery*? You want to take me to a graveyard? Now, in the middle of the night, after . . . after you . . . after that man . . . ?"

"Look, Molly, nothing's going to happen to you, okay? Didn't I just prove that back in town? I didn't let that bastard haul you off, did I? I think you ought to trust me."

"But, Cruise, why a cemetery? I'm so tired. I just saw a man killed right before my eyes, *don't you understand?*"

"Try to keep your voice down. Have a little respect."

Molly glanced around the area suspiciously. "We're already in it?" She moved closer to him. "Oh, God, we are."

He began stepping carefully across the slightly raised mounds of sandy graves. Some of them were ringed with rocks bleached white from the sun. He trailed his fingertips along the tops of rough-hewn granite headstones that leaned precariously this way and that. He heard Molly following at his heels.

"Dead's not so bad," he said in a quiet voice. "You're young. You don't know. You think dying's the worst thing that could ever happen to someone. You have to make friends with death, Molly." He dropped his voice even lower. This is how he sometimes talked to himself, the way he was instructing her, a confident tone because he knew what he was talking about, a reverent one because the subject was the most serious man ever discussed.

"If my enemy had killed me tonight instead of me killing him. I'd be here, in this ground, tomorrow. Before the roosters were crowing they'd have me under six feet of dirt. But by then it wouldn't matter, Molly, not at all. It's not dying that's frightening. It's living. It's *how* you choose to live. There are so many ways to lose yourself, to sell your soul. But once you're dead, all the choices are gone, it's over then. Dead is peace. Life is chaos."

"Cruise, don't talk like that. I'm scared. Let's go back."

He spun around and took her into his arms, drew her into an embrace, held her tight. She struggled for just a moment, then quietened so that he felt her heart stampeding against his chest.

"Molly, there's nothing to fear."

He felt her warm breath through the cloth of his shirt. She hadn't moved. She breathed through her mouth. Her heart still raged against the imprisonment, but she was doing a fine job of suppressing all instinct to push away or run from him. He loved her then completely, unconditionally, loved every molecule of her, would have died in her place, would have taken down dragons, ruined kingdoms, thrust swords through any and all warriors to protect her.

"Sshhh," he whispered. "Slow now. I told you there's nothing to be afraid of. Not me. Not this place. Not the dead. Not the past because it won't haunt you, Molly, unless you let it."

She began to tremble. It radiated outward from inside

where her heart could not pace itself. Her small arms shook, her back, her legs, her head on the fragile stem of her neck. He pulled her even closer, wrapped his big arms around her slight body so that she would not fall from his grasp.

"Sshhh. Hush. Hush. Get hold of it. Catch that thought that's trying to run away with you and hold it down. I brought you here so you'd understand. You cried so hard. So long. And for what? You didn't even know him. What if it had been me? Would you have cried that way?"

He didn't expect an answer. She couldn't have answered had she wanted. He knew what she must feel, must think. They were at the turning point now. If he'd let her stay in the hotel room without trying to reach her, she'd have been lost to him forever. Despite how the murder should have appeared to her, she had recognized something of his real purpose; she knew in an instinctive way that what he had done was not entirely connected with saving her from a savaging. She had reached conclusions he thought beyond her maturity. If she allowed it, he could forestall a disaster: her burial in this foreign ground.

"Molly? I'm not going to hurt you and I'm not going to let you be hurt. Do you believe that?" His practiced lies came so easily.

They were at the crossroads, her answer pivotal. In the next seconds what transpired depended entirely on the girl in his arms. He would either lift his hand to his hair and for the second time this night withdraw the knife, or he would loosen his hold and escort her back to the hotel. Life hung in the balance, in the eternity of time between his words and hers. If she knew the severity of the situation she'd not just tremble, but quake so hard she'd shake herself apart before his eyes.

"Molly? Do you believe me?"

A night breeze ruffled her hair. She had stopped breathing. He could still feel her heart throbbing against his body. Must he stop its beating? Must he do away with her so soon, oh, so soon before he had even found a way to know her? That would be such a pity, nearly more than he could bear. Only once before did a witness of his get to him the way Molly was now. He had wanted time with her, a relationship however strange and warped, however fated to end. But she had given the wrong answer to his question. And she had died sooner than she should have or needed to.

She let out her breath. She inhaled. She said, "Yesss."

Cruise smiled into the dark beyond the top of her head. He could feel the dead all around them sleeping in their graves, giving up a collective sigh. They would not be asked to welcome a new member among them tonight. Not until tomorrow when the family of Riaro brought him in a plain wooden casket and lowered his cold body into their company would they be disturbed in their slumber.

"Let's go back." He let her go, turned her from the cemetery, and pushed her gently on a path between the graves back the way they had come.

She did not talk again on the walk to the hotel. He let it be. She'd passed his test and he was well pleased. He must not push his luck. It was jubilation enough that she'd just saved her own life.

"Get some sleep," he said at her door.

He stood in the hallway and stared down the corridor at a window opening onto the silver lightening of the morning sky. He felt a chill that raised goose bumps along his arms. It wasn't the night that should frighten people so much. It was those scorching, blinding sunny hours where everything was laid bare to the eye.

It had been a long night. He meant to sleep it off. If

he didn't wake up for eighteen hours he wouldn't be a bit surprised.

In his own room he slipped off his shoes, took his belt from the loops of his slacks, and fell onto the bed without drawing back the covers. He couldn't sleep yet. His mind turned over the kill the way a farmer with a shovel turns over rich earth for spring planting. Down one row, up another until an entire patch of ground has been tilled. His thoughts took him down the street, into the conversation with Riaro beside the Rockola, down the street again after his prey, then up close, tight shot of Riaro's look of betrayal, his comprehension of his dilemma, his sprint for freedom.

The fight. The suction of Cruise's fist as he withdrew it from Riaro's torso. The fall. The quick death. The blood . . .

Molly stood shivering in the dark just inside the door of her room. She listened breathlessly for Cruise to leave. Bands of moonlight marched across the floor from the far window.

He was insane. That's all she could think. It was the sole explanation for what happened tonight. Even though the Mexican had pulled a knife, it was Cruise who pursued him, Cruise who ripped open his belly and left him to die in the street.

Then that creepy little walk outside of town to the cemetery. All the weird talk of the dead being better off. The strange pledge of loyalty to his ideas that he demanded from her before he would let her go. She had been so afraid she thought she might wet all over herself. That or faint outright in his arms. She knew what he wanted to hear and suspected violence had she not said it. She knew she must agree with him.

If he wanted to make her feel safe and secure, he had gone about it like no other man would have. He committed murder without a qualm, apparently without any remorse whatsoever. He had been composed enough to enter the cantina afterward and wash his hands. His actions were like those of a mechanical man, a computerized automaton with a fairly intelligent brain, but a soul made of chips and soldered connections.

What had she done taking a ride with him? She knew with a certainty that came from intuition rather than any past experience beyond the scene she had witnessed tonight that he was extremely dangerous. He inspired a fear in her that left her wordless.

She didn't know how long she had been standing next to the door straining to hear any sound. Surely Cruise had left by now. She must escape before he woke at dusk to drive them out of town. She had to call her father and ask what she should do. She needed help. She had to get away from Cruise before something terrible happened to her. Something fatal.

She wanted to reach out a hand to the door and open it, but for long seconds her arm felt paralyzed. She knew that uncontrollable desperation shimmered right at the edge of her thought processes. She also understood that if she wasn't careful, if she wasn't strong and diligent in containing that fear it could permanently disable her.

If she'd only not taken a lift from Cruise. If only she'd not fallen into his web.

Home. She had to call Daddy. She had to ask him what she must do to save herself.

She made her arm move, forced her hand to close over the doorknob. She turned it, moved to the crack and peeked out, let out a breath when she found the hall empty.

Wait! She needed to take her clothes bag. She rushed

across the room to the bath and snatched up her things. Colgate toothpaste, orange toothbrush, blue bottles of Finesse shampoo and conditioner. Secret solid stick deodorant. *He'd said she smelled like baby powder.* It caused her to shiver inside to think she'd been attracted to him for when he finally took her into his arms, she knew her life was in jeopardy. It repulsed her now that she had thought of him as a potential lover.

Then in the bedroom she found her purse on the dresser, threw the hot pink hairbrush into it, snapped it shut. Stuffed her dirty clothes into the blue bag, zipped it, hurried again to the door.

Couldn't get her breath. Couldn't think. Paused at the open door, clutched her purse and bag in her arms. What if he was near the elevator?

She stuck her head into the hall and looked. No. He wasn't there. He had gone to his room and was asleep by now. If she didn't find a way to control her thoughts, she'd never make it out of the hotel.

She drew in a deep breath and stepped into the hall. Closed the door behind her. Walked along the carpeted hall to the elevator. Saw that it wasn't in use. Punched the down button. When the doors slid open she jumped. The noise was unbearable. Surely everyone in the entire hotel could hear the cables of the elevator working as it came to fetch her. She was ready to turn and run the opposite direction. For just a second she imagined Cruise in the elevator staring down at her sadly. Saying something crazy like, "You're not going anywhere, little girl." She *must* get her imagination under control.

She ran inside the elevator and pushed the button for the lobby. She had to find a phone, get someone to help her. She hadn't any idea how she was going to do that, but she must.

Empty lobby. No one behind the registration desk. She flew across the room, stood up on tiptoe to look behind the desk and into a hallway that led off from the area. "Anyone here?" she called. She looked behind her, saw the elevator doors closing. Had someone called for the elevator? Was it Cruise? Oh, God. Oh, God.

"Hey! Anyone?" No one came forward. It was a ghost hotel. She didn't see a phone on the counter or behind it. She couldn't get high enough, even by standing on the brass foot rail, to see over onto the back of the counter.

In the lobby again she wandered around looking at the flocked wallpaper. Where were the pay phones? Didn't they have them here the way they did in the States? She went a little ways down two separate hallways that must have led to the closed dining room and the bar looking for a phone or someone to ask. *Damn.* Nothing.

The doorman was missing from the door. She ran out and down the long wide steps to the sidewalk. Sunrise painted the east a dusty pink-violet. Birds sang morning chorals somewhere along the red-tiled rooftop of the hotel. All the stars were gone and the moon was no more than a smudge in the sky.

She'd find something open. A store. A cafe. She'd beg them to let her use the phone.

It was eerie to listen to her lone footsteps on the sidewalks. Now that day was coming she could see what the town really looked like. It wasn't a place she'd want to spend any time. Weeds grew to the edges of the sidewalk. Paper cups and beer cans littered the curbs along the poorly paved street. The storefronts were dust-covered and looked hurriedly painted. Everything had a temporary look to it as if the people could pick up and leave on the spur of the moment. It was more of an encampment than a real town.

At the cafe where Cruise had told her to wait all the chairs had been turned upside down on the tabletops. A mangy gray cat sat beneath one of the tables eating something that looked green and moldy. The hungry feline hissed as Molly neared so that she had to go to the edge of the sidewalk to avoid an attack.

"Bitch," Molly whispered at the cat. "You're no help unless you happen to know where I can find a phone."

The cat growled and showed its teeth, hair rising along its spine. Molly went on down the sidewalk, eyeing the locked doors, the barred and shuttered windows. The farther away she got from the imposing structure of the hotel at the end of the street, the easier she found it to breathe. But everyone was asleep. She hadn't yet seen a soul on the street. Every bar was closed. Curtains fluttered in open windows on second floors.

At the corner she turned left. More closed shops, cafes, bars. Ahead, though, she saw houses. Since this street ran north and south, on one side the houses were in shadow, on the other weak morning sunlight threw the shacks in relief. Some of them looked as if they might fall down when a strong wind came. The roofs were made of every imaginable substance from sheets of corrugated tin to raw planks in varying lengths and widths. She stepped up her pace. She'd knock on a door, find someone with a telephone, call her father . . .

. . . she thought she heard someone walking behind her. She whirled around so hard her hair covered her eyes. She pushed it out of the way and stared back where she'd come. She saw no one, but she was almost sure she wasn't alone now. Someone else was up, moving about the town. She waited for him to turn the corner and follow her to make sure it wasn't Cruise, but she couldn't hear footsteps any longer. She turned back to the task at hand. Might as well try any door, she thought. It was a good possibility that few of the Mexicans had private telephones, but she must try to find one regardless. Until the stores and cafes opened she hadn't any choice.

She crossed the street to the nearest house and knocked loudly. She heard animal sounds and wondered where they were coming from. It was a *hea-hea-hea* sound, not like a cat or dog, but some animal she didn't recognize.

She started to knock again when the door opened. It swung back on great noisy hinges. A little boy in white briefs stood looking up at her. His eyes were big, wide awake, black as soot.

"Please, do you have a telephone?" She pantomimed using a phone, holding the receiver in her hand to her ear. If they didn't understand her English she'd move on to the next house. She hadn't any time to lose.

The boy was moved gently aside by a man. His thick black hair rose in a three-inch pompadour and sideburns grew down each brown cheek. He was bare-chested, but wore a slouchy pair of brown pants that he held up with one hand. "Senorita?"

"I need a phone. A phone? Telephone." Again she pretended to be dialing a phone, lifting a receiver to her ear. "I have to call my father in the United States. In Florida? I'm in trouble and I need . . ."

The man hadn't moved or given any indication he had understood her. She stopped talking when a gray and white spotted goat nudged aside the man's leg. It stuck its triangular head up at her and bleated plaintively. She saw the pink tongue, the white even bottom teeth, the black marble eyes.

"Shoo!" the Mexican said, pushing back the goat with his knee. "Come in, lady," he said to Molly. "I have a telephone for you to use, please. It's early, *sí*? We were sleeping."

"I'm so sorry to bother you, and I wouldn't except it's really important. But you do have a phone? That's great. Thanks a lot. I couldn't find a pay phone anywhere in town . . ." Again her sentence trailed off as she entered the dark little house. A fetid smell assaulted her and she wanted to gag. The reflex hit her throat, the contraction came, but she forced herself to breathe, to control the urge. She looked down and saw the floor was made of earth. She had accidentally stepped into goat dung. She scraped her rubber-soled sneaker in the dirt to get it off. All around her swarmed goats. Big ones with horns. Smaller ones, the females, she supposed. Baby ewes, downy-haired, little perked ears, all those shiny marble eyes. There must have been a dozen of them altogether. Some were of one solid color, others were speckled, patched with browns or grays or blacks. When her vision adjusted to the lack of light inside the house she saw not only goats, but people—the man's family. A woman sitting on the side of a drooping cot in a cotton nightgown. Three children. All boys under the age of ten including the little one who had answered the door. They were trying to get the goats away from her and corraled into one corner of the room. An old man and an old woman, probably the grandparents, were buttoning shirts and fastening pants and skirts, slipping on sandals. The room was a circus, crowded, smelly, close, and disorderly. Molly couldn't speak.

"In here," the Mexican said, leading her by the hand through the goats and children, through a printed cotton curtain into what appeared to be a kitchen of sorts. There was a brick oven in an outside wall, wooden counters along two other walls, pots and pans hanging from the rafters, a huge pottery bowl of flour. The smell of grease and cooked food drowned the scent of the goats from the other room. Next to a big water barrel with a tin dipper hanging from the side stood an old stool and on it sat an ancient black dial phone, the kind Molly had seen only at antique markets. The telephone wire also went up to the open rafters, was looped on hooks across the room to the open window. It evidently hooked up directly to a pole outdoors.

"Amazing," Molly said.

"It is, is it not?" the Mexican said, his bare, hairless chest puffed with pride. "Not everyone can have a telephone." He took the receiver, listened for the dial tone, then smiled and handed it over. "It works. It always works unless we get a lot of rain."

"Wonderful."

"This will be collect, *sí*?"

"Oh, yes, it'll be collect. Thank you. Thank you so much." She took the phone, waited for him to return to the front sleeping room. When he did not, she shrugged, and dialed the operator. It took several minutes to explain to the operator that she wanted to make a collect call to the United States, to Flor-re-da, and to give her the number. The Mexican watched, his face beaming, his smile flaring his cheeks so that the sideburns stood out on his face like the ties on a woman's bonnet.

Finally Molly heard the phone ringing on the other end of the line. The connection had gone through. It continued ringing. Ringing. "C'mon, Daddy," she whispered. "Answer the phone."

After an interminable time the long-distance operator came on and said the party was not answering. Molly almost said she knew that, she could hear, for God's sake.

When she replaced the receiver in its cradle she was near tears. She wondered what time it was in Florida. Maybe her father was out for a while. If he'd been sleeping, the ringing would have wakened him.

"Bad news?" the Mexican asked.

"I got through, but no one answered."

There was a racket in the sleeping room. Goats stomping and bleating again, children speaking unintelligible Spanish. Someone called a name and the man pushed back the curtain. Rather than enter the room, however, he stayed where he was, blocking Molly's way. She had meant to follow him. Maybe she could get him to help her. Since he spoke English and was so kind, maybe he could find her a way back to Texas before Cruise woke up at sundown.

Suddenly the man turned and took her arm. He led her forward through the curtain. She didn't think to resist.

"What is it?"

Cruise stood towering over the assemblage. His shoulders kept the sunlight from entering through the front door. He stood silently, his gaze never leaving her. Goats pressed against his legs and nibbled at the cuffs of his slacks. The children were at their mother's side, unmoving.

Molly's heart sank. She tried to pull free of the Mexican. "Let me go!" She might leap out the window in the kitchen.

"I didn't know she was your girl, Senor Cruise," the Mexican said. "She asked to use the phone. I could not say no."

"Come with me, Molly."

"I don't want to go with you. I want to stay here."

He smiled at that. He looked at the Mexican. "She wants to stay here."

"Oh, no, oh, no, she cannot do that." The Mexican faced her. His hair had gone wild in disarray from the shaking he was doing to his head. "You can't stay here. You must go with Senor Cruise."

It was impossible. She hadn't any way out. She hadn't

even made it to the edge of town. He must have followed her since she left the hotel. It was his footfalls she had heard behind her.

"You can't stay here, Molly," Cruise said. He crossed the space between them and took her hand. The Mexican held out her arm as if it were a gift, as if to say, *Take her, take her and all the trouble that comes with her.*

Molly was jerked out of the small house and into blinding sunshine. She squinted her eyes, tried to keep up with Cruise's long strides down the sidewalk and into the street. She wanted to scream, but the people here knew Cruise, they feared him, they gave in to his wishes. Her screams, she realized, would do her no good in this place.

"Who were you calling?"

"Cruise, I want to go home. I never should have run away from home, I know that now. I don't want to be on my own."

"Yes, you do. You left home and you aren't going back. Once you leave home, it's forever. Now. Who were you calling?"

"My father."

"What did you tell him?"

Before she could stop her tongue, she had told the truth. "He didn't answer." As soon as she said it she knew it was a mistake. She should have lied and said she told him where she was and with whom. *Damn it to hell.*

"That's good," Cruise said. "You don't need your daddy. You've got me."

All the way to the hotel Molly tried to soothe Cruise's anger. It seethed beneath the surface and deepened the tone of his voice. It made him abrupt with her, jerking her over curbstones, up stairs, into the waiting elevator. Nothing she said was working.

"I didn't want to have to do this, Molly." He had her in

her room and dropped her into the chair.

"Do what?" Punish her?

"Tie you up during my sleep time." He stooped to the floor and picked up nylon lengths of rope.

"Where'd you get those?"

"As soon as you left this room I brought them here."

"You're going to tie me to the chair?"

"It's all your fault." He tied her ankles first, kneeling, head bowed. Sunlight came through the windows and lit his brown and silver hair with a halo of gold. She stared at his hair, at the back of his head. She knew he had a knife there. It was unbelievable, but she'd seen him take it from his hair.

Molly wouldn't cry. Not in front of him. Not in front of a crazy man. She wouldn't fight him either, not now when she hadn't any chance of escape. She'd give in. She'd endure.

"I'm disappointed that you lied to me. Everything would have been all right if you hadn't lied," he said, tying her hands in her lap, then looping the rope through the arms of the chair.

He made her secure in the chair and then he lay down on her bed. He covered his face with a pillow, sighed into it, and soon was still.

That's when Molly cried just as quietly as she could while wondering what was to become of her.

In El Paso, Mark Killany found a Budget Inn just off the freeway and inside the city limits. The queerest feeling had dogged him for hours. He felt Molly was in some sort of distress. It was nuts because he'd never heard of a father being so close to his daughter that he had premonitions about her. Mothers, yes. Women were born with built-in radar. Especially when it came to their kids—knew when they had fallen and scraped a knee, knew when their diapers were wet, later on could read their feelings the way a blind man lays his hands on a face and reads the contours he finds. But fathers didn't talk about those things, never admitted to them, wouldn't have known what to think had they ever experienced them. Yet here he was with this gnawing in his gut. The worry spread out like a cancer taking over his body.

He couldn't sleep. Exhaustion rode him so hard he could hardly walk, but he couldn't get to sleep. He tossed, turned, got up for a glass of tap water from the sink in one of those flimsy plastic glasses. Lukewarm. Metallic tasting. He had forgotten to fill the ice bucket.

He turned on the lights and paced around the room making a path from the dressing table past the beds to the door and back again. Circling. Worrying.

Maybe he should get back on the road.

Maybe he shouldn't. He did need sleep. Didn't want to fall asleep behind the wheel and take out a young family with a bunch of kids sleeping in the back seat.

Nothing could be done about the premonition except live with it. He wished he had someone to talk to. Anyone. The agitation was unbearable. He dressed, grabbed the room key, and left for the motel restaurant. El Paso was lit up like the White House Christmas tree. He couldn't see the star cover overhead for all the lights in the city. People didn't sleep much here. The coffee shop was crowded. He chose a booth and drank coffee. He watched the entrance door. For what reason he didn't know. Molly wasn't going to walk in and plunk herself across from him. It wouldn't be that easy.

Might never see her again.

He had to squash that thought, an ant rolled between his thumb and forefinger.

A bum came in the door. Dirty chinos, ragged high-top tennis shoes, the black kind basketball players used to wear when Mark was in high school. The bum wore two shirts over an undershirt. An orange-and-white-striped polo beneath a long-sleeved blue-and-purple plaid lightweight flannel rolled to the elbows. Hanging open. Belt too big, the tongue drooping down the front of the guy's fly. It looked as if it had been chewed by a big dog. Mark figured the man for a wino rather than a crackhead. Crackheads had the haunted look in their eyes that demanded instant fulfillment. Winos just looked beat and dejected.

Mark caught his eye. Motioned him over with a nod of his head to the seat across from him. The bum shuffled through the restaurant. He wiped the back of his not-too-clean right hand under his nose, slid into the booth, nodded back.

"Want something to eat?" Mark asked.

"I could do justice to a hamburger, man."

"Right."

The waitress took the order for burgers, fries, milk, and apple pie for dessert. The bum frowned when Mark asked for two milks, but the expression left as quickly as it had come. Free food was free food.

"You get around El Paso much?" Mark asked.

"Some. Got to stay on the move, man, you know how it is."

"I'm looking for my daughter. She's a runaway. You might've seen her. I know it's a slim chance, but I have to ask." Mark took out his wallet, slipped Molly's school picture from the plastic casing, pushed it across the table.

The bum looked at it hard. Then he shook his head. "Nope. Would have remembered that hair. Never seen her."

Mark took the picture back and put away his wallet. He sighed audibly. "I don't know what I'm going to do."

"Good kid?"

"The best. We just didn't see eye to eye."

"Old story, man."

"Yeah, I know. Must get boring hearing it."

"Mostly I hear it from the kids. Lot of them come through here on the way to Cali-forn-i-aye. Some of them never make it."

"I can imagine what happens to the ones who don't make it."

"You might imagine it, but the real thing's worse. Sometimes lots worse."

"I'm glad I'm buying your dinner. You're cheering me right the hell up."

"I'm sorry, man, I can see you're lost without that kid, and I don't mean nothing, but I got to speak the truth, don't I?"

The food came and the bum ate ravenously at the burger. Mark didn't think he took his eyes off the plate a second. He never stopped chewing until every crumb was devoured.

"Here, finish mine." Mark pushed his half-eaten burger and fries across the table. The bum nodded his thanks and did away with the food in a few bites. He even downed the dreaded glass of milk.

"We get apple pie too?" he asked, a milk ring around his mouth.

"Sure. When's the last time you ate?"

"Oh, man, I don't need much. I don't get this hungry often. I eat enough."

Mark kept his comments to himself. He didn't know why, but he felt a lot better after feeding the guy. He thought he was against handouts to bums on general principle. On the general principle that they ought to go to work. But he knew now he didn't really believe that hard-line bullshit.

This was a human being with a deadweight around his neck. He needed charity. Hope. All those biblical commandments or whatever they were.

He signaled over their waitress and said they wanted the pie now. Two big slabs came spread out on huge saucers, slices of apple thick and long as Mark's thumb tumbling out of the flaky brown crust. He relished eating it just as much as his companion did. When they finished he ordered coffee for them.

"Man, that was the best damn meal I think I ever had. This place has got a good cook."

Mark smiled, felt himself relaxing from the inside out where that worry cancer had eaten at him.

"Sure wish I'd been some help about your girl. She's awful pretty."

"And awful young."

"Thirteen?"

"Just turned sixteen."

"That's a bad age, all right. I was out on my own at sixteen too. It ain't no kinda life, man."

"I was able to track her to a truck stop in Mobile, Alabama. Since then I can't get any breaks."

"Mobile, eh? Truck stop. Why don't you try the Metro, man?"

"What's that?"

"Biggest truck stop in El Paso. Gets hundreds of trucks a night. Everybody stops in there. It's like a fuckin' shopping mall. She riding with a trucker?"

"No, some guy in a blue Chrysler. Picked her up in Mobile. Of course, she could be riding with someone else by now . . ."

"Well, hey, man, I'd try the Metro, I was you."

"Where is it?"

"Go back east on I-10 about three miles. Watch on your

right off the freeway for a great big green Metro sign. You can't miss it, man."

"I'll do that, friend, thanks." Mark stood with the meal ticket.

The bum slid out of the booth after swallowing down the last of his coffee. He held out a grubby hand to Mark. "I wanna thank you proper, man. That was a helluva nice thing you done."

Mark took his hand. Once he'd paid the bill and was outside the restaurant, the bum was gone. He was going to offer him a ride somewhere, slip a twenty to him. Too late. Well, at least the guy was full and that was something.

He walked back to the motel, unlocked his car, and sat behind the steering wheel. Metro. Big green sign.

Maybe she was there.

He wasted an hour hanging out at the biggest truck stop in El Paso. He showed Molly's picture to everyone he could. Waitresses, shopkeepers, counter persons, gas jockeys. Came up empty. He even called the phone number for the tour service down into Juárez, asked if they'd taken a redheaded girl. Nope. Took a redheaded woman in her fifties, though, they said. She was a bottle redhead, pretty obvious too, but no kid.

By the time Mark packed it in and returned to his room at the Budget Inn all he wanted to do was crawl between the sheets and sleep until the Second Coming. The Metro Truck Stop had tired him more than his day's driving. All those people. All that commotion. It was like Grand Central back in its heyday. He didn't know how the truckers lived that frantic a life. He pitied them.

Tomorrow he'd hit the road again for New Mexico.

Maybe she was there.

THE FIFTH NIGHT

Cruise got up in the day twice to untie Molly to go to the bathroom. She whimpered some, but he'd warned her against too much noise. She wanted a gag, that was all right with him. She didn't. She was quiet while he slept.

When the sun set, Cruise woke for good with a raging headache. Moving around in the day did that to him. Gave him migraines that started in his sleep. He'd wake with a dull, heavy, bloated feeling in his right temple. Then before he could shower and dress the headache came out in the open, a dozen angry fists swinging a dozen sledgehammers against the inside of his skull.

He staggered around the room trying to get rid of the pain before he drove from town. He kept his right hand mashed into his right eye socket where the pain was the worst. He knew this didn't help it any, but it seemed to ease the pressure on his one eye.

"When are you going to let me go?" Molly asked, squirming in the ropes.

"Don't talk. My head hurts."

"Yeah, well, that's too bad. My hands hurt. My legs hurt. My butt hurts."

Cruise was across the room before she finished. He loomed over her, hand gone from his eye for the moment.

His face looked carved from the wood of a hard, old tree. Hickory. A gnarled oak.

"I *told* you my head *hurts*. You talk again I might make *you* hurt. You understand that, Molly? You got that written down yet?"

She nodded, eyes downcast.

"Fine. Don't forget."

He went back to trying to walk out of the barrier of pain that surrounded him. He stopped once to phone for room service. "Send up two Cokes, they're in those little bottles, right? Make it three Cokes then. And send someone to get me a decongestant. Hell, I don't care what kind. Sudafed. Dimetapp. Some goddamn thing for sinus, whatever the fuck you can find. And hurry."

Ten minutes later he was swallowing two little white tablets that he hoped were what he asked for. If it turned out to be some of Rodriguez's speed or other druggie shit, he'd kill the desk clerk, hang him from the lobby chandelier. He drank two of the small bottles of Cokes as chasers. He'd save the other bottle for when he felt some relief. Sometimes decongestants worked, sometimes not. If it was a sinus headache, they helped. If it was a true migraine, nothing helped short of suicide. He'd have to return to bed, cover his head with a pillow, and not move a muscle for hours until it stopped throbbing.

Now and then he glanced over at Molly. Damn shame about her. Too fucking smart. He ought to do her right now, here, get it over with. Pick up another witness somewhere else. Over in Arizona, maybe.

He stopped walking, stared at Molly from the one uncovered green eye like a cyclops considering eating her for lunch. Weighed everything in the balance. His time investment. The stories he'd told. The money he'd spent. The *effort*.

She stared back unabashedly. Fire there, smoldering like molten lead in her gray flinty eyes. He really liked that. She wasn't completely intimidated. She'd seen him kill and could still look him in the face with defiance. Great little kid.

"What do I have to do to make you behave?" he asked suddenly.

"What do you want with me, Cruise?"

"I just want you with me."

"It doesn't make sense," she said. "You don't even know me. I'm a hitchhiker. You're just a ride."

"Not anymore. I'm living my life and you're my witness."

"Witness?"

"Exactly."

"To what?"

"My life. I just told you."

"Doesn't make any sense."

"Doesn't have to. It does to me, that's what counts. But now you're rebellious. I don't know if . . ."

"You expected me to be some kind of angel? Some kind of heartless monster like you?"

"Shut up." He grabbed the other side of his head and swayed on his feet. The pain. The pain! Trying to knock him off his feet. Trying to drop him to the floor with a roundhouse slam to his temples. He cried out, "Ahhhhh . . ."

Stood absolutely still, held his breath, tried to center himself. If he could put himself into his stomach muscles, get out of his head, he could beat this thing.

He had to get to the bed. He stumbled over his own feet trying to reach the mattress. He felt Molly's eyes boring through him. Nothing mattered but to lick the pain. He couldn't stand up anymore. His knees hit the mattress; he fell forward onto his outstretched hands, eyes tightly closed. The jar from the fall thumped through his head like a galloping Clydesdale. He pulled himself onto the bed, groped for the pillows. Found one, placed it carefully over the back of his head, buried his face in the sheets.

Oh, God. He didn't know if he'd live through it.

And if Molly said another goddamn word, he'd cut her head from her body.

Molly watched him pace the room like a staggering drunk, clutching one eye and the side of his head. Migraine, she guessed. She couldn't summon an ounce of pity for him. She'd been tied upright in the white satin chair all night. She'd had plenty of hours to think over her situation while her hands and feet began to tingle, her butt turned to stone. Witness, hell. She was a hostage, pure and simple. She was trapped. If she struggled too much at the wrong time, if she said the wrong word, if she moved when she should be motionless, she thought Cruise might kill her. She didn't just *think* it, she *knew* it even though Cruise had not made a specific threat.

That didn't mean life was hopeless. It just meant she'd made her first and worst mistake on the road, on her own. She hadn't contracted a sexual disease, fallen under the power of a pimp, been gang-raped, or starved to death. She'd done far better for herself. She'd taken a ride with a maniac. Hopeless, no. Dangerous, yes. Life-threatening, assuredly.

She didn't know any of the rules. At first she thought Cruise was a regular kind of guy, like her father, but not as strict. Then with the stories and the truck stops she thought he wasn't much like her father at all, but a more exciting sort of man who knew about worlds she didn't know existed. She found the life attractive, the man exotic. Now she knew the truth, the shocking, mind-numbing truth, and she thought she shouldn't let it cripple her or she was lost. If she gave herself over to fear she'd make the wrong move and she wouldn't survive the repercussion.

One time when she was a girl, must have been eight or nine years old, she came up on a tangle of coral snakes. They lived in Hollywood, Florida, just miles down the shoreline from Dania where her father lived now. She'd been running from her friends in a game of hide-and-seek, running down a worn path they took through a patch of trees between their houses. There was a giant magnolia tree with its limbs poised over the path. She remembered the double-fist-sized creamy white blooms hanging heavy and fragrant from the canopy of wide shiny deep green leaves.

The corals, Florida's deadliest snake, owned their piece of ground. It might have been a mother snake and her offspring, or corals mating, she didn't know why there were so many in one spot, but they were irrefutably there when she came racing like a tornado down upon them. Molly recognized the bright bands of color the second she spied them. But she was running too fast to stop. Had she tried, she would have landed right smack in the middle of venomous and instantaneous death. She hardly had time to formulate a plan. Instinct took over, the will to survive. She couldn't, and therefore didn't, slow her pace. She saw the snakes coming at her faster and faster although it was her moving in their direction instead of them moving at all except to squirm one on the other, a deadly circle of red, yellow, and black. Her bare feet made two easy targets. Then without thinking of what to do she was flying, literally airborne, rising into the air, taking wing, bounding from the spongy beaten-down grass high up over the corals, one short scream escaping her mouth as she sailed cleanly over the threat. She landed a few feet beyond them and as soon as her feet touched down she was gone from the scene, moving like wind, the thought of the corals just behind her supplying enough adrenaline to carry her straight down the path and out again into her friend's newly mowed backyard where she halted out of breath, her face white as a magnolia blossom, hands on her knees, hunched over, her head falling almost to the ground. She was whispering, "Thank you, God, thank you, God, thank you . . ."

She never told anyone about the close call. Her father wouldn't have let her play outside again for fear of her getting snake-bitten. Her friends wouldn't have really believed it. None of them at that time had ever seen a coral snake, though they had all been warned about them. That was Florida, after all, parents had to prepare their children for snakes, stinging scorpions, spiders, jellyfish and sharks at the beach.

She remembered what she'd done to save herself from the corals in the pathway. She let instinct take over. It had delivered her once from certain death. It could again if she would simply trust herself. Making plans was what she *wanted* to do, but everything she thought to do to extricate herself from Cruise was something she knew he'd know about before she even put the first steps into action.

He had had experience at this before.

He had had *witnesses* before.

What had become of *them*?

She frightened herself so badly with that one question her hands trembled where they were tied together in her lap.

She thought she knew what became of Cruise's witness victims.

The same thing that happened to the Mexican man in the street the night before.

The same thing that would have happened to her had she panicked and landed in the midst of the coral snakes when she was a kid.

She thought she could already feel the torture of fangs sinking into delicate skin, the slow burning sensation of poison seeping into her bloodstream.

She must learn to fly once more in order to save her life. She must grow invisible wings and perform a miraculous flight above the danger lying in wait on earth.

Cruise didn't sleep, but he dozed as the pain subsided in his temples. When he felt he could move his head without crying out, he pushed off the pillow and rose from bed. He tested himself by walking to the bath counter to wash his face. It seemed he would live.

He noticed Molly hadn't said a word to him. She tracked his movements, her eyes following him, but she didn't speak.

"We'll be on our way now," he said, coming to untie her. He knelt to the side of her feet as he undid the ropes. He repressed an urge to run his hand up the back of her calf to the shadowed warm spot behind her knee. When she was completely free, she rubbed both her wrists and ankles before trying to stand.

"Are you all right?"

"I'll be okay."

"Grab your bag. Follow me to my room so I can get my stuff."

Molly did as she was told. She walked with a temporary limp. He glanced behind him as they moved down the hall to the next door. Inside he had her stand in the middle of the room while he gathered his things. "Hungry?"

"Yeah, a little."

"You haven't eaten all day. I bet you're starved." When

she didn't reply, he shrugged and led her to the elevator.
They hadn't seen any of the other residents in the hotel and
didn't on this trip to the lobby. Cruise waved good-bye to
the desk clerk, called out, "Tell Adolpho I'll see him again
soon."

The night was full dark by the time they reached the
Chrysler. Cruise had brought along the last bottled Coke
he had ordered from room service. He drank it down before
starting the car. "Warm Coke. Just what the doctor ordered.
I'll get you something to eat in Juárez. Think you can
hold out?"

Molly nodded.

He wanted to act cool. Courteous. His moods kept changing faster than the weather in Texas, but he was trying with
all his might to court Molly's favor. She didn't *have* to be
a prisoner if she'd just shape up.

"So you're not going to talk to me, huh?"

"Are witnesses supposed to talk?"

She sounded as if she just wanted to know. She didn't
say it with any sarcasm.

"You don't have to. I'm not particular."

"Good."

Great. She was in her hardass mode. She fidgeted and
fussed with the collar of her blouse. Miss Rebel without a
cause. He could live with that, actually preferred it.

Once they were outside of town and in the desert land
that lay between Adolpho's city and Juárez, Cruise felt like
telling a story.

"I knew a couple of women one time . . ." He paused
when he heard Molly sigh. "What? You don't want to
hear it?"

"I don't care."

"Don't be like that. Let me tell you about these friends
of mine."

"Whatever."

"They were driving down from Boston. The woman in the passenger seat had short black hair. She had her cat with her, a long-haired black cat she carried in her lap. They were passing lots of semis, you know, and these guys are all staring down into the car. It's about dusk, that gray time when things aren't too distinct." He peeked a look at Molly, saw that she appeared interested in his tale despite herself. He continued, "Well, the woman is driving and she's talking and they're discussing the cat. The cat hears its name, gets a little rambunctious so the driver reaches over and starts rubbing the cat's fur. Before you know it they've got truck drivers honking their horns and cutting up like crazy. Some they pass are swerving a little in their lanes, then they're laying on the horns. 'What do you think they're carrying on about?' the driver asks her friend. She's still petting the cat in the other woman's lap. Suddenly it comes to her. 'You know what?' she asked. 'I bet they're looking down in the car and you've . . .' She started laughing hysterically. 'You've got black hair,' she said. 'And I'm reaching over there petting a black cat. It looks like I've got hold of your . . . your *pussy*!' "

Cruise laughed like crazy, and Molly stared at him with a blank look on her face. He thought maybe she didn't get it. He sobered, stared down the road ahead. Molly wasn't going to be any fun from now on. She'd be a challenge, though, and he liked that just as well.

He had to maneuver the car around the worst potholes to keep from ruining the undercarriage. He had hoped he could cheer Molly up, but it wasn't working. The petting-the-pussy story was about the funniest one he knew. If she didn't find that amusing, nothing was going to bring her out of the doldrums.

"You won't have to be tied up if you'll just cooperate," he said.

"How long are you going to keep me?"

Well, well. He might get a dialogue going after all. "Not long," he promised.

"You've killed people before last night, haven't you?"

Cruise shrugged. She knew and didn't want to know.

"Doesn't it mean anything to you?"

Cruise smiled, but he knew the beard and mustache would hide it. "Sure, it means something."

"Why do you do it?"

"Why did you run away from home?"

"It's not the same thing!"

"I didn't say it was."

"Then what's the point? Leaving home has nothing to do with killing people. God."

"Here's the connection. You left home because you felt you had to, didn't you? Well, didn't you?"

"I guess so . . ."

"That's why I kill. I have to."

"Why?"

Cruise made an exasperated movement with his right hand. "I just told you. I have to. You changed your life, I change mine."

"Is that it?" she asked. "Killing is some kind of . . . some sort of . . . *change*?"

"I guess that describes it pretty well."

"But, Cruise, you can't kill people for a reason like that. It's dumb. It's . . ."

"Crazy?"

She was silent. Maybe she knew she'd gone too far. Cruise admired her restraint. He wasn't angry with her, in fact he found the conversation intriguing. When they probed this way, he had a good time with them.

"Most people think it's crazy," he admitted. "I don't think so. It's just a difference of opinion. And my reasons are reasonable to me."

"I've heard about people like you," she said. She didn't spit the words out, but they were coated with slime just the same. It sounded like it made her sick to say them.

"Like me? There's no one like me, Molly. Don't make a mistake in judgment."

"You're right. I don't think there's anyone like you."

He smiled to himself again. Now she was catching on. Not understanding, but at least feeling the slightest empathy for his actions. It was a beginning.

"There's Juárez. I'll stop for tacos or something."

He had to watch her at the border. If she tried signaling to the border guards, he'd have to kill her. It could be a messy business. He couldn't tie her, they'd see. He had to make his warning convincing. He didn't want a misadventure spoiling the trip.

In Juárez he parked the car near a portable stand covered by a rainbow-colored umbrella to shield the sun in the day, the moon at night. These were roach coaches, ptomaine domains, but what the hell. He wasn't in the mood for going into a four-star mariachi-band restaurant.

"Get out of the car," he said.

"Why?"

"Do what I tell you," he said, not unkindly.

He came around the front grille and walked Molly with him to the food cart. "What do you want?"

"I don't care."

"Be that way." He ordered tacos, bean and red chili burritos, and two canned Cokes from the cart tender. "Lose that sombrero, friend," he told him when he paid the bill. "You look like a clown."

Back in the car Molly said, "That was mean."

"You've seen me meaner. Here, eat your dinner." He handed her a taco and a burrito from the sack.

They sat in the car with the windows down watching the passersby on the street. Unlike Adolpho's city, Juárez had a sprinkling of Americans intermingling with the natives. Nearly all of them carried bags with their purchases poking from the top. Clacking wooden snakes. Hand-carved walking canes. Polyester lace tablecloths. Embroidered dresses. Leather goods. Multicolored blankets. Cheap stuff they thought were real bargains.

The place was running over with pedestrians. They haggled with shopkeepers, ate colored flavored ices from paper cones, begged on street corners, and picked pockets.

Cruise finished off the food, the Coke, and turned in his seat to face Molly. He had to lecture her. She wasn't going to like it. She had told him that's all her father ever did, lecture.

"They're going to stop us at the border. They'll probably inspect the car. They'll ask where you were born."

"So?"

"Don't get smart with me. I'm talking to you."

"I can hear you. Talk already."

"If you make a squawk, if you give any signal that something is wrong, if you say one word that puts me in jeopardy, I'll kill you where you sit." He heard her intake of breath although she wouldn't face him. He saw her jawline tighten down, the milky skin smooth against the bone. "You know what I can do with my knife." He moved his hand to the back of his head. Touched his hair as if smoothing it down. He knew she could sense his movements without looking directly at him. "I don't want to have to do that, Molly. But no one's ever taking me to jail. Ever. I promise you that. So if you get the urge to make a play, suppress it. Before you can make a move, blink an eye, utter a word, I'll slit your throat from ear to ear."

Molly looked down at her hands in her lap. She had them clutched together in a small knuckly ball. "I get it," she said, her voice barely audible.

"You're a good girl. Now let's get moving. I hate fucking Juárez."

He watched her closely at the border crossing. It all went peacefully. She trembled a little and her voice cracked when she said where she had been born—Dania, Florida—but other than that, it went fine. Once on the road in the darkness he said, "You performed that duty as well as could be expected, I'm proud of you. I think I'll tell you a story about a guy I knew once who crossed over into Mexico to get him a whore for the night . . ."

He settled into his driving and storytelling. Molly was still going to be the best witness he'd ever taken.

The miles rolled away. I-10 took them past Las Cruces, New Mexico, and back into the night. There was Deming, then Lordsburg came next and was soon behind them. They were across the state line into Arizona. All Cruise *ever* remembered on his travels across New Mexico was that the rest areas, the pickle parks, were pristine as sun-bleached bone. He filled the gas tank at a Chevron station off the freeway just east of Bowie, Arizona. He kept watch on Molly. She asked to go to the bathroom when he replaced the gas nozzle. He walked her to the rest-room door on the side of the station and waited outside for her. When she exited, he held her arm, pushed open the door, checked the stall walls, the floor, the mirror over the sink for any notes she might have left. He knew all the tricks. The girls he took almost always tried to leave behind messages. Molly didn't.

"You knew better, didn't you?" he asked, smiling genially.

"Knew better about what?"

"Never mind. It's not important." He didn't want to give her any ideas she didn't already have.

He sent her to the car while he paid the station attendant for the gas. She was in his line of sight every second.

On the highway again he gave her the news. "We're getting off the freeway about seven miles from here."

"Why?"

There was a high panic in her voice. He loved being able to produce that shaky, unsure note. "I'm taking Route 666 north to 70. We go through Globe, then we get a bunch of little shit-kicking roads north to Flagstaff. We're stopping off to see my sister. And my father," he added.

"What's your sister's name?"

"Evelander. Lannie. Not that it matters. She's not going to help you." He saw Molly visibly sag in the seat. There was no point in letting her hopes rise just to be deflated. Lannie *wouldn't* help her. He'd taken little friends by her house before. She was too scared of him to lift a finger without his permission. Lannie *knew* him. Her house was the only place in the world he could crash without fear of discovery. It was his safe house, his haven, the single rest stop in all of America where he didn't have to worry about running into someone he'd have to kill. Lannie looked straight through the kids he brought through on his constant trips across country. She rarely even spoke to them. And she *never* asked him to untie them or let them go free. She just knew it wasn't a request he'd honor.

"Does Lannie make a habit of murdering people too?" Molly asked abruptly, startling Cruise from reverie.

Cruise was left wordless for once. He didn't find the question funny. It was just odd. No one had ever asked him such a thing about his sister before. The thought had never crossed his mind. Lannie *kill*? He would laugh if he wasn't so shaken by the query.

"What makes you ask something like that?" He wanted to sound angrier, but he couldn't get any backbone in it. The kids surprised him sometimes. You'd think he'd get used to it.

"Well, if she wouldn't help me out, maybe she helps you do what you do."

He realized she had phrased the reply without using the words "murder" or "kill."

"Lannie's not in this." he said. "Now let's drop it."

"I don't want to drop it. What about your father? He know you go around cutting people open? That you keep hitchhikers as prisoners so they can watch you work?"

"My father . . . doesn't know anything."

"Why not? Can't he see what you're doing? Is he blind?"

"Molly, that's enough." He nearly reached across the car to smack her across the face. His arm trembled with the effort it took not to hit her. That cold rage that came over him when he did kill now crept closer. It wrapped him in its frosty sheath, coated his mind with a rind of ice. He clenched his jaws. His hands tightened on the steering wheel. He saw he was weaving across the dividing line on the highway and had to bring the car into his lane again.

Something about his changing demeanor must have leaked into the car between them because Molly didn't repeat the questions. She stared out the window as if she'd never asked them, as if the answers didn't concern her one way or the other.

Cruise fought to halt the fury that was trying to possess him. He didn't want to kill Molly. He knew he had to. One day, one night, sometime. But not now, not if he could stop the avalanche of his emotions.

He clamped the wheel, took the exit for 666 north, his gaze scanning the roadside for something, for someone on whom to vent the building power. He drove for thirty-two miles to the Highway 70 turnoff at Safford in a trance Molly would not have been able to penetrate had she tried. During the next hundred miles that took them to the copper-mining town of Globe, Arizona, Cruise concentrated his whole being on driving the Chrysler. He listened to the wind whistling past the lowered windows. He was intoxicated by the drone of the big engine, the swish of the tires on pavement, the steady hum of movement through space and time. Overhead he saw there was cloud cover. The moon peeked sporadically from the shifting rims of black fortresses. It looked like rain, smelled like it. There was a sharp taste to the cooling mountain air. They were entering the Mescal Mountains. Once outside of Globe they'd travel into the Sierra Anchas and the Mazatzals.

Arizona didn't get more than two inches of precipitation a year normally. Cruise didn't know how the trees in the national forests were able to grow. If it rained tonight he didn't expect much. A sprinkle. A light shower.

He was wrong. He came into town just ahead of a gully-washer. Lightning strobed the heavens delineating Globe's tall mounds of coppery dust against an electric-blue backdrop. Thunder pealed over the forested mountainsides and rolled down like boulders into the empty two A.M. city streets. Firs shivered crazily in the wind. Bits of paper and litter were flung into the air, plate-glass windows shimmered from the wind's force, a child's red and green ball rolled from a lawn across the street ahead of them.

He heard Molly wondering aloud where they were. He refused to answer. He wanted to ask why she didn't read the sign at the city limits, but fuck it, let her stew. Let her be frightened. He had become distanced from her on the drive from Safford to Globe. She was no more to him at the moment than a rag doll with a voice, a dog with a bark, an animal with a whine. Given the least provocation he could pull over and do her without a minute's regret.

He found his turn for Highway 88 north just as the rain let loose. At first it was rain. Big splattering drops that split open on his windshield like fat grapes. Five minutes after he had the windshield wipers going the rain turned to hailstones. The pummeling sounds on the roof, hood, and trunk of the car sounded like a truckload of hard-boiled eggs being dumped over them. Cruise got his window up in time, but Molly was making little squeaky noises as she brushed off the hail while trying to get her window cranked shut.

That was when the wind picked up. The trees covering the slopes of the mountains began to dance insanely in the headlights. The hail was slanted straight at them, missiles in the cones of the car lights, striking the windshield with enough force to make Cruise wince and hunch his shoulders over the wheel. There were no other cars on 88. They might as well have been alone on an alien planet where the weather had turned mean and meant to beat the shit out of any machine that dared move about in it.

Cruise slowed, drove snaillike on the narrow two-lane until he reached the Theodore Roosevelt Lake. It gleamed black as an oil slick to his right. The wind had kicked up frothy crusts of waves that beat on the shoreline. Hail pockmarked the water.

"I'm pulling over," he said.

"What is this? What's happening? Is it a tornado?"

He heard Molly, but he didn't want to talk to her. He thought perhaps it *was* a tornado, but he couldn't understand it. The tornadoes he'd been acquainted with in his cross-country travels were experienced from inside motel rooms or restaurants. He heard reports on the radio of that kind of weather looming, he always got off the road. He knew a tornado wind could pick up a car and send it flying through the side of a building or dump it down in a cornfield smashed flat as a dime. If this *was* a tornado, he'd be goddamned if he was going to drive through it. They'd have to wait it out.

Molly had her seat belt off. She was turned to her window, hands flat against the glass. With the motor stopped, the headlights off, the world outside took on a nightmarish quality. They could hear the wind shrieking in a multitude of infernal voices, low, high, harsh, whispery. The lake waters slapped angrily against the shore. The hail had stopped, but now rain again poured down hard and fast, sheeting the windows with gray. Lightning still strobed and lit the scene. Once he saw the lake foaming and boiling like a caldron over a hot fire. Once he saw trees on a mountainside leaning almost parallel to the ground. The Chrysler rocked on its tires. It shook them in their seats and had Cruise's top teeth rattling against his bottom molars.

"Jesus Christ," he whispered.

"What're we gonna do?" Molly repeated over and over.

Cruise didn't know. They were at the mercy of the storm. If a wind came down and plucked them from the roadside and hurled them into the lake, they probably wouldn't know anything until they were sucking water. He leaned forward and tried to see out the top of the windshield. He wanted to sight the motherfucking tornado before it got them, but the rain was too hard, he couldn't see anything but streaming water. His imagination took over. He *thought* he saw a funnel reaching down out of the blackness to snatch them from the earth. He *thought* he heard a freight train and that's what they always said preceded a tornado touching down.

The girl was nuts, trying to open the passenger door. What was her name? Molly! Irish girl, red hair, that was the one. He was more and more confused as the wind raged around the car and shook him where he sat.

He *knew* he couldn't let the girl out of the car. That was absolutely out of the question. A big negatory. The wind would take her away from him. The lake would cover her over and he'd never see her again.

He bounded across the space between the blue cloth bucket seats and grabbed her shirt with both hands. Fabric ripped at the seams. He held on for she had the door open now and wind and rain sliced into the car wetting his hands, his forearms. He grappled with her and had her around the neck, hauling her back inside. The door slammed shut from the force of the wind. The bang of it made the pressure in his eardrums close. He swallowed hard to clear them. He held her back against his chest, her head in the crook of his arm. All he had to do was snap it. Easy. Be rid of the nuisance of her. She'd been trying to escape. It wasn't the storm she wanted to flee. It was him.

He heard her weeping. "Do that again and I break your fucking neck." When she didn't say anything he said, "I should do it anyway. Save myself trouble later on."

She gasped as his arm tightened down. *"No!"*

He let up a little, but not much.

"I won't do it again!"

"I know you won't." He pushed her away and reached behind him to the back floorboard. He felt the loops of rope he'd brought along. He found one end of the rope, brought her hands together, and began tying her securely. He passed the rope through the hole in the door armrest. She wanted to get out again, she'd have to take the goddamned door with her. The whole goddamned car.

While busy with Molly the wind dropped and the rain fell to a soft shower. The sound of the freight train was gone and in its place was an eerie stillness with the gentle patter of raindrops as punctuation on the roof.

"It passed," he said, breathing heavy.

His arms were still damp from the rain. Molly sat quietly subdued, roped into submission. The windows had fogged from their breathing.

A rap came at Cruise's side window. He jerked away and stared out. Molly let out a yelp of surprise.

The rap came again and someone had hold of the door handle trying to open the door.

"What the fuck?" Cruise rolled down the window while holding the door closed by grasping the armrest.

A face came forward out of the dark. It was wet, the hair plastered in bangs across the broad forehead. It was a frantic red bloated face with a double chin beneath it belonging to a man who needed to lose at least a hundred pounds. His eyes were dark circles, his nose small and pointed. His lips worked long before anything came from them. He was like an actor in a foreign movie, his words dubbed in and unsynchronized with his lip movements.

"My car!" he screamed. Rain sluiced down his cheeks like tear tracks. "My car turned over. I stopped! But the wind turned us over. My wife ... my wife's caught ... can't get out ..."

Cruise pushed open the door and crawled from the bucket seat. He stood several inches taller than the fat man. "Where?" he asked, feeling the first droplets of rain soaking into the back of his shirt.

"Down here. I saw your car lights, saw you pull over just before that wind hit. Please help me."

Cruise followed behind the waddling fellow. He looked like a duck in his proper element. Cruise noted he wore a sloppy suit in a dark color. It was soaking wet. The cuffs of his pants dragged the ground and his heels stepped on them. When he turned back once to gesture, Cruise saw he wore a diamond ring on his right hand.

The car was just around a bend in the road, hidden from view by the forested mountain. It was on its side in a steep ditch, the undercarriage facing the highway.

"I don't know how to get into it," the man was saying. Screaming. The wind had stopped, the rain was gentle, the clouds were parting and letting through the moon, but this man was out of his head and he couldn't stop screaming. "She's on the other side!" He went around the front end of the car and pointed at the ground.

"Let's try to push it back on its wheels," Cruise suggested. He and the fat man put their shoulders to the roof of the car. It was a white Ford Escort. New. Light.

The car moved, tilted, fell with a resounding crunch into the gravel lining the roadbed. The windows on the side they faced were broken into spiderwebs. The fat man rushed to the wedged door and tried to open it. He couldn't. He was screaming still when Cruise went to the driver's side door and opened it. He leaned in. A small woman, dark hair thin as spaghetti swirling around her face, lay with her torso on the seat, her legs and hips crumpled into the floorboard area. She looked dead to him and he'd seen a lot of dead people. She wasn't moving or making any sound. He thought her eyes were open. Her mouth was. Her bottom denture lay on her unmoving chest.

Cruise felt the man behind him, trying to pull him out of the way. Cruise backed off. Stood watching while the man crawled into the car on his hands and knees. His tremendous belly got stuck between the steering wheel and the seat back. He was still screaming and crying and Cruise knew then the woman was lifeless.

Cruise felt beneath his hair for the knife. He pulled it gently from the Velcro patch. He stood with it in his hand until the fat man extricated himself from the wrecked car. When the other man turned to face him, that's when Cruise took a few steps to circle him, got behind his wide back before he could move again, grabbed the wet hair of his head, jerked him backward until the throat was exposed.

The screaming turned to a coughing, a gurgling. The little hook on the end of the sharp blade had severed the carotid artery and a few fatty neck muscles. The man jerked in Cruise's big arms. His blood warmed Cruise's skin where he'd caught him around the chest to hold him up. He held him until life drained out and the man was dead weight. He dropped him unceremoniously to the pavement. Stooping, he reached inside the coat pocket and slipped out the wallet. Took the cash. Wrenched the ring from the man's thick finger. Kicked him out of the way. Inside the car Cruise searched the front seat for the woman's purse and couldn't find it. Finally he gave up and shut the car door.

He'd have to wash himself in the lake. He thought maybe he'd do it right at the edge of the shore near the Chrysler so that Molly could see him naked.

He'd have to hurry. Another car might come along anytime. Cruise thought that would be a definite inconvenience. He also thought he felt much better with the fat man dead. The ice that earlier encased his brain had warmed and melted.

Molly was safe for a little while longer.

Molly's wrists were rubbed raw where the thin yellow nylon rope circled them. She tried like hell to get herself loose when Cruise left the car to help the fat man. Had she been successful, she could have disappeared into the woods where Cruise would never have found her.

She tried everything she could think to do. She twisted her arms until her elbows groaned, trying to get her fingers on the knots in the rope. She jerked and hauled, yelling out each time when the rope burned into the flesh of her wrists.

She even scooted from the seat and knelt on the floorboard to face the armrest trying to get a hold on the knots, but nothing she did worked. She merely succeeded in tearing up the skin on her wrists and crying until she felt sick to her stomach.

She was just able to get back into the seat before Cruise reappeared by her window. He scared her, standing there in the dark, the moon over his shoulder. She didn't know what he was doing, what he wanted. She reached up tentatively and wiped the fogged window. She was afraid suddenly that he wanted to rape her and was screwing up his courage to do so. But after a short time he stepped away from the window, walked toward the lake while shedding his clothes in the moonlight. Rain still came down, but it was nothing like the storm earlier. This was a light drizzle that sent trails of water slipping quietly down the windshield.

Molly watched, hypnotized by Cruise's actions. He stripped right to the skin. She saw his white buttocks, his wide muscled shoulders. She saw him walk right into the water until it was up to his knees. He turned then and began dipping the water over himself with his hands. Splashing himself. He was too distant for her to see his face. He looked like a nature god of the wilderness with his long hair dripping onto his broad shoulders, swinging free around his face as he bent to dip the water. What sort of bizarre ritual this was she could not possibly imagine. He had been wet from the rain, but why was he bathing in the lake?

God, what was she going to do to get away from him? She'd made that one effort during the height of the wind and rain when Cruise seemed most vulnerable. She thought she could get the door open and be gone before he could react. The stunt almost got her killed. She had felt her wind being cut off by his thick arm. Black dots appeared before her eyes from lack of oxygen. Her neck still ached from the strangling she took. She knew she was lucky to be alive.

Then they'd both been stunned by the rap on the window and the appearance of the fat man. He was bellowing about his car being wrecked, something about his wife being trapped. Cruise wasn't gone long. Molly wondered if the woman was okay. If they'd gotten her out.

She saw Cruise starting back up the slope to the car. He picked up his clothes as he came, held them modestly in front of himself. He circled the trunk, opened the driver's door, withdrew the car keys. He went again to the trunk and Molly watched out the rear window until minutes later the trunk lid was lowered. Cruise was dressed again. He had gotten into dry clothes.

She waited as he climbed into the driver's seat and started the engine. He had brought a wet scent into the car. His hair still dripped lake water. "Did you get the woman out all right?"

"She was dead."

Molly bit her lower lip. They drove slowly around the curve in the road and she saw the white Escort in the car lights. She also saw something—was it a body?—on the gravel lining the road next to the car.

She turned her head, looking back, trying to be sure.

"He's dead too," Cruise said.

"What . . . why . . . did you . . . ?"

"Yes," he said simply.

Molly couldn't look at him any longer. She stared instead ahead at the white dividing lines in the road. "I don't know how you can do that," she said when she was able to speak.

"Why not? He wouldn't have been happy without his wife anyway."

"How do you know that?" She spoke in a dull monotone. She thought all her indignation had been sapped; thought she might be losing touch with her deepest emotions, or at least losing touch with the necessity to express them.

"It's a gift I have. Knowing."

Molly couldn't stand hearing what he had to say anymore. Everything he said was a torture to her. He was playing God, the God of Death. Being crazy was worse than dying, she thought. Cruise was already crazy and now she feared she might be losing her mind too the way she kept thinking of him as a nature god, a death god. There was only so much shock she could endure before she turned into an inhuman being who couldn't be shocked. Someone just like him.

Despair at her situation set hooks into her brain and deadened it the way Novocain killed all the pain in a rotten tooth. She didn't want to feel anything. Maybe that's what going crazy meant. You stopped feeling. The appalling truths became commonplace. The heart shriveled to a lump smaller than the tiny nubs that were her breasts.

Mark Killany was nearly to the outskirts of Tucson with the car radio tuned to a local station when he heard the first reports.

Man robbed and murdered, found beside his wrecked car near Theodore Roosevelt Lake. His wife was dead too, apparently from being thrown forward into the windshield when the car overturned in a ditch during tornado weather. It was the couple's son, eleven-year-old Brian Delham, who had been relatively unhurt in the back seat who found his father. He told the police about the man who came to help them. The man with long hair, a beard, and mustache. The man who killed his father. Hiding on the floor of the car, Brian had watched the car the murderer drove as it left the scene heading north. It was a blue Chrysler, the boy said. He was positive. It was old. Big. He didn't get the license plate number, but he'd never forget the killer's face.

Mark sped to the next exit ramp and made a U-turn that took him east again on I-10. He had trouble breathing. He cranked down the window, drank in great heaving drafts of fresh air. The radio announcer said the murder occurred on Highway 666. Mark had seen the exit for it miles back. He had to get there. He had to get in touch with the Arizona highway patrol. He wanted to tell them about Molly. That she might be with the killer. If it was the same man he'd been following across country, the same man the hooker in Mobile identified, then he might still have Molly with him.

Or worse yet, he might *not* have her with him. He could have . . . murdered her too. The boy didn't say anything about a girl being in the car.

"Shit," he wailed. "Dammit to hell, shit, shit, shit."

The speedometer needle rose past eighty, ninety, hovered there. Mark didn't care if he was stopped for speeding. He had to get to 666 and Roosevelt Lake. He had to tell someone about the danger Molly was in. His girl. His baby. The blue Chrysler.

Lannie Reed lived in a modest three-bedroom house on a dead-end street in Flagstaff, Arizona. It was a working-class neighborhood where some of the people couldn't find work or else they made a salary that didn't cover all the expenses. Oil drip spots from worn-out cars marred the driveways. The Big Wheels and bicycles of the neighbor children were broken or rusted and lying forlorn in the weedy yards. Plastic garbage cans sans lids were stacked at the curbs where wandering packs of homeless dogs knocked them over for the sparse loot they contained.

Some of the homes were empty, windows broken or boarded over. Blue cardboard HUD warning signs were taped to the windows of sagging garage doors.

Cruise pulled into his sister's driveway. He parked next to a twelve-year-old brown Chevy station wagon with ripped seats and a dented front fender. Once the engine was off, ticking away its heat in the early morning hours, Cruise began untying his witness. She moaned as he slipped the rope from her wrists.

"I'll have to hobble you once we're inside, but for a few minutes I'll let you stay free so you can go to the bathroom. I'll get Lannie to feed you too."

Molly grunted. She hadn't talked to him since the lake incident. She was an unsatisfactory companion the way she'd argue with him, get her smart mouth running, then suddenly clam up and give him the silent treatment. Her presence was wearing thin, so thin he thought he'd made a mistake not leaving her floating facedown in the lake back on Highway 666.

"C'mon," he ordered, pulling himself wearily from the car. She tried to make a break for it, he'd still be able to catch her before any harm was done. She could scream around here for an hour and not more than two people would look out their windows to see what was going on. No one wanted to get involved. Too many of the residents had speed labs in the kitchens and marijuana gardens in the bedrooms.

It made Cruise sad that Lannie had to live in a place like this. There were lots of neighborhoods in Flagstaff where decent people lived, but it cost too much, more than Lannie could afford. Still, it wasn't right his sister lived this way. Broke his damned heart. Sometimes he sent her money he scored. It was never enough.

Molly came around the car, a docile little sheep. He marched her before him to the recessed doorway. In the cement entry lay a black plastic machine gun and a cap made of camouflage material. One of Lannie's kids left his junk out. There wasn't any way to make them mind. Lannie had given up trying a long time ago. She had five kids, stepping stones, from Sherry, who was the toddler in diapers, to Wayne who was ten, the eldest, the probable owner of the gun and cap.

Cruise tried the doorknob, found it locked. Didn't blame her. The street was a war zone what with the druggies, the teenage burglars, the unemployed. They'd lift their grandmother's girdle if they thought there was any money in it.

Cruise tried the doorbell. He listened, couldn't hear it ringing inside. He pounded finally on the door.

"Let's wake them all up," he said to Molly. "Get those little toads of Lannie's into high gear before sunup."

It took a while, but eventually the door creaked open on a safety chain. A woman wearing a red chenille housecoat looked out.

"Don't frown. It's me," Cruise said. "And a friend."

Lannie shut the door, lifted the chain, then opened up to them. She stood back in a dark hallway, one hand holding closed the robe. Her glasses had slipped down on her nose and she peered over them like a schoolmarm.

"You look like shit, Lannie." Cruise moved past her down the hall, pulling Molly behind him. They came out into a living area stuffed with Salvation Army and garage sale furniture, toys scattered on the matted dirty carpet, clothes draped everywhere, old newspapers stacked on every conceivable surface.

Cruise wrinkled his nose. "Home sweet home," he said.

"I don't need your bullshit, Cruise. What do you want?"

Lannie slouched into the room and cleared a place on the stained and worn orange upholstered sofa.

"Don't you want to meet Molly first? Molly, this is my sister, Lannie. Lannie, Molly. She's Irish, you can tell by her hair. She doesn't want to stay with me now, so watch her."

"Goody. Another one of *those*."

"Where's Daddy?" Cruise moved toward another hallway that led to the bedrooms.

"He's sleeping, what do you think? We don't usually get up around here before dawn in case you forgot."

Cruise paused, his back to the room. "Is he worse?"

He heard Lannie sigh the way she might with one of the kids when they asked too many unanswerable questions. "He's not going to get better, Cruise. You already know that."

Cruise nodded. He moved on down the hallway until he came to the door of his father's bedroom. This is where his father had slept for the past ten years. Lannie wouldn't put him in a home. She knew Cruise would have killed her if she tried.

He opened the door slowly, his fist swallowing and squeezing the doorknob. Breathed in the smell of age that bathed the room with its aroma. Old clothes, old skin, old air going in and out of old lungs.

Feeble light from the one window in the far wall made the bedroom appear watery and insubstantial. There was too much furniture in the room. An iron bedstead, unpainted and gray as lead. A bedside table covered with a lamp, a Bible, bottles of vitamins, tubes of salves. A standing wardrobe made of dark cherry, the mirror on its front cracked right down the middle. A stuffed easy chair, torn on the arms. A metal tube-legged kitchen chair, seat in canary-yellow. Rips in the vinyl. A battered chest of drawers, flaking white paint, the top stacked with newspapers and folded clothes.

Cruise approached his father's bed. He stared down at the old man. Here lay the monster of his dreams, the master of his past, the fearsome right hand that so often struck him low. He didn't look much changed except for the skin on his face and hands that lay atop the sheet. The skin had been ruddy and weathered and tough as oiled leather. Now it was papery white and thinly veined with blue. His father still retained his thick brown hair, tinged gray on the sides. He still had the massive forehead, the large nose that dominated his features, the narrow mean lips.

Where the real change had come with age was in the old man's brain. He'd been diagnosed as suffering from Alzheimer's disease the week Lannie took him into her home to care for him. His mind was a quicksand pit where you could throw in anything and get nothing back. He forgot his name. He forgot to go to the bathroom, how to hold his dick to take a piss, how to wipe himself. He forgot how to feed himself, forgot where he was, who he had been, what he had done.

Cruise reached out a tentative hand and touched his arm. The old man woke immediately, eyes swiveling to the side of the bed without moving his head. "Who?" he asked.

"Hi, Daddy. It's Cruise."

"Who?" The old man came up onto his elbows to squint at Cruise. "Who are you?"

"Your son. Herod, remember?"

"I don't know you. Who are you?"

Cruise reached behind him and caught the back of the kitchen chair. He dragged it close to the bedside and sat in it. He held his father's hand in both his own.

"Don't worry about it," he said. "I know you, that's enough, isn't it?"

"Where am I?"

"You're at Lannie's house. You've been here for years, Daddy."

"I'm hungry." He smacked his lips.

"Lannie will cook breakfast soon. Why don't I sit here and tell you about a few things while she does? Wouldn't you like that?"

The old man stared at him the way he would a stranger. Cruise began to tell him about his latest trip across country. He told him, in detail, about the Lot Lizard who called herself Minde. How she'd almost gone with Dirty Old Man and how he, Cruise, got to her first. How he'd already prepared a shallow grave outside of Charlotte. How fiercely Minde had fought for her life. Then he told him about Molly, picking her up at a truck stop in Mobile. What a pretty girl she was, so naive, so young, so trusting. He told him how much it meant to him to have company along. How lonely he got without *someone* at his side.

He told his father about Riaro, about the visit to the cemetery after he killed him. He told how Molly tried to call her father, how he'd almost missed finding her in time. He brought the old man up-to-date on his life since the last time he'd seen him. He ended with the story of the tornado, the rap on the window, the way it felt to kill the fat man who jiggled and struggled as he died in his arms.

When he finished, Cruise reached into his pants pocket and withdrew the diamond ring his last victim had been wearing. It was the first time he'd really looked at it. There were six big diamonds encircling a round center stone. It was a beauty. He slipped it onto his father's hand. "Here, this is for you. Isn't it nice? A real diamond, I think."

The old man held it up to his face, inches from his nose. "What is it?"

"A diamond ring. Lannie said you lost the other one I gave you. It doesn't matter. You can lose it. I'll get more."

"Pretty," the old man said, admiring the sparkle as he turned the stone back and forth on his finger.

"Yeah. I knew you'd like it."

"I'm hungry."

"All right. Get up and I'll take you to the kitchen."

"Where is it?"

"I'll take you." Cruise helped him from the tangle of covers, brought the slippers from beneath the bed for his feet. He guided him to the door and down the hall.

Molly sat in a rocking chair across from Lannie. Her eyes were red. Crying. Always crying. They did that so much at Lannie's house. Why would they think she'd help them escape? She knew better.

"This is my father." He smiled as he showed off the old man to Molly, but it was a wisp of a smile, a shadow. And it made him ache in his chest.

Molly had begged her. "You have to help me. Your brother's crazy. He's killed people. He'll probably kill me."

Lannie pursed her lips and shook ash-blond hair from the frames of her glasses. "Don't waste your breath. I can't do a thing."

"Why not? You know what he's doing. He has to be stopped."

"Not by me. I never could stop him. Daddy couldn't stop him. The only thing that will end it is a cop's bullet."

"Are you afraid of him, is that it? He wouldn't have to know . . ."

"He'd know the second I touched the telephone."

"But why haven't you told before? When he left, why didn't you call the police the first time you knew for sure?"

"You don't understand. Cruise is like a flood or an earthquake. He won't be stopped by me turning him in. They'd never catch him. He's too smart. He's been doing this for half his life."

Molly tried to think. Half his life. If he was about forty, that meant twenty years of killing and he hadn't been caught. She couldn't believe it. "Twenty years?" she whispered.

"Longer."

"But if you don't *do* something, he's going to . . . he'll . . ."

Lannie turned away her face. She picked at lint on the red chenille. "I can't help you," she said. "I *won't*. He helps pay for Daddy's care. I couldn't do it without him. I work like a dog just to pay the mortgage on this dump. Who's going to take care of my kids if I don't? I have to have someone come in when I'm working. My no-good bastard of a husband left me when the last one was born. I can't leave Daddy alone. It takes money."

"You're no better than he is," Molly said. Her cheeks flamed and tears rushed to her eyes. "Those aren't excuses. There *is* no excuse for what you're doing. You're as much a killer as he is if you don't try to stop him. They'd make you an accessory, you'll go to prison."

"So I'll go to prison. It can't be much worse than what I'm in now."

Cruise walked the old man into the room and Molly turned to face her executioner. He proudly introduced his father. When she saw Cruise smile, she said boldly, "Your son's a murderer."

She waited for the old man to react. She expected him to turn on his son. Instead he blinked stupidly and murmured, "I'm real hungry."

Molly's mouth dropped open. Lannie stood from the sofa. She stepped over the laden coffee table and made her way to the kitchen. Molly heard her opening the refrigerator door.

Cruise placed the old man carefully on the sofa where Lannie had been sitting. He patted his shoulders, settling him in. When he turned back to Molly he wasn't smiling.

"He's got Alzheimer's," he said. "Leave him alone."

"No wonder you come here. No one hassles you. No one cares enough."

She flinched when Cruise moved across the room and grabbed her by the arms. He spoke into her face. When she tried to turn her head, he shook her until her eyes rolled in their sockets. "They care!" he said, his green eyes darkening to a drab hazel color. "My father loves me!"

He dropped her into the rocker, turned on his heel to his father. "You love me, don't you, Daddy? Tell her!"

"I don't know, I don't know. Who is she? Where am I? I'm hungry . . ."

Cruise lay on Lannie's unmade bed unable to sleep. Molly was bound to the faucets in the second bathroom at the end of the hall. She sat in the tub. He told her she wanted to pee, she'd have to do it in her clothes, he wasn't coming to see about her until he was ready to leave. It was his way of saying *fuck you*. He thought she probably got his drift.

He reflected that Molly was right, he liked it in this house, he came back because no one cared enough to do anything about it. Even Lannie's kids didn't give a damn. They got up, the three oldest ones dressed for school, ate breakfast, and were out the door to catch the bus. Said one word to him, hello, that was it. The two little ones, Sherry in diapers hardly knew him, and Judy, the three-year-old, didn't think much of him one way or the other. Unca Cruise, Judy could say. But she never came to him or hugged his neck. She talked to her baby doll and poured water from a toy teapot.

Then there was Lannie. Broken like an aggressive dog you kick until it hides under beds when you walk in the room. She had about as much spirit as a june bug.

That left Daddy. Brain like grapefruit pulp. Who did he love? Who had he ever loved? It sure wasn't Cruise or Lannie or any of the others, not even his mother. His father hadn't known how to love anyone, hadn't the capacity. He made a living, he fucked his wife, he raised his children to fear him. That's all his life amounted to. A duty to persevere, never mind having any fun, feeling any joy, experiencing any hope. That made him one of the strange imposters who could never live by society's rules. Cruise grew to love him if only for that reason. He wasn't like other men. He viewed the world one way while other men saw it another. Cruise thought if his father really knew what his son had done with his life, he would have admired it. Before he came down with Alzheimer's he made no remark to dispute Cruise's feelings. He never made any remark at all. Cruise took that for approval.

Cruise always felt belittled and powerless as a kid, but he didn't blame Daddy. Nothing in a young person's world was under his control. His father had that iron fist, that razor strap, those chains. That's what fathers were supposed to do. That was the job entrusted to them.

Cruise wanted more than anything to possess the same power his father wielded. He thought for a while he'd never find a way. It wasn't enough to get some woman and raise kids the way his father had done. He wanted to go beyond that narrow scope, break out into the wider world where his actions determined whether men would live or they would die. His father was satisfied with punishment. Cruise wanted to wipe out the lights behind the eyes, take away the years people had coming to them, rob them of the future. In the hierarchy of control, his chosen way was at the pinnacle.

He was a man made in his father's image.

He could sleep if he honestly believed that.

• • •

Molly thought her bones were going to rub holes through her skin. If she had more padding she wouldn't be in such horrible pain. Cruise tied her wrists to her ankles before looping the rope around the faucet handles of the tub. He ended by taking the rope up from them to the showerhead. Even if she managed to get herself undone from the many knots around the stainless-steel faucet handles, she'd still be fastened to the showerhead.

The bath cloths Cruise had wrapped around her wrists and ankles to take some of the friction off her skin were beginning to slip loose. The yellow nylon rope dug into her flesh like a hundred stinging wasps. She cried for a while, cried until she started getting sick to her stomach and had to quit.

She cataloged her surroundings. There was a Rorschach blotch of rust around the lever in the tub that closed off the drain. As she stared at it the shape brought to mind an airplane, a bouquet of flowers, a casket, and a baby in a crib.

There was a bathtub ring. Lannie wasn't any too meticulous in her housework. The tub looked as if it hadn't been scrubbed in a month or more.

The caulk sealing the tub into the wall and the caulk around the square egg-yolk-yellow tiles were growing patches of mildew. A douse of Clorox would cure that, Molly knew, but maybe Lannie didn't. From her biology class study on fungus, Molly remembered how the mold looked under a microscope. Thin and furry like little thousand-legged insects. Truly appetizing.

There was a constant drip from the tub faucet. It had no recognizable rhythm. Not enough beat, couldn't dance to it. Just an irritating *drip, drip, drip* that kept the drain wet. After a while, Molly stopped even hearing it, but she could smell the faint chlorine scent that rose from the drain, and there was a dampness that hung in the air of the tub area.

Around noon Lannie came into the locked bathroom and offered her a drink of water from a coffee mug that had red hearts all over it. Molly drank the tepid fluid gratefully. She begged to be freed so she could use the toilet, but Lannie just shook her stringy hair and left again.

"Are you really going to let me wet all over myself?" Molly yelled.

She heard the key turn in the door. They must have used the bathroom as a holding cell before. She suspected it was Cruise who had put in the new burnished silver doorknob with the outside locking mechanism. Or maybe Lannie locked the old man in here so she could get some peace and quiet. She wouldn't put anything past this family. They were all bent in some unimaginable way.

The next time Lannie came with water, Molly refused to drink. Already her bladder was full to aching and they obviously weren't going to let her out of the tub until Cruise woke. She'd be damned if she'd soil herself. So she wouldn't drink. Or eat. Not that food had been offered her since the burned bacon and scorched eggs Lannie served up at breakfast.

Molly had another day to think. While Cruise slept in Mexico she'd decided she must be careful or she'd get herself killed. She still thought that, even more so now. The murder of the man at the lake horrified her much more than the Mexican's death. She could still lie to herself about the Mexican. Try to believe Cruise was in his warped way protecting her. But when he killed the fat man at the side of the road, she knew for certain that her first suspicions were correct. Cruise killed without motive, randomly, whenever he felt like it, and it meant no more to him than if he were snuffing out marauding ants at a summer picnic.

Sitting all day in the tub, shifting her weight from one bony hip to the other, she had time to think over everything after she had finished noting the grime around the toilet bowl, the mildew in the caulking, the dead bugs caught in the cover over the fluorescent bar light that hung above the bath mirror. She dissected her decision to leave home. No use lying to herself. She loved her stodgy father with his old-fashioned ideas of discipline. What a spoiled baby she was for not trying to cooperate with the counselor who advised her to go easy on her dad, try to understand his position, that although he was tough on her it was because he loved her.

She hadn't tried to work it out. She thought, well, her life was set into stone, it would never change. She wasn't stimulated by any of the subjects at school, she didn't have any really close friends, she pitied herself for not having a mother, and she gave her father hell for being who and what he was as if he could change more easily than she. She saw now that people probably didn't change once they were adults. Her father was a Marine, and although he had retired, he would always *be* a Marine, a lifer. He thought kids no different than his boot-camp trainees. They had to be whipped into shape. They had to learn duty and responsibility and how to take orders. Now she knew that was a mistake he'd made, but from the perspective she had in the bathtub of a strange house, captive of a killer, she figured her father's method of child raising, mistaken as it was, seemed highly preferable to the present situation she found herself in.

She'd suffer boot camp any day compared to one night on the road with Cruise Lavanic.

And if adults never changed, that meant Cruise was locked into murder as a way of life. His sister was imprisoned by her own circumstances and her deathly fear of her brother. Even the old man was lost, his mind held hostage by deterioration of his brain cells.

But *she* could change. Molly Killany was not an adult, not by a long shot, she realized the truth now. She was a kid who thought she knew it all, thought she could get out in the world and create a brand-new life for herself. Thought she could take care of herself, stay out of danger's way. Stupid, stupid, stupid.

The first thing she had to do—and she thought this the most mature idea she might have ever had—the first thing was to admit to her helplessness and ignorance. She didn't know anything about killers or how to keep one from taking her life. She was not wise, not experienced, not smart enough to be on her own. She needed help from somewhere or she was doomed.

Okay. She admitted to those sins. But what could she do about finding help? Lannie wasn't going to do anything for her. Not one single thing. If she was sorry for her, she hid the fact pretty damn well. Molly thought something had gone wrong with Lannie's emotions. They had jumped the track to disappear into a dark muffled place where she didn't feel anymore. Whereas Cruise's emotions were always at the edge, ready to explode into enough rage to take a life, Lannie admitted nothing to faze her.

So the sister and the father were out. That meant Molly had to stay alive until she got close enough to someone else who might help her. A gas-station attendant. Another motorist. A waitress in a cafe. A passing patrol car. She must gain the attention of someone along the way who could come to her aid.

There was just one problem. She didn't know how long she had left. If Cruise had killed for all those years, had he also taken kids like her on his many death trips? If he did, what happened to them? Easy to answer that. Since none of them had ever turned him in, they must be unable to. They were dead.

That's what she was going to be if she didn't get lucky real soon.

She hung her head, rested it on her upraised knees. It didn't matter that much anymore about her physical comfort. The tub was cold, but it wasn't as cold as a grave. The mildew, the chlorine scent, the steadily dripping faucet—they were just slight irritations. The ropes hurt, but they weren't going to kill her. Her bones ached, her muscles were cramped, but she was young, strong, healthy. The discomfort was not so unbearable. She was hungry, but she wasn't starving.

She'd find someone. She'd stop giving Cruise a hard time. She'd keep her mouth closed, her smartass comments to herself. She'd do exactly what he wanted. She'd try to enter into conversations when he wanted to talk. She wouldn't say anything to upset him.

There had to be help somewhere if she lived long enough to find it. She was too young to die. She hadn't done anything so wrong that she deserved to die.

She would make her own luck and get out of this alive. The other alternative was unacceptable. Dying wasn't on Molly Killany's agenda this year.

THE SIXTH NIGHT

Cruise woke clammy cold with sweat. He smelled a sweet stench rising from his body as if he had perspired all the Cokes he had consumed over a lifetime.

He had been tortured by one of those nightmares that were flashbacks from his childhood. This one had been so vivid that even now he brushed his arms to get off the dirt.

He and his two older brothers were playing outdoors. Their parents were in town shopping, leaving them alone for several hours. It was a Saturday, summertime, suffocatingly hot. They were bored, the juvenile wildness rising in them to such heights that they felt impelled to whoop and holler as they chased one another around the frame house. Lannie came onto the front porch yelling for them to stop acting like "wild Injuns," but they ignored her warnings.

Tiring of the game of chase, rolling and wrestling on the grass in the backyard, Cruise thought of something to cool them off.

"Let's dig holes and get in them," he said. "That's what dogs do to get cool. It's better than walking all the way to the creek to go swimming."

Orson, fourteen, and Edward, twelve, immediately agreed to a hole-digging expedition. They found shovels in the toolshed. They made shallow holes to begin with, but that didn't seem satisfactory to Cruise. "Let's dig them deep enough we can squat in them and then cover each other up to the necks!"

That suggestion was happily adopted. The holes grew deeper. The earth around them cooled the air by several degrees as they stood in the holes throwing out dirt over their shoulders into huge piles.

"I'll bury you two first," Cruise offered. His brothers hunched themselves into the holes and laughed uproariously while Cruise shoveled the dirt on top of them. When nothing but their heads were aboveground, Cruise squatted and asked what it was like. "Isn't that cool? Like being in a 'frigerator, ain't it? Wasn't I right?"

Orson and Edward both agreed it was indeed cool to their hot, sunburned skins. It was superduper. It was swell.

"Here, y'all bury me." Cruise hurriedly dug his brothers out until they could wriggle free and pull themselves from the holes, dirt falling from their pockets and around the waists of their pants.

Cruise couldn't wait. His skin felt oven-heated. Sticky sweat fell from his forehead into his eyes. Sweat ran into his ears and slipped snakelike down the back of his neck. He jumped into the hole and gestured for his brothers to cover him over. Orson and Edward had him half-buried before Cruise saw the exchange of sly looks. By then it was too late. "What's up?" he asked. "Don't do anything mean, okay? I didn't hurt y'all none. And it was *my* idea. Wasn't it my idea?"

He was trying to get out, worried about the shared look between his brothers, but they were working faster now, filling in the hole quicker than he could find a purchase out. "C'mon, y'all, I changed my mind. I don't *wanna* be buried."

"Well you *are*," Orson said. He scooped dirt around Cruise's thin neck, then stepped near enough to make his brother flinch. He grinned evilly, foot held in the air before he lowered it to tamp the dirt down with his bare feet.

The pressure set in on Cruise's chest. He thought maybe he wasn't going to be able to breathe. "I want *out* now!"

"Not yet, Herod. We got a surprise for you." Orson snapped his fingers at Edward. Edward ran from Cruise's restricted field of vision.

"Where's he going?" Cruise wanted to know. He felt cooled off, that's for sure. Felt his blood congealing. He was nine. His older brothers often played cruel tricks on him. He knew this was going to be one of those times. He just hoped they wouldn't bury his head. One more shovelful and he'd be underground completely. They'd dark the hot, hateful sun from his eyes for good.

Cruise heard his destiny before he saw it. "It's the lawn mower!" he screamed. He heard the *clackedy-clack-clack* of the push mower as the blades rolled over the ground in his direction.

"Yeah! We're gonna mow down your head." Orson looked fit to be tied. He jiggled on his tiptoes and waved his arms for Edward to hurry.

Lannie came out the back and saw in a glance what was happening. "You boys quit it right now. Put up that lawn mower before someone gets hurt."

"Somebody's gonna get hurt! And it ain't us," Edward squealed, bringing the mower around so that Cruise could see it.

Cruise's vision, ground level, gave him an impeccable view of the sharpened blades of the push mower. They sat still now, gleaming, bits of cut grass clinging along the curved metal surfaces.

Sweat rolled down and stung Cruise's wide eyes. A grasshopper flopped onto his forehead and he had to shake vigorously to make it hop off again. "Make 'em stop, Lannie, make 'em stop!"

"Edward, get away from there," she called.

Edward and Orson looked over their shoulders to see their sister coming down the back steps, furious red spots on her pale cheeks.

"Oh, you don't let us ever have *any fun*," Orson said.

He ran to Edward, pushed him over a little so they could both hold on to the mower's push handle. They glared down at Cruise, demented and determined.

"Scared, huh? Remember the slivers of soap you put in our soup last week? Remember that squashed frog you put in Edward's bed?"

"Stop it, stop it, stop it!"

"Let's back up to get a running start," Orson said.

The two boys quickly backed away until they were near the rear of the house. They were making the sounds of revving motors. "Varrooommm. Varrooommm! VAARROOMM!"

Lannie was running now, trying to reach them.

Cruise saw it all in slow-motion agony. Lannie coming into his peripheral vision, her feet slapping the ground. Edward and Orson pushing down hard on the mower handle, the blades whirring, chopping, the grass flying from the rear to cover his brothers' feet. He could already feel the crunch and explosion of the blades hitting him square in the face. He struggled mightily. He jerked his shoulders, clawed at the dirt with both hands, tried turning his torso this way and that to get free of the prison of earth. He arched his neck, the tendons tight with his long-drawn out scream.

That's when he woke sweating and brushing at his arms in Lannie's bed during the twilight hours.

His heart knocked madly against his rib cage. His mouth was open in a silent scream of terror. In the darkness of the bedroom he thought he saw his brothers bearing down on him with the killer machine. Then there was a snap in the air and he was sucking in rapid breaths, his head between his hands.

Lannie saved him that time. He never knew if Edward and Orson really would have tried to mow down his head as if it were a fat watermelon. She stopped them inches from his paralyzed face, the blades halting magically. Cruise fainted that day. He didn't wake until they had him dug from the hole, lying on his back on the green, freshly mown grass. The sun scorched his eyes. He thought he might be dead. He had hated the sun from that day forward. His tortures happened in the daylight. People left him alone at night.

Lannie had to help him walk into the house and bathe. His bladder had loosened in his fright and there was mud on his legs. He could have told his father and gotten his brothers beaten for their stunt, but he never told and neither did Lannie. It was an unspoken code between the children that tattling was verboten. They were punished enough. They wouldn't bring down extra wrath on one another's heads for any reason.

Cruise wondered why he'd had that particular nightmare tonight. He might have had the lawn mower dream ten times in his whole adult life. It always left him so tight he thought he might burst from his skin. He wanted *out*. Out of the hole and away from the danger. *Out* of harm's way. *Out* of the family that drove him crazy in the beginning.

He came onto his feet unsteadily and felt his way in the dark to Lannie's bathroom that was connected by a door to her bedroom. He left the light off, urinated into the toilet. In the bedroom again, he sat on the side of the bed trembling.

Had to do it. Had to release the pressure, the anxieties. Might kill everyone in the house if he didn't.

He reached beneath his long hair for the knife. He held it in his right hand and turned over his left hand until the palm was up and the wrist and inside of his arm was available to the blade. He was thinking of nothing but finding relief. All his nerve ends screamed for it. He sat making short decisive cuts in the skin between wrist and elbow. He switched the knife to his left hand and began operating on his right arm the same way. Blood oozed from the cuts and dripped onto Lannie's sheets.

It was the first time he had ever done this. He thought that it helped immensely. The feeling of tightness escaped through the slits in his flesh like air seeping from a bicycle tire. He wouldn't die; he hadn't cut into the veins. He wouldn't get infected; he knew how to disinfect the cuts and bind them.

He just felt better.

He'd have to remember this remedy when his fears and his anxieties grew impossible to bear.

For a while he wouldn't have to kill anyone, though if he hadn't already dispatched Edward and Orson to their deserved rewards, he would find them right now and take off their heads *again*. In a slower, more torturous way.

Just the way they'd tried to take his. The scummy bastards.

8:15 P.M. Cruise stood next to Molly in the open door. They were ready to leave. He had to move her by holding on to her arm. Her wrists were too badly burned by the ropes for him to touch without her crying out loud.

Lannie's children milled around getting in the way. Lannie had the baby in her arms. Her hair fell over one eye and she squinted from her glasses. She looked tired. Haunted. What right did she have? She just took care of a bunch of rug rats and his father. She didn't really have anything to complain about. He gave her money to help out on the bills. She didn't have to look so bad if she'd wash and roll her hair, put on some unwrinkled clothes that weren't so stained with baby shit and throw up.

"Thanks, Lannie. Tell Daddy I'll be back," he said.

Lannie shrugged.

"I know he'll forget. Tell him anyway."

"All right." She shifted the baby onto her opposite hip bone, shook the hair from her eyes. Cruise saw she wasn't wearing a bra beneath her shirt. Her breasts sagged like pennies in a sock.

"Remember what I told you," Molly said to Lannie as he hustled her outside.

Cruise put her into the Chrysler and slammed the car door. He didn't care what she told Lannie. Wouldn't do her any good. Lannie'd never turn him in. He waved good-bye to his sister.

Flagstaff at night was a dead town. All the stores were closed down. Not many drivers on the streets. He filled up the gas tank at an all-night service station, checked the oil and water and tires. Doing these chores, he kept a careful watch on Molly. She never moved from the front seat. She didn't even glance toward the cement box where the station attendant sat in a metal folding chair reading a muscle magazine.

From the station he drove to the turnoff for 17 south and took it. They'd go to Phoenix, take I-10 down to Eloy where he'd pick up I-8 to San Diego.

"You think getting Alzheimer's disease is a bad way to go, right?" he asked Molly.

"It's pretty bad," she said softly.

"There's a thousand ways to die. For most people first the heart goes bad."

"You mean they get heart disease?" Molly asked.

"No, I mean when the inside of a person changes, when the landscape gets all black and stinking. I had an old aunt when I was a kid. My father's sister. She was widowed, and maybe that alone was too much, the overload that blew some of her circuits, that blackened the landscape in her bloodred heart." Cruise maintained his speed at fifty-five heading down from the mountains into the plateau where he'd find Phoenix. He repeated in his thoughts what he'd said to Molly. *Bloodred heart*. It was a comforting vision that leapt to mind. The rhythm of the tires on pavement lulled him as he told his story.

"My mother told us Aunt Maddie was senile, but it was more than that. I saw the deterioration happen over a period of years while I was growing up. She wanted *something*. I think she needed someone to care about her.

"She had sons. Four of them, all rotten apples, every one. Her husband had taken a long time dying. It was Parkinson's disease, I think. He just got weaker and more frail, his hands shook so bad he couldn't hold a glass of water, his head shook like it was a flag blasted by a high wind. Maddie loaned him so much of her energy just to keep him going that she didn't have any left over for her boys. They were wild, always in trouble. One of them attempted suicide. They found him in the chicken coop hiding underneath the hens' nests. Maddie stitched his wrists herself and bound them in white gauze."

He paused and looked down at his own arms. The bandages were hidden by the long-sleeved shirt he wore. Molly didn't know about that. No one did. When Lannie asked about the blood on her sheets he told her he had had a nosebleed in his sleep.

"The boy who tried to slash his wrists was never right again. Then the youngest one, Randy, started stealing. Money from his mother's purse, the family silver—what there was of it. Finally he was breaking into houses and carting off the neighbors' televisions. Two of the boys joined the army together. One was drunk on patrol in Vietnam and ate a Claymore. The other one struck his C.O. and was thrown out of the service for insubordination. He runs a junkyard in Jersey. Lives in a shack with a pack of stray dogs last I heard of him.

"So Maddie finally lost her husband, then the boys forgot her, and she was left alone.

"Daddy tried to check on her when he could, but she got to where she was hateful to visitors. Once we moved to another house and he went by to see Maddie. 'You want our new address and phone number?' he asked. She wouldn't look at him. 'No,' she told him. 'You don't?' 'No,' she said. He just walked out shaking his head; there wasn't much he could do with her by that time.

"After that Maddie went down fast. She saved everything, turned into a damn old pack rat. She had shelves of paper grocery bags. Empty jars and cans. Newspapers. Buttons. Lace. Ribbon. Vases. Her house became a garbage dump of useless things. Drawers overran, countertops were heaped with things, she couldn't walk through it all without tripping. Roaches were so thick they scattered every time she made a move.

"Her heart soured the same way grapes ferment in a stone crock. It turned black as night and shriveled to a tight little ball. She wouldn't come out of the house or let anyone in.

"She died one night in her bed. They found stacks of old cloth and clothes she'd worn fifty years before—all this stuff piled on the bed with her. Scattered around her were boxes of photographs and shoe boxes of old shoes, even a tin coffeepot on the bed with her, all this stuff leaving a tiny space for her to curl up on the mattress to sleep her last sleep.

"I guess since she didn't have anyone left to monitor her behavior, she collected things around her to keep some kind of watch. Her house was so stuffed with junk we could hardly wade through it to her bedroom."

He remembered the sharp smell of collected and forgotten things. The old dried grape smell of his aunt lying in the bed, molting like a snake losing its skin.

"That's one way to die," he concluded the narrative. "Mad as a headless chicken. All alone in the world, living out some kind of dream you think might save you."

Cruise waited for Molly's response to his story. When she didn't say anything he said, "You're too young to know what it's like being alone in the world."

She glanced at him, saw him waiting for a reply. "I guess so," she said.

"I mean, you *think* you're alone now, taking this hitchhiking trip across country, but you see you've got me. Before me you had your dad. Real loneliness is the killer."

"Is that why you wanted me along?"

He liked her tone. She had dropped the smartass sarcastic comebacks and seemed to really be listening to what he was saying.

"That's one reason," he said. "I have someone with me, I don't figure I'll wind up like my aunt Maddie. Or Lannie."

"Lannie works hard."

Cruise made a sound of disbelief. He rested his left arm on the window. The wind pressed against his shirtsleeve, against the bandage, reminding him of the slits in his skin. It wasn't unpleasant. "Lannie," he said, "turned into a fucking zombie. She used to sing."

"She did?"

"Like an angel."

"She doesn't sing anymore?"

"Only to herself. She could have done something with her voice. She could have been somebody."

"Not everyone can be somebody important," Molly said. "We can't have a world full of VIPs."

Cruise looked at her. Sometimes the kids knew more than he gave them credit for. "Everyone could try," he said. "Don't they owe it to themselves to at least try?"

Molly wouldn't answer him. She stared forward, her hands lying palm up on her lap as if she were airing the raw places on her wrists.

"We got us a world full of zombies," he said, trying to find the words to explain his philosophy. "There's more people who are just like Lannie than not. They don't give a goddamn anymore. They let themselves get beaten down. If they'd follow their instincts, if they'd *listen* to their desires . . ."

"Like you?" Molly asked abruptly, interrupting him.

"Yeah, like me, you're fucking right like me. Even like you."

That got her attention. She shook her head slowly.

"People need to do what they feel they have to do. Like you did. Like I do. But most people, they're all tied down with fears and they keep these unspoken rules and regulations in their heads. They get an impulse, they don't follow up on it. Someone told them it was wrong, or it would ruin their reputation, or they'd suffer from it. People will look and point, they think. People will call them names. People will laugh. So they'd rather play it safe, take no chances. They end up like Lannie, stuck in a two-bit job where the paycheck won't cover the expense of living, no husband, five kids crawling all over the broken-down furniture."

"And your father to take care of," Molly added.

She'd left him wordless at last. Was she trying to tell him something?

"Someone," Molly said, "has to take on the burdens. Lannie's doing that. If she were a real zombie, she'd walk out on the kids and the job and your father. She wouldn't care about protecting you."

Cruise thought about it. Thought about it so hard he noticed he was squinting his eyes at the lines in the road. It didn't fit in with the way he thought of Lannie, how he blamed her. It made her sound heroic, but who could ever picture his sister as a heroine? She'd asked for the burdens and accepted them. She let them wear her down until she was devoid of any personality of her own. Was Molly trying to say something about *him*? Was she razzing his ass for not living up to some debt the world said he owed? Well, fuck that. What did a sixteen-year-old kid know about anything?

"Some of us know how to live a life," he said, defending himself. He sounded fierce, couldn't help it. He felt the kid was criticizing him. "You have to stay free. You stay free, you remain outside the rules. You can do anything you want and get away with it."

Again she didn't respond. He thought she was acting in a mysterious manner. She should be arguing with him and she wasn't. Just about everyone disagreed with him when he said you could get away with murder if you wanted to—even though he was irrefutable proof that you could. Molly seemed to be trying to point out flaws in his opinions without making him angry. Trying to manipulate him? He didn't like that. He *hated* that. No one ever manipulated Cruise Lavanic.

He didn't have to listen to her. He didn't have to let what she said raise doubts in his mind. His beliefs weren't dictated to him by stupid fucking teenagers.

He drove to Phoenix without speaking again. The crusty wounds on his arms itched. He thought they might be bleeding a little. He hoped so. He felt tight all over the way he had felt after waking from the nightmare.

An urgency filled him with the jitters. It felt just like a horde of roaches crawling from his innards out to the muscle sheaths covering his bones. They wanted *out*. He needed to lessen the tension so that he wouldn't burst and fly off in a million pieces.

He guessed he'd have to kill someone after all.

Mark Killany spoke to the homicide detective on the case.

"What makes you think this is the same man?" the detective asked.

He wasn't very cooperative. Mark pegged him right off as a man who had trouble dealing with authority. He had taken those types into boot camp and turned them every-which-way-but-loose until their brains were settled into place. This man probably hadn't been in the service. He was too young to be out of diapers when Mark was kicking butt *all over* Vietnam. He was too young to be detecting more than the smell of his own bad wind. He was a fucking know-it-all with an attitude.

"I'll tell you again." Mark said wearily. He hated repeating himself. If people didn't get the drift the first time what was the point? "The kid at the wreck said the guy was driving a blue Chrysler. My man was driving a blue Chrysler." Mark was ticking off the common elements on the fingers of his right hand. Square in the detective's face. Next he'd punch out his lights if he didn't get no satisfaction as Mick Jagger would say. "Second. Kid said the guy had long hair, down to his shoulders, and a beard, and a mustache. Guy picked up my kid in Mobile was described to me the same way, hair, beard, mustache. Third. I've been following this bozo across country. If he took the turnoff at 666, he'd have been at the scene about the time your killer was there."

"Hey, there's a million blue Chryslers. There's ten million guys with long hair." The detective wasn't convinced. "Besides. The kid didn't say nothing about a girl in the car he saw leave."

"It was dark! That kid was sitting in a car that had just been wrecked and his parents were dead! His fucking mother was sprawled out in the front seat with a broken neck. What do you expect, a detailed book report?"

"Look here now. We're searching for this son of a bitch, we've got roadblock checkpoints, we've got out APBs, we're running some checks on the M.O., and if we find him and we find your girl with him, we'll be careful to try to get her out of it unharmed. More than that I can't promise you. Meanwhile I suggest you go cool off somewhere and let us get on with our jobs."

Mark itched to slug him. Right in the pink snout in the middle of his face. He was a piggy-eyed young man with a layered haircut, tassels on his loafers, and a row of four, count 'em, four pens in the pocket of his fashionably starched pastel shirt. He wasn't going to be any help.

"I'm leaving right now," Mark said, going for the door. "And when I call back from the road, you're going to tell me what's happening, isn't that correct? You're going to let me know if you pick up any suspects or you see my daughter?" He stood with his hand holding open the door, looking back.

The detective glared. He took a pack of Marlboro from

the desk and shook out a cigarette, lit it as if he had all the time in the world.

Mark waited. Wanted to kick the door shut and throw the chairs through the wall, but he just waited while the nerves jumped in his neck and the veins throbbed in his temples.

"I guess we can accommodate you that much. But keep this in mind." He dragged deep on the Marlboro, blew out the smoke across the desk. "You get in the way, you can be hauled in on charges of obstructing law officers from performing their duty. We even stop you for speeding, they're gonna know your name, Mr. Killany. We don't hold with former Marines who want vigilante justice here in Arizona. Not even a smidgeon."

Mark wanted to tell him he didn't "hold with assholes" either, but thought it best not to let the words slip past his lips. He left the door open and stalked through the Globe, Arizona, police station without looking at anyone. Outside at the curb where his car was parked he couldn't keep his anger under wraps any longer. He slammed the parking meter with his open hand, marched to the car, and jerked open the driver's side door with enough force to make it bang back shut so he had to open it again.

It took everything he had not to squeal his tires as he backed into the street.

He was going to Flagstaff. They were headed north. They might be in Flagstaff. He'd find Molly if he had to scour the state for the next six months.

The frightful image of the dead man alongside the road in the rain superimposed itself on the windshield. He hadn't seen the man. He'd been told by one of the investigating patrol officers what the scene looked like. Fat man, obese really, a three-chinner. Slumped onto the pavement next to his car, the door standing open. Neck sliced wide, "looked like a can opener did it," the officer said. Rain coming down, not bad, just enough to keep washing off the blood so they could see the raw neck muscles in their flashlights. The man's son sitting on the trunk when they drove up. Little kid, about ten. "Wet as a duck-hunting dog." Wore glasses and they were shattered, but he still wore them. Couldn't see his eyes. Boy talked in snatches.

"He killed my dad," he said. "Didn't look in the back seat. I was in the floorboard just coming to. I felt the car fall down, I guess they turned it back on its tires. It made my head hurt. I was looking for my glasses when I heard my dad screaming and crying. He was inside the car, but I couldn't get up from the floorboard yet. Then when I did . . . I saw out the side window this man . . . and he grabbed my dad from behind . . . and he caught his hair and jerked his head back . . . and . . ."

Mark cringed as the patrolman repeated the boy's story. He shook his head now to clear it of visions of dead men.

He had to keep the radio on, tuned to local stations. He'd call back to Globe every four hours. They were going to get tired of his harassment before this was over. They were going to know he meant business.

But nobody was going to stop him.

It was just east of the outskirts of Yuma, Arizona, that Molly saw a chance to signal for help. During the long, tense night Cruise had driven them down from the forested mountains of Flagstaff to Interstate 8. It was two-thirty in the morning. Molly had stayed awake without any trouble. She'd slept as much as she could when tied in the bathtub the day before. She couldn't sleep anymore when Cruise was awake. He might decide to get rid of her, and she'd never know until he had the knife to her throat.

They hadn't talked much all night. When first leaving Flagstaff Cruise told her about his Aunt Maddie. When he began berating his sister, Molly spoke up on her behalf, and that's when she noticed Cruise was in trouble. He kept feeling his arms as if something were crawling on him. She didn't know why he was wearing a long-sleeved shirt. It was a mild night and they had driven out of the storm area long since. They had to keep the windows rolled down for fresh air or they would have suffocated.

Molly thought Cruise might be keeping something from her, some secret he didn't want her to know about his arms. He began driving one-handed, touching, caressing the other with his free hand. Then he'd shift hands on the steering wheel and rub and caress the other arm.

She was too afraid to ask him what was the matter. She could tell he thought she wasn't noticing his actions. But she watched him from the corner of her eyes, watched his every move, fearing that he would pull the knife from where he kept it hidden in his hair.

Now she'd not yet figured that out. How did he keep the knife there? She knew he had it; she'd seen him whip it out when in the fight with the Mexican. Did he glue it or something? Did he tie it there with string? Beat the shit out of her. The important thing was that she knew about it. She watched for it.

She *didn't* know what was wrong with his arms. Maybe they ached. Maybe he was having the first symptoms of a stroke. Didn't the arms hurt before a person fell down clutching his chest? That's what they did in the TV shows and the movies.

God, she wished he'd have a stroke. She wished he'd zonk out and die at the wheel. She was ready to take over driving if that happened. She kept herself taut, ready to spring across the Igloo cooler and grab the wheel if he lost control.

In Phoenix he refilled the gas tank at a small truck stop

off the freeway. Molly looked for someone who might help her, but the pumps were empty. A trio of trucks idled in the back lot, the drivers nowhere to be seen. There appeared to be just one cashier and one waitress inside. She asked to go to the bathroom again. Cruise walked her through a side entrance. The ladies' room was right there, too far from the cashier to say anything. When she finished, Cruise returned with her inside the bathroom to check for messages she might have left. He was a careful man. But that's not the way she was going to do it. What the hell, even if someone found a message, she'd be too long gone to benefit from it.

Cruise seemed to know she wouldn't throw some kind of out-and-out fit, create a scene. She wasn't nuts. She knew how fast he was with his knife.

No. When she found an opening she wasn't going to scream and run. She meant to be subtle about it, get attention without Cruise noticing. All she wanted was for someone—preferably a man—to come over to them to ask some questions. She figured Cruise wouldn't kill someone right out in the open where there would be witnesses. He was too much of a snake to do that.

She saw her chance near Yuma. Cruise had the CB on listening to the truckers. He was still doing something with his arms, and that was beginning to worry her ungodly. He couldn't seem to keep his hands off himself. In the past hour or so he had even stopped caring if she watched him. He stared straight ahead at the road, squeezing and squeezing his arms through the shirt. It set her teeth on edge.

The CB interested Molly. If Cruise got out of the car to pump gas she might be able to get the mike and say something over the trucker channel. She worked it out in her head. She'd say . . . *I'm Molly Killany and I've been kidnapped by a man driving a light blue Chrysler. He's*

killed some people. Someone call the highway patrol. Tell
them he murdered a man near a lake south of Flagstaff.
We're on I-8 headed for California. Help me, please!

That's what she'd say. She had it rehearsed in her mind
and she was ready. It was like learning a poem to say before
the class in literature. You say it over enough in your head,
you can repeat it in your sleep.

But it wasn't the CB that presented her chance near
Yuma. It was a man dressed in Wrangler jeans, boots, and
a cowboy hat.

Cruise pulled off a freeway exit and took the feeder lane
until he came to an all-night Pick 'N Save.

"I've got to have a Coke," he said. "I'll get some to put
in the cooler. You want anything?"

She thought fast. She hadn't eaten all day. This was the
first time since Lannie made breakfast that Cruise had
thought to offer her food.

"They got sandwiches in there? Those cellophane-
wrapped ones?"

"Probably." He unbuckled his seat belt, had his hand on
the door release.

"I want a ham and cheese. A bag of potato chips. A
banana if they have them. Maybe a doughnut or a package
of cookies. I'm pretty hungry."

Before she knew the real Cruise, before the killing, she
thought Cruise would have grinned at her with his perfect,
pretty smile and kidded her about being a hog, about getting fat eating that way. But now he didn't crack a smile
or make any cute remarks. He shrugged and got out of
the car.

"Don't try going anywhere," he warned, slamming closed
the door.

He had not tied her up again since they left Lannie's
house. She wanted to believe it was because he felt sorry

for her bruised and battered wrists where the rope had cut into her, but it was no doubt because he felt she was under his control now. Without him saying it aloud, she knew he wouldn't hesitate to kill her. Even if he had to chase her first, he'd kill her.

The Pick 'N Save blazed with fluorescence. The clerk, an older woman in a green uniform with white pockets and trim, was alone in the store. Early morning shifts were the pits in convenience stores. The Stop 'N Robs.

The minute Cruise was inside hunting down Molly's supper, a red Toyota short-bed pickup truck drove into the slot next to the Chrysler. Molly looked over and saw a man in a cowboy hat turn his head and smile at her. He was about Cruise's age, early forties. Nice face, rugged, the smile a little crooked as if he had had a few beers. Not as big as Cruise, but big enough, and just as tall as her captor. His jeans fit so tight that when he descended from the truck, her gaze automatically went to the rounded lump in his crotch.

He was no more than two feet from her open car window. She glanced fearfully to the front of the Pick 'N Save trying to see Cruise. He must have been on a far aisle. She looked back at the man and the words jumped out. "Can you help me?"

The cowboy hesitated next to her window. He stared down at her, puzzled. "How can I help a pretty little thang like you?"

Molly looked at the glass windows of the store again. Where was Cruise?

"Listen, I have to tell you fast. The man in the store has a knife, he hides it underneath his long hair. He's killed two people and he has me prisoner. I think he's going to kill me too." It came out all in a rush, words tumbling together, syllables running together.

"You what?" the man asked, leaning over a little to better understand. "Kidnapped you?"

"Please. Listen. He's dangerous, he's a killer. If he knew I was telling you this he'd kill you too. You've got to have some kind of weapon. Don't you understand? *I'm being held against my will. I'm going to die if someone doesn't help me.*"

"Motherfucker." The man stared at her a few seconds longer as if weighing her honesty on an invisible scale. He turned to the truck bed and leaned in. He returned with a metal baseball bat in his hand. "Where *is* that motherfucker? We'll straighten this out before you can say jackshit."

Molly pointed toward the store. Now that she'd told someone she was shaking all over. She wanted to open the door, get out of the car, stay close to her rescuer, but she couldn't get moving. It was like when she was scared in the Mexican graveyard and Cruise grabbed her. She couldn't stop shaking to save her life.

The man had left her as soon as she indicated Cruise was in the store. He was over the curb and halfway to the door before Molly heard the voice calling him back.

"Hey, you!"

Cruise! He wasn't in the store any longer. He was somewhere behind Molly's head, she hadn't seen him come out. It must have been when the man went for the bat. She leaned out the car window to see. There he stood at the back bumper all coated in white fluorescent light. He looked deadly grim. Without looking directly at her he said, "You caused this, Molly. And I know you knew better."

The cowboy had turned at the voice. He stood on the sidewalk hefting the bat. "Little lady there says you're the motherfucker holding her against her will. That true?"

"I'm the motherfucker. Come and get me."

That was all the cowboy needed. He was moving down the curb, between the vehicles, heading for Cruise at a pace that would have frightened most normal men. All Cruise did was back away from the bumper a few steps so the cowboy could clear the passageway.

Molly got her hand on the door release and jerked it up. Locked! When had she locked it? She felt for the lock button and lifted it. She heard them talking behind the car, but couldn't hear what they were saying. She had the door open. Had her feet on the pavement, was standing free of the car when the battle began.

The cowboy swung the baseball bat so hard it whistled through the air above Cruise's head. He had ducked, danced back another few steps. They were in the middle of the parking lot. Molly turned and ran for the store. She hit the door so hard it crashed loudly against a stack of boxed 10W-40 Penzoil and sent some of the loose cans tumbling and rolling across the floor. The female clerk came up from behind the counter where she'd been crouching to cut into a carton of cigarettes. Her eyes were wild with sudden alarm. "What is it?"

"Fight outside. Call the cops quick."

The clerk dropped the box-cutter. It clattered on the tile floor. "Uh . . . uh . . ."

"Do it now! Where's the phone, for God's sake, let me have it!"

The clerk was too petrified to speak. She glanced to her left. Molly came around the end of the counter and found the phone sitting behind a display of gum. She had the receiver in her hand, her finger on the nine button when Cruise came through the door for her, his knife hand dripping the cowboy's new blood.

"Put down the phone, Molly."

"No!"

Cruise vaulted the counter and had the clerk around the neck before Molly could glance down at the phone to push the one-one that would connect her to emergency services.

The clerk screamed and the screeching of her panic filled the empty store with a sound that reverberated from the shelves.

"Drop the goddamn phone."

Molly let the receiver fall from her shaking hand. "Don't hurt her, Cruise, she didn't do anything."

"I won't hurt her," he said, breathing hard from his exertion. "I'm going to kill her."

Molly lurched forward, reached for the woman's out-stretched hands, saw the woman's pleading eyes.

Saw Cruise take her by the hair and cut her throat with one swipe of the knife in his fist.

Saw the blood gush out and river down the green uni-form with the white pockets, staining it all one shade of bright red.

Saw the woman's eyes again. The fear stuck there, imprinted there forever.

Saw the woman slump to the floor at Cruise's feet as if she were a toy animal who had lost its stuffing.

Molly stood over her, head hanging, tears falling onto the inert body until Cruise took her around the counter and out the door and placed her gently into the Chrysler.

As they pulled away from the store, Molly saw the cowboy in the headlight glare. He lay on his back, the tips of his boots pointing in opposite directions.

Molly couldn't see his neck, but she knew it was cut. She couldn't see the blood, but she knew it pooled beneath his head.

She couldn't bear to look at Cruise driving the car onto the freeway ramp, but she knew he was there.

She didn't think she'd ever get away from him.

• • •

Cruise crossed the state line into California. He drove fifty-eight miles to where 86 south crossed the freeway. He took the exit ramp.

"Mexicali," he whispered.

Before he reached the border crossing he had to bathe. There was blood all over the front of his clothes, some of it his.

He saw a side road leading to a subdivision of "ranchettes." The archway sign hanging over the gravel entranceway said "Hondo Estates." Cruise thought if these people really believed they could *ranch* on one acre, they'd buy anything. Although the per capita income for California was one of the highest in the nation, following only Connecticut, New Jersey, and New York, the people living along the border barely scraped a living from the arid soil. They could call California the Golden State all they wanted. They could give the state motto as Eureka, meaning "I have found it." But those living in the Hondo Estates knew a different California. One of rattlesnakes and lizards, cacti and blue burning seasons that scorched the brain and cracked the earth into a jigsaw effect.

There was another side road to the right before he ever reached the first boxy ranch house sitting woebegone in the distance. He turned down the road. The Chrysler bounced through the potholes, spewing gravel behind the tires. The shocks and springs squeaked in protest. The headlights bobbed up and down, highlighting a landscape that looked bomb-blasted. It was a desert without a rose, sand without a sea, low scrubby vegetation that clung to the earth without the encouragement of rainfall.

"Where are we going?"

Cruise heard the barely controlled desperation in Molly's

voice. She thought he was taking her out into the desert to die. He could let her think that. Or he could still her worry. Because she had been so much trouble back in Yuma—it was *her* fault he was covered with alien blood—he decided to let her fret.

When he thought they were far enough off the main road, he stopped the car, turned off the headlights. The night was quiet the way it is out in the wilderness before dawn. The last time he had stopped this way the tornado wind and rain and thunder was deafening.

The silence was a welcome respite. Cruise felt he had been driving for eons. The inside of his head jingled and jangled from the aftermath of the Yuma killings. A muscle in his jaw twitched spasmodically. He put his hand there to hold it motionless, but when he took his hand away it jumped again, playing to its own symphony.

Molly had not said anything more. Bitch tried, he'd kick her out of the car, then kick her some more until she couldn't speak again.

He opened the car door. The overhead dome light came on and made him twitch. He stood outside the closed door looking over the roof into the far reaches of empty desert. He could see an occasional car passing on the highway. It was the early part of the morning, the late part of the night. Not many drivers going to and from Mexicali, Mexico.

He looked at the sky. Not a cloud. The stars so bright, so shining, they looked near enough to gather and pocket. The moon riding low, a silver-white nimbus radiating a cold hazy aloofness that caused shivers to break out on Cruise's wounded arms.

He stepped away from the car and found the key that would open the trunk. He stood with his hands resting on the upraised trunk lid wondering what he had wanted. *Oh, yes, the bottled water*. He was sticky damp with blood and he must get clean or he would go mad. He could smell himself. He gagged, swallowed hard, reached in for two gallons of the purified water. He set them on the ground near his feet, lay the car keys on the fender.

He leaned down and opened one of the plastic jugs. He stood again, lofting the jug over his head, feeling the chill thrill of water cascading down over his closed eyes. He stopped, lowered the jug. He had to get out of the clothes. He had to bury them once the water had cleansed him of the scent of old caked blood. He disrobed, slipping out of his shoes and socks, kicking the slacks from him, throwing the shirt from his back. He stood in his jockey shorts beneath the star-studded heaven. He saw the wet, clinging gauze bandages on both arms. He ripped at them until they were on the ground. Again he took up the water jug and poured it over him. When it was empty, he took the second jug and used it to wash his chest, his belly, the wounds on his arms. The flesh there split open and clouded the water as it rolled down his elbows.

The first time he had murdered someone, *two* someones, he had to throw himself in the creek to make the blood disappear. It was the first and last time he had killed people he knew. He waited until he was sixteen. He had suppressed the urge for seven years. He had waited patiently since he was nine years old, since the day Orson and Edward tried to run over him with the lawn mower in the backyard.

He toyed with the idea of murder the way a cat toys with a mouse. He dreamed of it. Planned and plotted. Giggled over his secret at inappropriate times.

Since his brothers were older than he, his murderous thoughts were not carried out until he was sixteen and had come into his growth. The muscles of his arms and legs thickened and grew strong, he had reached most of his adult height of six feet four inches; he was just as much a man as either of his brothers. He knew he could take them.

His method was the knife, even then. He could have sneaked his father's shotgun from the bedroom closet. Or he could have put rat poison in his brothers' food. Or he could have burned them alive. No, dead. Burned them *dead, dead*. But in all his years of planning the deed he had never considered any method more just, more *intimate*, than a knife to the throat. With a gun you had to stand away from your victims. With poison you never laid a hand on them. With fire you had to manipulate too many elements, gasoline and matches. These were all oddly impersonal ways to take a life when a knife was a handy weapon, when it afforded him close contact, when it demanded that he really *meant* it. You could accidentally shoot, poison, or torch a person. There was nothing accidental about cutting a throat.

He talked Orson and Edward into a fishing trip. Orson was nineteen, Edward twenty-one. They were both working at the sawmill, bringing home paychecks and paying their father room and board. They had girlfriends and cars and they thought Cruise—*Herod*—had long forgotten the little trick with the lawn mower. Cruise knew what they thought. That because they were children at the time it didn't matter, it didn't count. They thought he'd believe they wouldn't have hurt him anyway, even if Lannie hadn't intervened. It was a joke. A prank. A scary bit of nonsense. Harmless play.

But Cruise knew he had escaped death by inches, by centimeters, by seconds. He had seen their faces. Their expressions from that day were forever emblazoned on his memory.

They meant it. It was not a childish impulse gone awry. They would have killed him while he struggled to free himself of the homemade grave.

Cruise had the knife stolen from his mother's cutlery

drawer in the kitchen. It was the sharpest five-inch blade in the house. The handle was made of a dark wood dulled by years of use. There were three shiny steel rivets in the handle that he often covered over one by one with the pad of his right thumb.

They set out on a Saturday on another summer day much like the one when Cruise thought he was about to die. They threw fishing rods and two boxes of tackle into the rear of Orson's truck, an old 1965 black Ford. They drove to a favorite fishing spot on the river, the truck bounding down a narrow back lane through the thick Arkansas woods.

Cruise let his brothers josh him about being "a squirt who grew into a giant." He let them horse around the way they always did, popping the tops on cans of Budweiser, and talking about the pussy they were going to get off their girls that night at a dance being held in town. *How sorry* they were Cruise was just a kid yet and didn't know diddly about fucking girls. *How sad* it was he didn't seem to have the same kind of luck they did in attracting the opposite sex.

"You even *got* a pecker?" Orson asked, giving Cruise a knock on his arm to send him off-balance.

"Sure he does," Edward chimed in. "He's got a *wood-pecker.*"

They thought that was hilarious. They thought they were stand-up fucking comics.

Cruise let them make fun of him. He let them bait their lines and throw them into the gently flowing brown river. He let them lean back with their Lucky Strikes trailing smoke above their heads. And then he went to the truck to feel under the seat for the knife he had hidden there before the fishing trip.

"Where's Herod going?" Edward asked his brother.

Orson looked over his shoulder, frowned, turned back to

the river. "Fuck if I know. Take a piss maybe. How should I know what the kid's doing?"

"Hey, you jerking off, all this talk of pussy?" Edward laughed like a jackal.

Cruise pretended not to hear. The hate now was so great it was like a barbed-wire fence around his heart. It squeezed and pierced him. He bled inside, the hate turning his blood black and rich as the dirt they had scooped around his neck in the backyard when he was a trusting naive boy.

He came from the truck, keeping the knife out of sight behind his right thigh as he walked toward them lounging on the riverbank.

A pair of redbirds flew down and rested on a bush near the water. A slippery bed of pine needles carpeted the incline to the water's edge, and Cruise had to walk carefully to keep from falling. A cooling breeze wove through the treetops, making the leaves and limbs sing in soft chorus. Shifting spots of sunlight blinked through the forest and shone like a sheet of hammered bronze from the river surface.

"You gonna fish or what?" Orson asked, not bothering to turn to look at Cruise.

"He can't catch any goddamn fish, Or. He ain't got the co-or-din-ation," Edward said, laughing at the fun things he knew how to say.

Cruise had Orson by the neck, arching out his chest in struggle, before Edward knew what was really happening on the riverbank. Orson dropped his rod and grabbed for Cruise's strong, choking arm. "Fuck!" he screamed and that was all. He was holding his throat to halt the flood.

Edward scrambled onto his knees, moving toward them, hands out, Lucky Strike dropping from his wet lips, when Cruise finished with Orson and turned to bury the knife in Edward's stomach.

"Ah . . ." he said.

"What . . . ?" he said.

And Cruise was on him, knocking him backward to the ground, redbirds fleeing with a flashy rustle of wings, the sunlight playing over the tussling figures on the slick bank as they rolled thunderously toward the dun-colored water.

Cruise had a time with Edward. He was older, he wasn't taken by surprise, he wanted very much to live and catch a fish and go to town for the dance and feel his girlfriend's breasts beneath her dress.

In the end Cruise half drowned, half cut his brother to death. Once they rolled down to the river, he pushed Edward's face under the water while cutting frenziedly at his exposed Adam's apple. Edward sucked in water and blood instead of air. He groped blindly, his fingers pressing over Cruise's face, trying to find a way to stop the killing, the cutting, the cover of water.

Cruise muttered insanely, "Die, you bastard, die, you son-of-a-bitching fuck, die . . ."

When it was done Cruise climbed to his feet and looked down at his clothes. The T-shirt he wore was soaked scarlet. Mud and blood and pine needles covered him from the cuffs of his jeans to the roots of his hair. He thought there could be no greater hell than to spend another moment covered with the evidence of his crimes.

He dived headfirst into the river. He swam out to the center where the whirlpools formed. They carried him downstream. When he climbed onto the bank, he had to push his way through tangled undergrowth to where his brothers lay silent and staring upon the muddy, bloody bank.

He buried them quite a ways from where they died, in the woods where no one ventured save a few deer hunters during season. He took their rods and the fishing gear to the truck. Then he found a place where he could drive the truck over the side into the water. He stood fascinated, watching it float out like a black ship to the river center before it plummeted under.

He walked home. His clothes dried on the way. It was late afternoon when he walked into the house. When his parents began to wonder where his brothers might be he told them the first whopping lie of his life. "They said they were going to town early for the dance."

When Orson and Edward were never seen again Cruise's father inquired in town. No one had seen the truck. Or the boys.

The family fretted for a few days, but they didn't call in the police or fill out a missing person's statement. They had heard rumors that Orson's girlfriend was pregnant. They decided that was reason enough to abscond. Cruise thought they didn't much give a damn or they might have even decided, in their quiet talks in the bedroom at night, he had something to do with the disappearances. Either way no one made him pay for murder. It amused him to think, in the coming days before he left home for good, that killing was such an easy way to get things done. If the blood that covered him didn't bother him so bad, he thought he could probably do it again.

Later he found that he could.

He opened his eyes to the stars and felt a slap of vertigo that made him sway on his bare feet. He was standing in mud that squished between his toes, the empty water jug in his hand. He panicked, wondering how long he had been standing there dreaming of his brothers.

He dropped the jug and hurried around the car to Molly's side. She wasn't there.

He turned in a circle, looking for her outline on the desert. He saw a dark stick figure moving toward the west, toward the ranch houses.

Cursing his lapse, he ran to the trunk, threw in his soggy clothes and shoes, slammed it shut. He grabbed the keys from the fender and slipped into the car wearing only his wet undershorts.

He ought to run her down.

He ought to hurt her.

The cuts on his arms bled onto his thighs as he drove across the bare land toward the girl speared in his headlights.

Molly thought her lungs would burst. She could hear the car behind her, closing in like a bumblebee aiming at the lush heart of a flower. She ran harder, her feet slapping the firm sand with a flat crunching sound. She was too far from the houses! She'd never make it!

Oh, God, oh, God, he'd run her over.

She stumbled on the thought and fell flat on her face, knocking the wind from her belabored lungs. She gasped, trying to get air again. She heard the engine of the Chrysler roaring in her ears. It blocked out the world. She brought her fists to each side of her face, sucking in air finally, closing her eyes and her mind to what might happen to her in the next few seconds. She couldn't think of it, couldn't get her mind to conjure the image beyond the one of her lying helpless on the ground while the car sped across the sand straight at her body.

She screamed out, pressing her fists into the sides of her head, legs automatically pulling up to her groin, toes curling in her shoes, feet tucking toward her buttocks to present the smallest possible target.

She might have lost consciousness for a while. She couldn't remember hearing the car braking or the sound of the car door opening and closing or the touch on her arm. The first thing she did hear was Cruise's voice demanding . . .

"Get into the car."

She couldn't get up. She expected to be run over and that expectation had become real in her head so that now she didn't believe she was still whole. She lay there, exhausted, not enough air in all the sky for her to breathe right again.

She felt herself lifted, taken into his arms. Her head hung down and she still couldn't breathe, her chest sucking up and down like a bellows.

She was put into the car, but she kept slipping from the seat, her legs Jell-O, her arms like strings attached to her shoulders. He shut the car door and the sound rattled her teeth.

Shouldn't the third try have been the charm? she wondered idiotically. She tried to leave him in Mexico. In Yuma. This time she should have succeeded. He had been in some kind of trance. He had stood behind the car after pouring the water over his head, stood so long she thought he had fallen asleep. He didn't even move an eyelid when she opened the door and began running.

Shouldn't she have made it? Was her luck so bad or did she have any? But yes, she had luck left. He hadn't driven the car over her prone body. She had lots of luck, but it just wasn't sufficient to get her free.

Strength returned to her limbs. She was able now to lift a hand to her face and brush the sand from around her eyes. She spit. Sand granules were in her mouth, grating on her tongue. She stuck out her tongue and wiped it on the back of her hand. She wiped her hand along the leg of her jeans.

She turned in the seat a little and saw the trunk lid open again. Soon it lowered and she saw Cruise dressed in fresh clothes. A sky-blue shirt, long sleeves. Navy trousers. When he sat in the driver's seat, she cringed, moved closer to the door on her side.

"We're going into Mexico again," he said.

He turned the car around and returned to the bumpy road they had taken into the desert.

"This time there's no hotel room for you. I'll leave you tied in the car."

She almost wanted to thank him. Being bound seemed an infinitesimal annoyance compared to being run over by a big blue Chrysler.

They drove past the tired border guards without a hitch. Cruise showed them his driver's license, his car insurance. Molly sat with a docile look on her face, though her red curly hair was all in disarray, and there was sand on the front of her shirt.

In Mexicali, Cruise drove to the far side of town where he found cantinas open all night. Molly saw that he knew the people in this section of town, knew them as well as he had in the other Mexican town east of Juárez. They called to him as he drove up. "Senor Cruise! Amigo!"

They came to the car windows and watched curiously as he tied her with the yellow nylon rope. He looped it through the armrest, making it fast. Even if she could get out of the car, she was hobbled, ankles tightly tied together, and she wouldn't get anywhere. She'd be back on her belly again, in trouble and out of luck.

"Please . . ." she begged.

Cruise told her to shut up. He said, "I don't need you to witness this part of my life."

She didn't know what he meant. She expected to have plenty of time to think about it.

She didn't know the drunk Mexicans who had grouped around the car to watch her imprisonment wouldn't give her much time for thinking. She didn't know they wanted to have some fun with another of Cruise's young female hostages.

•   •   •

The murders at the Pick 'N Save in Yuma, Arizona, occurred between two-thirty and three A.M. At four-thirty Mark Killany heard the news on the car radio as he drove the streets of Flagstaff.

There hadn't been witnesses to the crime. But the throat slashings matched the way the murderer killed the obese Mr. James Comquest near Lake Roosevelt.

"Authorities believe the same suspect is responsible for both murder sprees," the news announcer said, "and that he's moving south through the state of Arizona. The highway patrol has alerted California state police to watch for any car resembling the one described as being driven by the killer."

Mark pulled over to the curb to listen. He held his jaws rigid in thought. Yuma. First the lake, then Yuma. Had the killer ever gone to Flagstaff, or even to Globe?

Consulting the road map spread on the bench seat of the car, Mark found the route that would take him south to Yuma. It was one helluva drive and he was tired. He needed a thermos of coffee to keep him awake.

He found a service station open. They had a small convenience store that carried thermoses. There were three on a bottom shelf. The boxes were covered with a patina of dust. Mark took one to the counter, slipped out the thermos. "I'm going to fill this with coffee. Add it onto my gas ticket, will you?"

He was on the way to Yuma by five A.M. Once there he'd call back to Globe, see if they had any information the radio newscast overlooked.

How long a head start did the fucker have anyway? He had killed Comquest the night before. A convenience store clerk and a customer tonight. It couldn't have taken him that long to get to Yuma. That meant he had holed up somewhere along the way. He might have slept in his car in a national park. Or did he know someone in Arizona who had taken him in? Did he just drive at night, sleep during the day?

Mark would have to throw some of these questions at the detective in Globe, gauge his reaction.

But the important questions none of them could answer were the ones doing chaotic things to Mark's mind. *Was Molly with the killer? Was this the same man she had taken a ride from in Mobile?*

The coincidence of the same kind of car and a man described the same way made him almost sure. Sure enough to follow the leads. To wherever they led him.

He had seen a film once on cable TV about a serial killer. He had a home in South Florida, drove a Porsche, owned his own business. He went into shopping malls pretending to be a photographer looking for models. He conned young girls to his car in the parking lot, then he kidnapped, raped, brutalized, and left them dead alongside the roads countrywide. About nine victims in all if Mark remembered correctly.

The scary thing about him, though, was that he took one girl from a mall and *did not* kill her. Instead, he made her stay with him on the road for nearly two weeks. Checking into motels together, letting her drive the car, even in the end trusting her to help him lure another young woman from a mall.

The psychologist working with the F.B.I. theorized he didn't kill this one girl because she'd been raped at age thirteen. When he raped and threatened to kill her, she was so traumatized, she didn't seem to care if she died or not. The other girls begged for their lives. That gave him the momentary thrill of having complete control and power. He killed then. But the girl he kept with him—her name was Tina—didn't beg for her life. It was what saved her.

Eventually the killer put her on a plane in Boston to send her home. Later he was spotted by an F.B.I. agent and shot with his own gun while they fought over it in the front seat of the car.

Mark remembered from the film that the psychologist believed Tina hadn't tried to escape her captor because she was suffering from the "Stockholm syndrome." Prisoners in World War II first exhibited the syndrome and it was documented in psychoanalytic textbooks. Some prisoners, it seemed, stopped caring whether they lived or died, were in such deep shock that they would not try to escape if given the chance. They were locked into a psychological as well as a physical prison, traumatized, tortured, and turned into shadows of their former selves.

If Molly was with a murderer, she wouldn't be with him under her own free will. Therefore, she was a hostage. Hostages died. Not many of them were as fortunate as Tina.

Drinking coffee from the thermos, driving faster than the speed limit, Mark worried about his daughter and what might be happening to her now. If she was with a killer, she wouldn't react the way Tina did. She hadn't been traumatized before. She'd try to escape any chance she got. And the hostage-taking serial killers of the world had little patience with the girls who wanted to survive.

"Shit," Mark said aloud. He poured more coffee into the thermos cup while holding the wheel with one hand.

It was still a long way to Yuma. If his hopelessness welled any higher, he thought he might drown in it and that wouldn't help Molly at all.

He wished he hadn't thought about the cable film. He had to harbor some hope that whoever Molly was with, the man displayed a modicum of forbearance. Without it Molly was lost.

• • •

Molly believed she was lost.

No matter how loud she called for Cruise to help her, no matter how much she tried to talk some sense to the men surrounding the Chrysler, nothing got any better. The best she could do was wait out the demeaning experience, try to think of something else. *Endure. Survive.*

Just as soon as Cruise passed through the portal of the cantina, Molly knew she was going to be in for a hard time. With Cruise out of sight, the man closest to the car window on Molly's side reached in and grasped one of her breasts. Mostly he got hold of a bra cup. The Nubs hid behind the stiff material of the padded cup like scared rabbits behind a thicket. When he twisted his wrist, the bra lifted from her chest. She wanted to laugh in his face. *Ha ha,* she thought, *you can't get me. I'm too skinny to get hold of, Mr. Prick.*

But she was wrong. She wasn't going to be protected from a mauling by the mere presence of a padded brassiere. Frustrated to find he had a handful of cloth, the Mexican grinned slowly before tightening his grip and ripping the front of her shirt down to her waist. Molly sat looking down at herself, furiously embarrassed, her skin blotching with red all over her chest and stomach.

"You get away from me!"

But they didn't speak English. Or they didn't care to. She heard a half-dozen tongues wagging, but not one word she recognized. Other men stuck their heads in the back window to gawk at her. Two of them crawled onto the hood and pressed their faces flat against the windshield. Their faces looked as grotesque as Halloween masks. Finally one of the men opened the driver's side door and slid into the bucket seat next to her.

If they would untie her she'd have a chance. She even held out her bound wrists to him, thinking if he wanted to rape her he'd have to get her onto her back first, and that meant untying her hands and feet. But again what she thought might be her protection was no trouble at all to the drunken group who had descended upon her like locusts.

They refused to untie her. Wagging of heads in the negative until the girl realized it was no use. That might make Cruise unhappy and no one wanted the American unhappy. No, they'd leave her bound hand and foot to the car door, the easier to play with her. The easier it was to terrify. She tried to claw, to spit, to bite, but nothing she did proved a deterrent.

Molly bucked and fought to keep the strangers' hands off her body, but it was a losing proposition. The man hanging halfway in her window had his head buried against her chest. His mouth kept slipping off her nipples onto her ribs as she tried to thrust him away. His mustache scorched paths that smelled of tequila across her naked skin.

Meanwhile the man in the seat next to her worked to unzip her jeans enough to get his hand inside. When he'd succeeded, the two leering faces on the windshield shouted with demonic glee.

Two men got into the back seat and leaned over the Igloo cooler to watch the proceedings. One of them tried to kiss her until she butted his chin with the top of her head.

This went on. It went on and on until Molly tired of fighting back. Already she'd drawn blood where the ropes held her prisoner. Her lip had split in the melee and dripped blood down her neck. One man had his mouth on her breast. Another had two of his fingers searching blindly inside her. Someone caressed the back of her neck and shoulders.

Molly couldn't scream, couldn't fight anymore. She went limp. A plastic doll would have been more sport. It took a while, but after some minutes passed and she showed no reaction to the probings, fondlings, and suckling going on, the drunken bunch tired of the game. They cursed her and one another. They took her face in their hands and shook it until her eyes rolled. The man with his hand inside her jeans caught her tightly there and squeezed to see if she would flinch.

She slumped into the seat, her limpness not a ruse, but an admittance of futility. She couldn't do anything. Her body was not her own while they worked so hard to possess it.

Let them have it. That's what she thought. *Let them have it if they want it so fucking bad.*

Soon she was alone in the car, the drunks staggering and laughing over the incident as they headed into the cantina and the music. They could spend themselves on the willing women inside.

Her blouse was in rags hanging off her shoulders. Her bra was torn apart in the center, the cups lying on each side by her arms. Her jeans were undone down to the tops of her bikini panties. She might be a fashion plate for a club that went in for body slamming.

She sat this way without one tear making a track down her cheeks. She had no way to cover herself, not with her hands tied to the door. She must remain half clothed until Cruise returned to the car to see about her. When that would be, she didn't know. Until then she was at the mercy of any man who happened by the car and saw her. She was an open invitation to any horny Mexican who came in or out of the cantina.

And that's just the way it is, she thought, at peace once she accepted her fate.

Her luck was still holding out even though it wasn't the best luck in the world. At least she wasn't dead. Or raped.

Not quite.

She didn't feel so good, though. She didn't feel *right* anymore. She could tell she hadn't been feeling all right again since Cruise killed the woman in the store. When he tried to run her down with the car something inside her really snapped. She thought she might be getting to a place where she . . . just . . . didn't . . . care.

A small black dog crept to the car and sniffed at the ground. Molly looked down at it and watched until it went away, limping. She listened to the sounds of music and laughter. She smelled the sick-making mingled aromas of spilled beer and cooking beans.

As the sky grew light and the sun began to rise, some of the cantina patrons came outside and trotted away, none of them paying any attention to where she sat staring through the windshield.

A skinny red rooster swaggered down the street crowing for a majestic dawn. The stray dog that sniffed the Chrysler earlier scurried out now from between two houses and chased off the lone rooster.

For a while the town seemed deserted. The music had stopped. The laughter was gone. No car passed.

Molly lay her head back on the headrest and closed her eyes.

Cruise would come for her when he was ready.

Until then she would try to sleep since the help she longed for wasn't available in Mexicali, Mexico.

The movie behind the closed lids of her eyes took her back to Dania, Florida, where once she had been safe. She sat in a starched white room where the plaster on the walls had been swirled to create circular patterns. The furniture was the best money could buy. There was a white leather sofa, a club chair to match, a blond coffee table bare of adornment. Across from this magazine-perfect arrangement sat Jason Harcraft, juvenile counselor, behind his mahogany desk. The desk so dark, so smooth and rich, dwarfed Jason, and made whatever advice he gave sound weak. Molly had a hard time taking him seriously.

"All teens rebel," he was saying. "It's a natural process of growing up. You have to break the bonds from your father so you can become an adult."

"So what's the problem?" She was a smartass even then, but it never got her into dutch with Jason. He was *understanding*. Too much so. He let her get away with murder. He was indulgent in the extreme. If she had taken a ballpoint pen from her purse and stabbed holes in his brilliant white leather sofa, she expected he'd *tsk-tsk* and ask her to sit in the chair so the holes wouldn't snag her clothing.

"The *problem*," he said, infinitely patient, "is your particular brand of rebelliousness is worrying to your father. We need to *modify* the methods you employ to break the parental bond."

"How do you suggest I do that, Jason?" He liked her to call him by his Christian name. Mr. Harcraft, he said, sounded like an airplane inventor. *She* thought it was because he wanted to be twenty again. He wore his thinning hair combed over the bald spot where the hair had receded on his forehead. It was sad. "My dad *is* a former Marine boot-camp instructor. We can't forget that."

"No." He stroked the front edge of his desk as he spoke. "We can't forget that, can we?"

Molly shrugged, bored. It was all sunshine and fun outside. She could go down to the beach and lounge in the sand, walk in the surf, pick a bouquet of wild hibiscus. She could go to the marina in Ft. Lauderdale and watch the million-dollar yachts steam into dock. Yet here she was stuck in a modern white office with an *understanding* man. Some days she thought she actually preferred her father over the mealy-mouthed Jason Harcrafts of this world.

"It is precisely because of your father's background that the two of you are having many of your disputes," he said.

"Meaning I'm as normal as apple pie."

He wagged his thinning cranium. "I don't know if I'd go so far as state you're behaving absolutely normally. You do have a certain talent to provoke your father into . . . uh . . . rages."

Boy, did she. She could look at him cross-eyed and he'd get mad. Why are you looking at me that way? he'd ask. What have you done that would make you look at me that way?

"He won't let me do anything," she complained. "He's worried about all the reports of drugs and sex in the schools."

"Yes, well, most parents are concerned about that."

"He doesn't know about the guns."

That perked Jason's ears. "Guns?"

She took on her cloak of ultra-cool. She knew something the adults didn't know. All the kids knew a thousand secrets that would blow the domes off the capital buildings in every city in the country. "Kids carry them to school." she said matter-of-factly. "Lots of kids. Lots of guns."

Jason leaned forward until his elbows rested on the desktop. "Why wouldn't the teachers know about it and take preventative steps?"

Oh, so he didn't believe her. They never did. The world kids lived in was so alien to adults that they couldn't quite grasp the picture. "The teachers," she said, "don't hang out with the kids. They see them in class, that's it. During lunch they go into the teachers' lounge, they stick together."

"Why are there so many guns in school then?"

"Guys carry them for protection. There are gangs. The Jamaicans. The Vietnamese. They get picked on so they go packing. Everyone knows. Some kid not in a gang wants to be tough or he thinks he might get hassled, he packs. He lets everyone know about it too. Even some of the girls carry."

"Doesn't it scare you?"

She shrugged, the cloak of cool firmly in place. "Not much. I'm used to it. Someone's got a gun and he asks to borrow a pen or paper in class, you don't refuse him. You just do what he says and it's okay."

"Hmmm." He was back to rubbing the desk edge. "It sounds as if school is a dangerous sort of environment."

She laughed. "It ain't Disney World."

"How do the kids at school hide all these guns?"

"The guys wear baggy overcoats, like raincoats, you know? I know one guy carries a sawed-off shotgun fitted into a special holster under his coat."

"Where do they get hold of these weapons?"

"Buy 'em off the street. Bring them from home."

He looked so saddened, so out of touch with reality, that she felt sorry for him. "You can't tell my dad."

"About the guns?"

"Right. If you do, he'll put me in a private school. It's no better there. The richer the kids are, the looser the rules. I'm better off in the public system."

"Is it the state of the schools that causes you to argue with your father?"

At last. Jason had found a pertinent question, something that went to the real heart of the matter.

"Not really," she admitted sheepishly. "He's just a pain in the ass sometimes."

"You can't try to compromise?"

"He's too tough. He wants too much."

"Might it be because he loves you? He wants you to be happy?"

She thought it over. "I guess so. But that doesn't make it any easier. He just won't give me any slack. He hounds me all the fucking time." She said "fucking" to test him. He didn't bat an eyelash. *Sooo* understanding.

"We'll talk again," Jason said, rising from behind the massive desk. Standing, he wasn't such a tiny man. He looked more human, not like some kind of circus freak who had wandered into a room full of outsize furniture.

She knew her time was over. She could go to the beach now, but if she was late getting home her father would give her the third-degree. He set his watch by her comings and goings. He was a hawk, she his scurrying, earth-bound prey.

Outside the glass-walled building in the afternoon sunshine, she paused on the steps to breathe in the fruity scent of a nearby flowering mimosa shedding its shrimp-pink blossoms in the breeze.

She might as well go home. Ask his permission. It would make things easier. She'd have to explain *why* she wanted to go to the beach, *who* she was going with, *when* she'd be back, *what* she planned to do when there. But maybe that was the kind of compromise Jason meant to encourage. Give the old man his chance to act out his role. Play along. Stop fighting the inevitable.

She did that until she couldn't do it anymore. She listened to Jason and his common sense advice until it was coming out her ears. She compromised until she wanted to scream.

And then she packed her things and hit the road.

And here she was, opening her eyes on an adobe cantina yellowing in the morning sun, hog-tied like some animal, clothes in tatters, her body a plaything for stinking, drunken strangers, hostage to another adult. One who wouldn't just yell at her for being out late or bringing home a B− or wearing her skirts too short.

She was smart all right. She was cloaked down to her toes in cool. She had swapped semifreedom with a father who loved her for imprisonment with a man who didn't know what love meant.

What would Jason Harcraft, the venerable counselor to troubled teens, have to say about that?

Cruise pushed at the girl's thighs and said, "Spread your legs more."

She wasn't much beyond Molly's age. Cruise liked her because she spoke good English. He didn't have to struggle with the language to get what he wanted.

She did as she was told and he sat back on his naked haunches to play with her. It was almost day and he had used her twice already. Soon he would order her from the room and sleep like a baby in a silken crib.

They had brought in a noisy box fan and installed it in the window for him. The breeze wove over their bodies, ruffling his long hair, drying all her natural juices so that her soft pink flesh felt like the petals of a rose. He stroked between her upraised knees until she moaned and squirmed. Girls her age were insatiable, couldn't get enough.

Suddenly he slapped the inside of her thigh hard enough to leave a palm print. She scooted away from him, hugging her knees together. Tears stood in her dark eyes.

"Just a little love tap," he said, grinning.

"It's not funny," she said in her quirky accent.

"Come here, baby. Let me make it all better."

She shook her head and long black hair fell around her brown shoulders.

He grabbed himself and smiled. "Don't you want this? Come on over here and help me make it work again."

Lust overcame her fear as he knew it would. This little backwater whore never failed him. She did it for money and she did it out of burning need. She relaxed her legs until they were out again on the bed beside him. He gently pressed her ankles apart and leaned over her fragrant core. "Ummm, so sweet."

She reached to the bed table and dipped the tips of her long fingers into a brass dish of golden honey. She let drops of it fall past his face onto her flat belly. She smeared it in a circular fashion all around until he began to slurp from her fingers.

"Now it's sweeter," she said, arching her back for him.

Cruise relinquished himself to taste and touch, everything in the room dimming at the edges as if a fog undulated over the sparse furnishings.

"You," he murmured, pointing behind him, "come join in the fun."

The second girl who had been napping in a chair against the wall woke immediately and sidled over to the bed. She wasn't nearly as pretty or willing as the girl on the bed, but she would do. She didn't understand a word of English. She took orders from his tone of voice, from how he pointed to what he wanted.

"On your tits." he said. "Put the honey there."

She covered her small budding breasts with the golden syrup, massaging her nipples until they stood out like small milk-chocolate cones. She lowered the top half of her body toward him.

Cruise leisurely tasted the two girls. The last time should be the best one. He had to hurry before the sun was too much higher in the sky. He couldn't concentrate when the room grew too light.

Mental flashes kept intruding so that his tongue slowed as if the battery powering it were losing energy.

Molly lying on the sand in the desert.

The convenience store clerk compliant in his arms until the knife worked a path through her throat.

The bottled water sluicing over his head.

Edward's face under the skim of river water, his mouth open in a last choking gasp.

Shit!

He pushed off the two girls lying side by side in the bed. He ran a hand over his face, pulled on his beard until it hurt.

"What's the matter?" the pretty one asked.

"Shut up. You just shut up."

He crossed his arms over his chest and moved his hands up and down the scabrous wounds. They needed opening again.

He might be able to get it up for a final session if there was blood on the girls.

He reached beneath his hair for the knife. Both girls looked at him in horror. They knew about the knife. They had touched it during their lovemaking as if it were an icon of luck.

"Don't worry. I don't want to cut you."

He spoke the truth. He wanted to cut himself to let out the worms of anxiety. They crawled beneath his skin in tormenting waves that would not . . .

Would not cease.

He made small incisions an eighth of an inch deep, two and three inches long all up and down both arms from the top of his shoulders to the inside of his wrists. The blood peaked and ran. He put away the knife when he felt that he could, and held out his dripping arms over the bodies on the bed that watched him in silence and increasing dread.

Cruise didn't see how they turned their faces away when he began to lick the red honey mixture from the brown succulent skin. He didn't notice when they turned cold as statues as he mounted one and kissed the other's blood ruby lips.

THE SEVENTH NIGHT

All day Molly blistered in the sun. Heat waves rose from the Chrysler's hood, wavering and blurring her view of the cantina walls. At one point Molly was forced to beg for water. One of the girls waiting tables inside was given the message by an old man pushing a grocery cart of aluminum cans. The bar girl came out with a tall bottle of Coca-Cola slippery with ice crystals. Molly thanked her profusely, her throat so dry and raw her voice sounded deeper than it really was.

The girl stood beside the car waiting to return the empty bottle inside. She appeared to think it the most natural thing in creation for someone to be held prisoner by ropes while the sun baked the town clean of pedestrians. She swiped at a cloud of black flies that hovered just at the window edge, but they came back, re-formed into the original configuration.

Molly tried to talk to the girl. She looked to be sixteen or seventeen, and she had a sweet Madonna face that did not smile. Molly wondered if the girl had ever known a situation that called for smiling.

"Will you untie me?" Molly held up her wrists as far as they would go. She lifted her ankles from the floorboard and let her feet thump down again. "Cruise won't let me go. Can't you help me? I want to go home. Wouldn't you want to go home if you were me?"

The Mexican girl stared off across the street behind the Chrysler as if she didn't understand and didn't care to. She tapped one sandaled foot in the sand, waiting for Molly to finish drinking the Coke.

Molly finished, gulping the last of the fizzing liquid down her parched throat. The rapid guzzling gave her a temporary bout of hiccups. She wouldn't turn over the bottle until she could make the girl understand. "You know Cruise, right? He carries a knife hidden in his hair, did you know that too?"

The girl reached through the window to take the bottle. Molly held it away. "No, wait! Isn't there anyone here who will stand up to him? Are you all so scared, you'd let me stay prisoner in this car all night and all day? You'd let him take me away from here and kill me somewhere, leave me beside the road? How could you live with yourself? How could you let that happen? Don't you have police? Someone who cares?"

Molly ran out of breath and sat hiccuping, crying now, her voice so pitiful that she had made herself miserable. There were deep half moons beneath her eyes. Her lips were rough and reddened, a split caked over with scab down the center of her bottom lip. Scrapes and scratches from the fall she took in the desert left red marks on her arms and face, burn marks were raised on the flesh of her chest where the man with the mustache rubbed against her. She had managed to drape scraps of cloth from her torn blouse over her breasts, but the breeze kept blowing them aside. She tried, but couldn't get her fingers to the zipper in her jeans. They still stood open so that the top elastic of her panties showed white against her ivory freckled skin.

"Look at me." She had to scream. The girl wanted nothing to do with her beyond supplying the cold drink. She wasn't listening.

"Will you just look what he's done to me?"

The girl flinched at the shout, but she continued staring into the distance.

Molly handed over the Coke bottle and lay her head on the window ledge. "Never mind then," she said quietly. "I don't care." And at that moment she didn't.

"You want . . . tamale? *Chalupas?*" It was the first words the girl had bothered to say. She *did* know English.

Molly didn't raise her head. She said, "I don't care. I don't care if I starve to death."

She heard her walking away, small bits of gravel stone crunching into the sand beneath her heels. Sometime later when the sun was high overhead and Molly fell into and out of bizarre dreams, the girl returned with three tamales wrapped in wax paper, and another icy Coke. This time she didn't wait for the empty. She left immediately for the cantina.

Molly wolfed down the food, grateful to have it. She needed to go to the bathroom. She wondered if she was going to get used to the feeling of bloat and fullness, wondered if her bladder would expand or if she might have to release it while she sat tied in the car seat. She had held it all day in Lannie's house, trapped in the bathtub. It was Lannie, upon untying her, who let her use the toilet right away, standing guard outside while Cruise called down the hallway for her to hurry, it was past dark, they had to leave.

In the sultry, stifling afternoon a little boy came by the car swinging a tin can tied by string to a stick. Molly called him over. "Hey, kid! C'mere a minute."

The boy was about six, big black eyes, a youthful and trusting grin splitting his face. The grin dissipated the closer he came to her. She knew she must look a fright with her hair uncombed and full of sand, her face tired and scratched. She thought the boy wouldn't be able to see inside the car, see that her clothes were ripped. But when he came closer, dragging the can behind him, he stood on tiptoe, hands on the window frame, and his eyes widened on seeing her naked breasts.

"Look . . . I . . ."

He was fleet as a startled deer, running from the car into the dirt street, disappearing between houses, his can rattling along the ground beside him.

"Damn."

Sweat rolled down her temples into her eyes and stung. She leaned down to wipe her eyes against the strips of fabric hanging from her shoulder. She wished she could hide the bra, could cover herself. She wished the girl would come back so she could beg her help just once more. She was sure she could convince *someone* to help her, if she only tried harder, pleaded with more zeal, cried more furiously, shouted longer and louder.

She thought this, kept her hope alive, until the sky darkened and the sun died in flames of red and gold glory. The skinny rooster strode the street again, crowing in confusion. Men laughed and made jokes when they came to touch her hair before entering the now lively cantina.

Cruise appeared in the doorway in the dull gray twilight. He looked rested and washed, his hair reflecting light from inside the cantina. He wore the same clothes, the long-sleeved blue shirt, the navy slacks, but something was different about him, and Molly couldn't put a finger on what it was. His upper body looked . . . bigger, maybe. No, it was his arms. He had Popeye arms. Arnold Schwarzenegger arms. They looked so thick they bulged and stretched tight the material of his shirt. How could he have done that?

Before he could get into the driver's seat, she said, "I have to go to the bathroom. I have to put on some clothes."

He sat down in the seat, leaving the car door open. It was the first time he had seen her partially unclothed and she blushed and looked down at her hands, ashamed of her nakedness. She hunched her shoulders, but that produced a slight cleavage that distressed her so she tried to relax. It wasn't her fault The Nubs were bare. It was *his* fault those men had . . . had . . . touched her . . . had done those things to her. He was the one who should feel shame. Nevertheless she ducked her head and tried pretending it didn't matter.

"Can I get a shirt?"

He reached behind him, his movement causing her to jerk sideways. He hauled her blue carryall into his lap and unzipped it. He drew out a T-shirt with pink flamingos imprinted on the front and a legend below that spelled out FLORIDA in lime green.

He threw the bag in the back seat.

"You'll have to untie me first."

"I'm going to. Gimmee time." He carefully unknotted the rope and slipped the loops from her hands. "You can take it off your feet yourself," he said.

She leaned down, her nipples brushing against her thighs as she took the rope from her ankles. She shivered as if a mild bolt of electricity had shot through her veins. Even her nipples were raw. She was going to bawl again if she thought about the men who molested her.

Her muscles ached, her back was a solid pain zone, her buttocks felt dead as stones. The T-shirt fell into her hands as she sat up. She turned her back to Cruise, wriggled out of the torn blouse, slipped the shirt over her head. She zipped the jeans over the pudge of her bloating stomach, sucking in as she did so.

"The bathroom?"

He nodded, and stepped out of the car. She opened her door, had a little trouble lifting her legs to the ground, had to lever herself from the seat by hanging on to the top of the door. Her legs felt wooden. Her bottom tingled and stung, coming to life. She groaned, took a step away from the car. Cruise stood back, giving her a chance to make it on her own.

"Where?" she asked.

"Go inside. There's a bathroom behind the curtains at the back, near the stairs."

She hobbled into the cantina, trying not to look anyone in the eye. Some of these same men had been the ones who assaulted her the night before. She didn't see the girl who brought her food and Cokes. She kept her gaze lowered, watching her footsteps as she shuffled across the room, the crowd opening a passageway as she moved through it. The noise in the bar died down to an uneasy silence.

"Damn you," she muttered at Cruise beneath her breath. "You bastard."

"Shut up. Just keep going."

"Damn you."

She made it without falling down, but her rear was a pincushion of new sensations. Past the flowered curtains, across a dark hall, past the shadowed stairs, into a dirty bathroom painted a shade of red she'd never seen before. Cruise shut the door for her, stood outside waiting. She had to lower the toilet lid with the tip of one finger, afraid of the splashes and dark spots around the rim. She couldn't hurry fast enough to get her jeans undone and stripped down her legs, she was dribbling water before she ever lowered herself to the seat. She never sat on public toilet seats, but this time she hadn't the strength to hold herself suspended over it. She covered her face with her hands in despair when she saw there was no toilet paper. All these small things might build to such a peak they destroyed her, she thought. The humiliation of it. The helpless feeling, the refusal of everyone to lend a hand to save her from Cruise.

She sat for a long time, long enough for Cruise to grow impatient and call for her to come out. She found brown paper hand towels to clean herself. She washed her face, though there was no mirror, and used a minuscule bar of soap to get the sand and grime from her arms and hands. The grains stung as they were washed across the scrapes on her arms. By the time she exited the urine-splattered bathroom, she could walk without imitating a cripple, and her kidneys had stopped hurting.

She held her head high as she pushed open the door to confront Cruise. This time he took her arm as if instinct told him she was in much better shape than when she'd come into the cantina, that she beared watching now.

"Some friends you have, Cruise," she said as they passed through the room and out the door. She tried jerking her arm loose, but he kept his hold.

"Only the best."

"Yeah, real high achievers with prominent IQs."

"Get in the car, it's late. No one cares about your bitching."

She sat in stony silence as he wove through the back streets into the middle of Mexicali. Would he really kill her if she jumped from the car at the border crossing and accused him of kidnapping and murder? Would he have time? Could he take two guards, various passersby, and her all at once?

The more she thought about it, the less she saw she had to lose. She couldn't depend on getting a stranger's help again. That hadn't seemed to work out; it just got people killed. She couldn't run away. He always brought her back.

If she wanted to get out of this alive, she'd have to take greater risks. Nothing less would do.

Mark Killany couldn't get an audience with any police officer who would tell him anything. They had gotten the word from Globe. They didn't believe he had a legitimate gripe. They didn't believe his daughter might be with the killer. And they had enough mayhem on their hands, they didn't need him in the way. That was the message.

All he thought he could do was listen to radio reports and follow the trail west. After leaving the police station, he drove to the freeway and found a restaurant. He had to eat. The sun lanced through the windshield where he parked in the lot facing the feeder road. He searched, couldn't find his sunglasses. He also couldn't stop yawning. He felt sleep grabbing at him like a pickpocket. Sneaking up, putting the touch on him, moving off a little, coming back for another try.

After breakfast, orange juice, more coffee—a last-ditch attempt to stave off sleep—he made his way to the car and collapsed in the seat. He sat rubbing his eyes with the balls of his thumbs. He didn't think he had enough energy to find a motel. He could sleep in the car. Maybe he could park it around the side in the shade.

He started the motor and put the car into reverse. He parked next to a black van in the lee of the building. Perhaps the occupant had decided on a quick nap too.

He scooted down in the seat until his neck fit comfortably against the headrest. His eyelids came down like weighted curtains. He didn't drift into sleep; it came over him like a crushing ocean wave, taking his consciousness with it.

In his dreams he saw a very large man, long hair, mustache, beard. The man was walking a swinging bridge across a deep chasm. He herded Molly before him, forcing her to take another step. If the rope bridge broke, Mark knew the man would let Molly fall into the rocky depths without trying to save her. He'd first save himself. Mark stood on a narrow path before the bridge calling out, "Molly! Molly, come back!"

He groaned and stuttered in his sleep, twisting in the car seat. His knees knocked the steering wheel. His neck slid off the headrest until his face pressed against the rolled window.

The dream renewed itself, played over again, an old film on automatic rewind. He saw the man. Molly ahead of him being prodded across the dangerous swaying bridge. Below the rocks lay in velvet purple shadows, beckoning.

He called to her, "Molly . . . oh, please . . ."

Cruise knew he was in trouble. He had never before wanted to harm himself. The fresh cuts on his arms were deep and would surely leave scars. Yet, it wasn't enough to let out his mounting trepidation. Nothing seemed to be of help. The visit to see his father. The whores in Mexicali. His witness.

Especially his witness. She was less than useless to him. Just as soon as he found the right place, he was dumping her. It was possible he didn't need witnesses anymore. He might not get lonely again. He had too much to deal with to keep a close watch on someone else.

There was something loose inside him, rattling around and causing him profound concern. Could it be doubt? He had never doubted before, never worried that what he did—the killing—might be unwarranted, an aberration. The day he buried his brothers, he thought he was free to do as he pleased. He would never again be threatened. But here it was back again despite his years of living by his own code. The threat that he was racing toward great pain and retribution. It was as if he had found a way to avoid it for only so long and now it had returned to mock him. To destroy him.

The doubt, if that's what it was, whispered about coming annihilation. Payback.

And he did not know why.

The uneasiness ate at him like a wildfire cancer. His arms itched intolerably. The girl at the cantina had bandaged them for him with a torn white sheet. He could hardly pull on his shirt over them. Now they burned and screamed to him to reopen the wounds. Let the blood flow. Release the balloons of grief welling beneath the taut skin before he exploded.

At the border crossing the frenzy to do something was upon him. He squirmed in the seat and had trouble keeping still. Looking normal. Appearing sober and sane.

"You feel okay, buddy?" one of the guards asked, peering in at him.

"Oh, sure. I feel fine." The words felt like shards of glass on his tongue. He thought he might have grimaced. He looked at Molly to keep his face from the guard's inquisitive view. She had her hands on her thighs. If they bothered to look very closely they would see the rope burns. He reached over and covered her left wrist with his hand. She opened her mouth as if to say something, closed it. Her eyes were in a panic, gray wolves fighting to get free of traps.

He knew then what she meant to do. His hand tightened on her wrist. Her mouth twisted and she let out a small whimper.

"Do you have anything to declare?" the guard asked.

"Nothing," Cruise said, keeping his gaze riveted on Molly, warning her not to make a move, not to say a word.

He glanced at the guard. "My daughter and I have been on a pleasure trip to Mexicali. We didn't do much shopping."

"Fine." The guard marked something on a clipboard he carried. "And where were you born, sir?"

"Arkansas. West Memphis."

"And you, miss?"

Molly turned to him. Cruise bore down on her wrist. She said, "Dania, Florida."

"Okay, drive on."

Cruise let up on the brake and eased forward in the lane. He had not let go of Molly. When they were past the crossing station he said, "You were going to tell them."

She whined a little, turning her hand this way and that to free it of his grip.

"Weren't you?"

She yelped when he applied even more pressure. He felt her small wrist bones grinding together beneath his palm.

"Don't try it again," he said, letting her go, throwing her hand away from him. "I'm tired of your bullshit."

She didn't speak. When he turned on the radio to search for an AM talk radio station, she slumped down until her knees were against the dash. Sulky little bitch.

On the hour during the newscast Cruise learned he was in real trouble. Not only did he need to get rid of Molly, not only did he feel as if at any moment he were going to fly apart if he didn't release the building pressure, but the radio informed him that the incredible, the unbelievable, had happened. He had left behind a living witness at a murder scene. On the lake. Where he took the fat man's life and his diamond ring. The man's son had been in the back seat. Why hadn't he checked? Why had he been so sloppy? It was the rain, the tornado. He had made a mistake. And now they knew he had been in Yuma, had killed there next.

There was a net out. They knew his car. They knew what he looked like. They thought he might have entered California.

For the first time in more than two decades of murder, he was a wanted man, hounded, on the run.

Molly had come back up in the seat, ears primed, listening.

Cruise said, "They won't get me."

"I think they will," she said in an even voice.

"Don't bank on it. Don't lay your money down."

When he reached Interstate 8 he turned east. They thought he was headed west. He would backtrack. He'd take minor highways where they wouldn't have the manpower to put up roadblocks. He'd pick his way back across Arizona and New Mexico. In Texas he'd head north, throw them off completely.

But first he had to ditch the Chrysler. A car he had driven for ten years. A car he loved.

"Goddammit," he swore, tapping the wheel with the heel of his hand. Molly jumped in her seat.

Where was he going to find another car?

A semi-truck overtook and passed them in the left fast lane. Cruise stared at the rectangle of lights that outlined the rear doors.

Would they be looking for a truck driver?

He started laughing, positively overwhelmed with his new idea. Molly wanted to try out as a Lot Lizard, didn't she? Wasn't that what she was up to when he found her in Mobile?

He sped up to trail the semi. He had to drive a steady sixty-five or seventy to stay in the game. The semi was perfect. A cab independently owned hauling a container trailer for a company.

"I'm going to want you to do something," he said when he could stop the laughter bubbling out.

"What?"

She was right to sound cautious. She wasn't going to like it. He saw that since he was driving faster, she had begun to grip the top of the door where the window had been rolled down.

"Wait and see."

"You can't tell me now?"

He shook his head. His hair moved and the Velcro patch pulled at his scalp. When he touched the knife to make sure it was secure, Molly crouched closer to her side of the car.

No. She wasn't going to like it at all.

It took some talking to get the driver pulled over at a rest area. He had to do it before they reached Yuma. Already he was taking chances driving the Chrysler on Interstate 8 in California. From the corners of his eyes he kept seeing ghost images of patrol cars coming close to him in the fast lane, readying to pull him over. When he looked square out the side window the ghost cops disappeared.

Again Cruise thumbed the CB mike. "She's a sweet girl, man. You won't be disappointed."

The trucker said, "Aw, I don't know. I got this load to deliver all the hell the way to Florida by next Friday. I don't really have the time for much recreation, come back."

"Hey, tell you what," Cruise said, sounding jolly as a pimp with the john in his pocket. "We pull over at the next pickle park we come to and if you don't like her, fine, man, be on your way. If you *do* like her, what's a few extra minutes in the sleeper? You can add it anywhere in your logbook. And I ain't asking half what she's worth," he added.

"Forty. I dunno. That's steep." Static returned to the channel. There weren't any other truckers on the road right now. The driver was bored, seemed tempted by the impromptu offer from a four-wheeler.

"Let you have her for thirty then, what you say?" Sweat had popped out on Cruise's forehead. He probably shouldn't have done that, could have blown the whole deal. Driver might wonder what was wrong with her, lowering the price that way. It was costing Cruise plenty to sound buoyant and trustworthy. It never had before. He didn't know what was happening to him, what was going wrong. He felt like a man diving from high cliffs, aiming for the boulders below.

A rest area sign leapt past in the headlights. Cruise didn't see the mileage. "There, you see?" he asked over the CB mike. "Gotta be fate, man. There's a pickle park up ahead not far."

"She of legal age?" the trucker asked. "I don't want no jail bait."

Cruise said, "She's fine, don't worry. We just need the dough, man, or I wouldn't be offering her in this sleazy way, right over the CB where God and everybody could hear. I just been a trucker, you know, and I trust you guys to do right."

"Yeah, awright. Let me check her out." The semi drifted off the exit ramp for the rest area. The Chrysler followed.

Cruise lowered the knife from where he had it resting close to the skin on Molly's throat to keep her from talking. He didn't trust her since the border crossing. She was out to fuck him, he'd seen that in her eyes. They got to this point, his witnesses, and they were more danger than they were worth. He had to spend too much time threatening to get his way.

He replaced the knife underneath his hair. He transferred the mike from his left, driving hand to his right and hung it in the slot. "You don't have to do much," he said to her. "Look properly seductive. When he's out of the truck and standing nearby, that's when I'll take over."

The truck parked in the trucker lane. There was one more truck already in the line, but it was farther up. The truck driver left three open slots between them for privacy's sake. Cruise parked in a space for cars. The light from the public bathrooms stained the cultivated lawn, but didn't reach to the parking places. He had to hurry before more four-wheelers found their way into the rest area. It was too early in the night for most of them yet.

He had Molly out of the car, his hand around the back of her neck, pushing her slightly before him as they crossed the tarmac to the rear of the truck. He circled to the side closest to the freeway so that if anyone came into the area while he was doing the job, they wouldn't see him. He had to take the chance of the other trucker parked in front looking in his side mirror, but it was unlikely. He was probably snoring in his sleeper.

"Please, don't do this," Molly said.

"You cry, you bitch, and I'm going to take off your fucking head. Now *smile*."

His arms. They itched so bad, he had to rub his left arm against his side. His right one, the one holding Molly, felt like it was going to explode from the bandages. He couldn't understand it.

Couldn't think of it.

Had to get the truck. He knew how to drive one. Maybe not this particular one, but he'd figure out the gears by watching the driver go through the motions.

The driver was down from the cab. He wore greasy jeans and an undershirt. He was black. Cruise hadn't known that from talking to him over the CB. Big fucking deal. They bled just as easily as white men. He'd taken them before.

"Hey, girl," the trucker said as they approached. He didn't have time to check over Cruise. His eyes swallowed Molly like a morsel of tasty cream dessert.

"I told you, man. Ain't she worth it?"

"What do you say, girl? You worth it?"

Molly choked trying to speak. Cruise stepped to her side, hand still on her neck. "She's still shy. Hasn't been in the business too long, you know how it is."

"Never had a black man, I guess," the man said and smiled. "Honey, all the stories are true. We all got bigger cocks than these white boys." He laughed out loud, throwing back his head.

When so engaged Cruise dropped his death grip on Molly and went for the knife. He had backed the black against the side of the truck before he had finished laughing. "What you doing, hey . . ."

"What I'm doing is taking your truck. You're driving us across the state line. I'll let you out somewhere down the way if you're real good."

"Hijacking my fucking truck? Why, you son of a bitch. I heard of you guys . . ."

"You've never heard of me. Now follow me back to my car to get my gear."

Cruise had him carry the luggage. He kept his hand on Molly's neck. Back at the truck door he said, "Get up in the cab."

"But, hey, everything I got goes into this truck. It cost me . . ."

"I'm not interested in your finances. Now *move*." Cruise took a tiny slice of the black's neck, enough to get the blood flowing, and the fear instilled.

The trucker yelled, reached up quick to feel the cut, came away with sticky fingers. "Okay. All right," he said. "Don't get nervous, okay? You can have the fucking truck. I don't want it that bad."

Cruise knew some of these truck jockeys stashed an arsenal. They were the National Rifle Association's hard-core supporters. Some even had Uzis, they were so nuts about preventing a hijacking. He climbed right behind the black to make sure his hands didn't go for a weapon. Once he had crawled across the gearshift and engine cover Cruise said, "Now get in the sleeper for a minute. Stow my gear. If you make a move, motherfucker, you're a dead man, won't bother me a bit."

"Take it easy, take it easy." The driver crawled over into the sleeper. Cruise motioned for Molly to climb up behind him. He had her follow as he moved onto the engine cover, gestured her into the sleeper with the driver, before he took the passenger seat. "Okay, come on out and drive this bastard."

The black made his way into the driver's seat. He shut the door. "This is a rotten thing to do to a working man. I've been paying on this rig for two years already," he said.

"Shut up and drive."

They crossed the state line into Arizona without notice. Cruise saw state patrol cars every few miles. *Real ones*, not phantoms. He slumped in the high seat so they wouldn't see his hair. It wouldn't be long before they found the Chrysler at the California pickle park and figure he'd hopped a ride with someone.

Cruise studied how the driver put the truck through the gears. Outside of Tucson he said, "Pull over at some place we can get some food."

"Whatever you say, Jack. You the boss."

"I also want you to drop this load."

"Now wait a minute . . ."

Cruise moved across the engine cover and had the knife out all in one motion. The thermos next to the gearshift fell over onto the floorboard with a bang. The driver jerked upright in his seat. The truck began to weave. "Whoa!"

"You don't want to argue with me."

"No, no, I don't wanna do that, don't get carried away with that knife, okay? I'll find a place. We'll drop the load, don't worry. No skin offa my ass, ain't my stuff."

"That's right. It isn't yours." Cruise slowly relaxed into the passenger seat after looking at where Molly was curled into a corner of the sleeper as far as she could get from him.

A billboard announced Guthrie's Truck Stop at the next exit. The black drove to it, Cruise watching as he changed gears and worked the clutch. He thought of something. "You got mud flaps on this rig?"

"Sure."

"Good. I want it legal on the road." He knew from hearing the truckers talk over the years that trucks couldn't go into cities without mud flaps. They were ticketed without them. That's all he needed, a cop pulling him over.

First he'd get rid of the load. They ever found out he had taken a truck, they'd be looking for one with a trailer. Next he'd get rid of the driver. He thought he could drive the rig without instruction now.

Turning into Guthrie's, Cruise leaned forward and looked through the wide windshield for a quiet place to park the truck and drop the load. He pointed to the rear of the building. "Back there, back row."

"Whatever you say."

The driver circled the big truck and began backing it into one of the last slots near the rear fence that bounded on open pastureland. When he had it parked and out of gear, Cruise watched how he pulled out one of the knobs on the control panel and a second knob popped out all on its own. He heard the gushing hiss of air brakes. He had to remember that.

Cruise told him to get out and unlock the trailer from the cab. He descended from the passenger side after giving Molly a hard glance. He watched while the man pulled the big rod that unhooked the trailer from the truck. He watched closely while he cranked the landing gear to the cement. There were big red and blue air hose cables to unlatch, an electrical connector to disconnect.

Inside the cab again the driver put the truck into first, gave it a little goose of gas. There was a thump and the cab rocked. He goosed it again and there was a clang as the rig came loose of its load.

"Good. Now let it sit while we get something to eat." The driver relaxed in the seat, breathing noisily.

"They're gonna hate losing this fucking load," he said. "I'm hauling a reefer full of California avocados. It was a damn good payload too."

"You make me want to cry. Now climb outta the cab. Molly, you stay put."

Cruise hurried around the front of the rig. He confronted the black man as he hit the pavement. "Let's go check the reefer first."

"What's to check? We're leaving it, right?"

"Just go." Cruise had the knife in his hand. The driver saw it, began walking to the rear of the trailer. There weren't any trucks parked in the back row with them. There was nothing beyond the hurricane fencing but yucca plants and prickly pear.

Just as the black reached the back doors and began his turn to face Cruise, the knife did its business. The victim held his throat closed, but blood pumped between and over his fingers. He looked like he was gagging, had a chicken bone caught in his gullet. What he had was too much blood and no way to swallow it all. He stood on his feet for what seemed like a long time, staring straight into Cruise's eyes. He didn't make any sounds. He didn't move his hands from his fatal wound. He stood there while blood covered the front of his white undershirt and soaked his jeans. Then suddenly he fell to his knees, the sound like walnuts cracking under the force of a hammer blow. He fell forward, Cruise backing out of the way just in time. The victim's hands were still around his own throat.

"That's what you get," Cruise whispered as the blood ran onto the lip of the pavement and over into the dry dirt.

No time to wash. Had to get the hell out of Arizona. Needed to make New Mexico before morning.

In the cab he took the driver's seat. Molly hadn't moved from her frozen position in the sleeper's corner.

"You're driving?" Her voice was shrill as if she knew what he had done, but didn't want to admit she knew it.

"Go to sleep or something. Leave me alone." He turned on the rig's lights, pushed in the buttons that released the air brakes, stomped the clutch, and got the transmission into first gear. As he drove from the parking lot, the rig too powerful without its load to haul so that it bucked and tried to get out of control, he wished he could have gotten something to eat.

He could smell some blood on him somewhere. He felt his shirt, but it was dry. He felt his arm that itched and there it was, that sticky wetness that drove him mad. He didn't know if it was his blood or the driver's blood, not that it mattered. It was going to drive him out of his mind.

A Mayflower rig driver parked next to the avocado reefer an hour after it had been dumped. In his rear lights as he backed into the slot he thought he saw something lying on the pavement near the fence. He went to investigate. He stepped in a puddle of blood before he reached the corpse. He didn't bother to check for a pulse. He knew the man was dead.

A news crew from Tucson picked up the story on the police scanner and were at Guthrie's Truck Stop with a mini-cam minutes after the first patrol car squealed into the lot.

Mark heard the report of the slashing near midnight. He slammed the brakes and edged over into the emergency lane.

"Tucson," he muttered between gritted teeth. "He's backtracking."

Mark waited for a break in the traffic, then bounded across the wide sandy space between the east- and west-bound lanes. He stomped the accelerator. He had slept all day and part of the evening hours before waking when the van next to him revved its motor to leave. He wasn't far west of Yuma in the state of California. If he drove like a son of a bitch he could get to Tucson and be behind the killer once again. All these changes of direction were mind-boggling. First the killer was going west on I-10, then north on 666, then south again to Yuma, then instead of west, he had turned back east.

Mark decided it was because he was trying to throw off the highway patrols. He was leading them on unpredictable paths.

The latest death happened at a truck stop. The identity of the man was not yet being released pending family notification, but the announcer did say he was a truck driver, carried his D.O.T. certification in his wallet.

What if the killer stashed the blue car and had stolen the dead driver's truck? They wouldn't say that on the newscast. Mark had to decide if it made any sense. It *sounded* right.

The killer probably didn't expect his victim to be discovered so quickly. He thought the truck would make good cover. If he heard the same reports Mark had heard on the radio, what would he do?

He'd ditch the truck or he'd get off the freeway system. Either way Mark would find him eventually. He would never give up now. Not since on the last report there was a busboy going off-duty who claimed he saw a girl in the cab of a truck in the back lot where the body was found. She was waving her arms, the truck-stop employee said. Just like she was in bad trouble, but for some reason couldn't lean out the window to yell at him for help. When asked why he didn't go see what she wanted, the boy replied, "She just went back into the sleeper, I guess. I started over to the truck and she disappeared. I didn't think nothing of it. I had to get home. How'd I know she might have been with a killer?"

That was Molly. She was alive. Now he knew for sure.

When he reached Tucson and saw the billboard for Guthrie's Truck Stop, he took the off ramp. He didn't expect to glean any new information from the personnel, and he was certain the police had already come and gone. What he did want to do was make a purchase.

He needed a CB.

He told her to climb into the passenger seat. She didn't want to. It felt safer in the sleeper, behind him where he couldn't see her.

There were smells in the sleeper, comforting homey scents of bedclothes and sheets that had been slept on, the pillowcase that held the aroma of hair oil. She hoped the man who created these distinct scents was not dead, but she knew. She knew Cruise. She didn't want to think about it much, sitting in the dark of the sleeper, sharing the same space the driver had used for his rest. It seemed strange that his personal scent could linger once his life was over. Possessions, yes, the person's clothes, shoes, his toothbrush, his shaving articles, this was to be expected and could be dealt with; they could be put away. But how would his family feel when they crawled into the coffin darkness of the sleeper and recognized their loved one's smell?

It was enough to break the heart.

Cruise insisted she take the passenger seat. She finally complied, too weary to give him misery.

She had tried to stop the murder. They couldn't say she hadn't tried. She saw the teenage boy walk out the back exit of the truck-stop restaurant and she fairly flew from the corner of the sleeper onto the center section between the front seats. She was afraid to roll down the window to wave, but she pressed up against the windshield and she tried to get the boy's attention. He glanced at the truck. He saw her! He stood holding a black garbage bag in his arms. He cocked his head as if in question. She waved wildly, shook her hands, pointed to the rear of the truck trying to signal that something awful, something permanent and deadly was taking place there.

Suddenly she heard the ring of footsteps on the rungs leading to the driver's door and she fell back, scooting fast as she could away from the windshield, burrowing into the sheets in the corner of the sleeper as Cruise climbed into the cab. She saw the boy dump the garbage bag, look her way once, shrug, and cross the parking lot to a battered black Camaro. He had not understood her pleas. He might have thought she was playing a joke on him. Or he might have decided she was a Lot Lizard and didn't deserve his attention.

As Cruise put the rig into gear and let out the clutch too quickly, humping the big growling machine across the parking lot to the feeder road, she despaired of ever finding someone to help her. She slumped against the buttoned and rolled brown vinyl walls of the sleeper, letting her chin fall onto her chest. She sat with her legs beneath her, the raw places on her ankles burning from her weight, and she wondered when she was going to die.

"Let's turn on the CB, see what the world's up to," Cruise said.

She would have rather he turned on the radio so that she'd know when they found the trucker's body, but it was long past the time she could suggest anything to her captor. He was fast losing it if his actions dictated his state of mind. There was something wrong, terribly wrong, with his arms. Not only did they look misshapen—too large and puffy—but she couldn't stand the way he massaged them, the way he held one, then the other out from his body as if they were alien appendages he had just discovered. And of course, the killings. It was as if a dam had broken and his thirst for blood rushed over to flood his senses. He wasn't cautious. Imagine overlooking the little boy in the back seat of the car at the lakeside when he murdered the child's father. How could Cruise have done something like that? If he had been killing people without getting caught for so many years you'd think he'd have looked in the back seat first. But he hadn't, thank God, or there would have been a dead boy alongside his parents on that dark rainy road.

He hadn't made much effort to hide the truck driver's body either. There. She thought of him as dead. She knew it was the truth.

He might have put him into the trailer, but Molly didn't think so. She hadn't heard the doors open or close. She expected he left the driver where he died, somewhere on the truck-stop property near the trailer. Maybe he'd be discovered soon and they'd know Cruise had stolen the cab. Wouldn't it be an easier vehicle to find than the Chrysler?

Molly felt herself perspiring despite the cab's air conditioner. She could smell her own scent mingling with those of the driver's. She had not had a bath in . . . two . . . three days. She couldn't remember the sequence of events, they were all becoming scrambled in her memory. She thought it might be a side effect of sleep deprivation. She didn't think she had slept more than an hour or two total in a couple of days. But then she didn't know for sure. She couldn't remember. The nights were fluid, running one into the other, time bent out of joint.

She wished now she'd not been frightened into submission at the border crossing. She had meant to make a break for it. She never should have looked into Cruise's eyes. He saw her resolve and took hold of her wrist. Had she said anything to the border guard, Cruise would have killed her first.

She didn't want to die. She guessed she would keep her mouth closed during any atrocity as long as she was assured of another hour of life. That thought should have scared her more than anything, but that's the way it was. In order to keep breathing, she did as she was told, she didn't speak up, she didn't even get a chance to warn the black man that he was doomed if he got out of the truck with Cruise.

It seemed a squalid way to die. In a truck stop. In the dark at the back of the lot.

She shivered, sweat drying beneath her shirt so that it stuck to her skin.

She thought she ought to talk to Cruise, find a route into his madness where she might influence him, but she couldn't find her tongue and couldn't make words form in her mouth. What could she say? What had she been able to say so far that changed anything he had wanted to do?

Nothing.

It was all beyond her ken, beyond her control. She mentally flinched over the word "ken." It was another word from vocabulary lessons like the word "chattel" that she didn't know she knew or would ever use. Ken. Range of knowledge. Beyond her range of knowledge and control. Way out there in the ozone layer floating into the hole over Alaska, drifting into space. *Beyond her ken.*

Ever since she got into the car with Cruise in Mobile she realized all choice had been out of her hands. She was out of her range. Lost in the depths.

She listened to the periodic static and sudden influx of voices talking on the CB about late loads and missing home and dispatchers who made them wait over weekends to deliver and clocking the miles and doctoring the logbooks before they hit the weigh stations and staying on the lookout for Smokeys.

It might as well have been a foreign language because they *didn't* teach her about loads and logbooks in school.

Besides which, the voices weren't talking to her.

He wanted to talk to her. He filtered the many voices coming from the CB, but didn't give them his direct attention. He wanted to tell Molly something about the cuts on his arms, but he didn't know how. Maybe just that they tortured him, that he felt impelled to do it again, to cut into the tightening flesh to let out the galloping fear. He wanted to tell her that ghosts kept following them. Indians on ponies keeping pace with the truck, their reflections glimmering off the side window as he drove. Edward sat on the engine cover between them, dripping sewage water from the gap in his throat. And in the sleeper lay the ghost of the black truck driver, whistling wind and gulping for air.

He had been anonymous. He was one of the elite, the chosen, a man above the law. Now they knew about him, those faceless peasants in their faceless jobs. They meant to cage him and judge him. He wasn't afraid so much as enraged that he had been found out in the end. He thought he never would.

He had failed to look in a back seat. He left someone as witness.

Maybe they even knew he carried the knife attached to the Velcro patch on his scalp. Oh, that made his arms flare with renewed itching. He scratched at himself and felt a scab come loose, tearing and pulling at the hair along his arm.

They could know it all if they knew a little. He put nothing past the police and their low cunning. He had been apart from society all his adult life. He picked up the kids for company, but they didn't count. Kids weren't quite flowing with the mainstream yet, especially not the ones he found on the road. They had turned their backs, just as he had, on the right life, the conventional path.

Now the world had found him out. They hunted him like he was a common fox on the run. The hounds were howling at his back.

He reached to turn down the squelch on the CB radio. The roar of the big rig's engine filled the cab. Cruise brushed aside Edward from the engine cover so he could see Molly better. "I want you to take a look at my arms the next time we stop."

She jumped at his voice. She must have been dreaming while awake. "What?"

"My arms are bothering me a lot. They feel so tight it's like they're covered with elastic bands cutting off the blood. My hands keep going numb."

"What's wrong with them?"

"I don't know! It started happening at Lannie's house. I tried to do something about it, but nothing helps."

"What do you want me to do about it? Maybe you should see a doctor."

He smiled sadly. "You know I can't go to a doctor."

"Cruise, this is no good, you know that, don't you?"

"What do you mean?"

"This running. Hiding. You can't escape now. They know about you."

"We were talking about taking a look at my arms." He turned to watch the road. From the corners of his eyes he saw the Indians, see-through apparitions on painted ponies that dogged the truck every mile of the way. In the sleeper Edward and the truck driver commiserated over their similar deaths.

It was funny. He couldn't see or hear the ghosts too well. They were muted in form and sound, but it was obvious they were there at the periphery of his hearing and vision. He didn't think that incongruous. He had always believed in them. The odd thing might be that they had never showed themselves before now.

"Okay," Molly said. "I'll look at your arms for you."

"Will you?" He sounded like a petitioner. He cleared his throat. He had a notion that the persona he had spent years sculpting was changing in several pertinent aspects. But then it would since the day had come that he was hunted.

"Sure," she said. "Why not."

"We have to get off this freeway."

"Why's that?"

He could tell by how she replied that she knew why. "You know why. They'll be looking for me. You said so yourself."

"I also said this was no good now, Cruise. You should think about that. They're going to get you sooner or later. You've killed too many people."

"More than you know," he said softly.

His arms were singing an improvised melody, a rhapsody in a minor key. He rubbed them each in turn while handling the big round steering wheel that kept the truck in the inside lane. Cruise could sense the mechanical beast lying in wait for the release of power. There was more horsepower beneath the cab than in a herd of wild Indian mustangs. If he wanted, if he dared, he could make the truck fly down the freeway like an eagle on a downdraft.

"Not yet," he murmured.

"What?" Molly asked, leaning toward him.

"Not yet," the ghosts in the sleeper chorused for him. "It isn't time yet."

"Let me tell you about a guy I once knew," he said to drown the whispers at his ear. He thought he saw Molly slump dejectedly into her seat, but that didn't stop him. He told her the story anyway to keep them both occupied during the darkest hours across the state of Arizona.

Mark had to have one of the truckers help him install the CB and antenna. It didn't take but a few minutes. "Channel Nineteen," the truck driver said. "That's the one we use. Channel Nine, that's the emergency channel the police monitor. Good luck, man. I'm going to tell everyone on the road about this son of a bitch. We'll all watch for him."

Mark was on his way again, the CB squawking and blaring as he drove east toward dawn. He thumbed the mike, said into it, "I'm looking for a bobtail rig. I don't know what kind it is, but it's dark blue. The man driving it is wanted by the police for murder. He's got my daughter hostage."

He let go the indentation on the mike and waited for a response. Static roared. He turned the little knob that had the word "squelch" beneath it. The static died into a ringing silence. Just as he was about to send out his message again, a voice came over the CB so loudly it sounded like an amplifier was on the dash. "What's your name? Whose this driver you're trying to find?"

Mark glanced into the oncoming lanes. He counted three tractor trailers. Ahead of him was one. He looked in the rearview mirror and saw another three cars behind. One of them was talking to him.

"I'm Mark Killany. I've been following the trail of a man who just killed a truck driver at Guthrie's Truck Stop outside of Tucson. He dropped his trailer and took the rig. An eyewitness saw my daughter waving inside the cab."

The voice returned fast. "This guy's bobtailing it, is he? And you don't know the make of truck? Was it a Peterbilt, a Mack, an International?"

"I don't know what it was. The boy who saw it said it had a snub nose. It was a . . . cabover, that's what he called it. And it was blue, dark blue."

"Probably an International," the disembodied voice said. "International's got most of the cabovers. What are *you* driving, come back?"

"I'm in a white Chevy, a Caprice."

"I got you in the rocking chair. I'm coming up on your left. I'll keep out an eye for the son of a bitch. He never should have messed with a trucker. We'll run him off the fucking road."

"Don't do that. My girl's with him, remember. At least she was when he was last seen in Tucson."

"Got it covered, Mr. Killany. Over and out."

A huge truck bore down next to Mark and honked as it passed.

Mark thought he might have a chance with the truckers helping him. He'd have dozens of pairs of eyes watching for the stolen rig. Someone would have to spot it. You couldn't hide a vehicle as large as a goddamn semi-truck. Not on the interstate highway system.

Every few minutes he'd send out his message over the CB. The radio was supposed to get out pretty good. The antenna carried his voice as far as two miles in all directions. He hoped to hear from someone coming west who had seen the blue bobtail.

He picked up the mike, depressed the button, began again to plead for help. At least this way he was doing something more than driving blind. He prayed to God it was going to do some good.

No matter what anyone said to the contrary, time had a way of speeding up. Cruise pondered the idea that he might be imagining everything, but discarded it finally. Time really was moving him into the slipstream. As he watched the white center lines in the highway they began to blur. While he drove, holding onto the rig's steering wheel with both hands now, cars zoomed past from the oncoming lanes until their headlights turned into one long beam of light the way he'd seen them appear in time-release photographs.

The engine shook and roared so that he constantly bounced in the air-cushioned driver's seat. He looked at the speedometer to see how fast he was going. Fifty-five. Is that all he was driving, fifty-five miles an hour? He tapped the face of the speedometer with his forefinger to see if it would change. No. It registered his speed accurately. Then it wasn't the truck that was taking him speedily forward. It was time that must be doing it, moving him so rapidly into the future that reality fell behind in his wake.

It left him a little short of breath. He never drank, never took drugs, but having tried both when he was younger he knew that time telescoped the way it was doing now. He wanted to believe that his perception was scrambled from some other influence—a mental one?—but that notion did not ring true when he tried it out.

Time. Speed. Moving him toward what?

"I've got to stop," he said aloud. Only then did he remember he had a witness along. He turned to her and said again, "I've got to pull over and stop."

She didn't say anything.

He took the next exit that loomed in the headlights. It led to a cross road and he turned north, taking a ramp over the freeway. He had trouble going through the gears. The truck jumped and leapt and spit like a bronco under loose rein. He saw no other traffic on the road. He found a way to slow the truck and pulled it over to the shoulder. He took it out of gear and hit the button that released the hissing air brakes. He sat still a moment. The white lines in the road had stopped moving past. The world had slowed. He sighed.

Think, he told himself. Hunted. Would know he had stolen the truck soon. Would know what it looked like. What *he* looked like.

He turned in the seat. All his bottled water was in the Chrysler, dammit. But he needed water to shave the beard and mustache. Truckers must carry water. He crawled onto the engine cover and searched the sleeper. In a deep shelf on one end of the sleeper he began pulling out crumpled paper grocery bags to glean their contents. One held two apples and an old orange that was beginning to smell. Another contained a box of crackers, a jar of peanut butter, a half loaf of crushed white bread. He pulled out another. He found two cans of Dr Pepper and a quart of mineral water. Ahhh.

From the other end of the sleeper he drew his travel bag and rummaged in a side zipper pocket for his razor and shaving foam. Holding the prizes to his chest, he backed like a crab into the driver's seat.

"What are you doing?" Molly asked.

"I'm shaving."

He rolled down the window and angled the rectangular side mirror until he could see himself in it. He found the switch on the dash for the inside lights and hit it. The interior was flooded with a yellowish light. He sprayed a handful of the shaving cream into the palm of his hand. He paused before slapping it onto the hair of his face. He wouldn't know himself once he did this. He'd be someone else, someone new.

They'd never recognize him. He might even cut his long hair.

No. He couldn't do that. That was going too far, asking too much. Where could he hide the little knife if he cut his hair? Impossible.

He lathered his face, grinning into the side mirror so that his teeth showed. Pulling a long face, he took off the mustache first with careful strokes of the razor. He cleaned the razor between swipes by pouring water from the quart jug over it outside the window. There went his hair onto the earth. His upper lip cooled in the night air. Naked. Naked now. Almost.

He began on the beard. He started at the top of his face, near his cheekbones, taking down the hair from first one side and then the other. It was a long process, delicate. He cut himself more than a few times unused as he was to shaving. Holding out his chin, he worked diligently and as carefully as he could to finish the job. As the skin of his face was revealed, a new man emerged in the side mirror. It was a man with a square, hardy face, sensitive lips, a strong

chin. It was a handsome man were it not for the cold look
of the eyes. They stared straight out upon the world without
the camouflaged face to disguise them. They were hard,
unrelenting, the eyes of a predator of the night. He thought
he saw the little man in the depths of his eyes, gesturing
to him, but he dismissed that with a wave of his hand.

Cruise turned to face his witness, to gauge her reaction.
"What do you think?" he asked.

He saw her bite her lower lip in contemplation. She
didn't want to say. He didn't blame her. He had seen the
new naked person's face, and handsome as it was, the cool
green eyes could freeze a flowing river within its banks.

"Never mind," he said, putting away the shaving gear in
the grocery bag and stowing it on the sleeper's bed behind
him. He ran a hand over the smooth cheeks and chin, trying
not to smile. He knew it would scare her even more if he
were to give himself over to the urge.

After realigning the side mirror, rolling the window tight,
and flicking off the interior lights, he sat with his hands on the
wheel while the engine idled like a chained beast. "Now let's
see if I can get this rig turned around so we can get back on the
freeway. We'll get off for good in New Mexico. It isn't
far."

He talked to hear himself speak. Did the words come out
easier now he had shed the facial hair? He thought that they
did. He *sounded* cleaner. Neater. Surer.

Would this change stop time from speeding beyond his
grasp? He didn't know yet. He hoped for all things to fall
into place the way they should.

Before grinding the transmission into first gear he said
to Molly, "I guess you're stuck with me to the end. I'm
going to need someone to see me through it. I wouldn't
want to be alone if they caught me."

He thought she might have sighed in relief, but he couldn't

be sure. By then he was hauling on the big wheel to turn the rig around in a half circle that would take them south again to the I-10 entrance ramp.

The next miles were covered in split seconds. A sign at the state border welcomed them to New Mexico. The white center lines blurred. The oncoming cars made one endless ribbon of colored light. The slipstream had him firmly in tow.

During the next hundred miles Cruise turned on the radio and found out the body of the truck driver had been discovered at the Arizona truck stop. They knew he drove off in the cab, leaving the trailer behind. Even as fast as he moved away from his pursuers, he knew they might catch him. He had to flee the freeway, get off I-10 completely. At Deming he took 180 north. When he saw the sign for highway 61 east he turned again, no true destination in mind except that of escape.

Mark Killany was twenty miles west of Deming, New Mexico, when he got a break. He had just broadcast his plea for help from the truckers for maybe the hundredth time without effect when the CB static broke up and a voice said, "Hey there, Killany, this is Gold Nugget. You talking about a blue cabover? Dark blue bobtail?"

"That's right. It could be an International. There's a man driving and my daughter is his passenger."

"I didn't get no look at who was in the cab, but I saw a blue bobtail about fifty miles back on Highway 180. I remember because not many trucks take that route. I was surprised to see anyone and when I sent him a hello, he didn't answer me. Must not have had his ears on."

"Highway 180? Where's that?" Mark could hardly contain his excitement. Fifty miles ahead somewhere!

"You catch it outta Deming. It heads north. This blue rig, now, it ain't on 180 no more."

"It isn't?" Mark's spirits dropped down like a sack of wet laundry falling from a high window. "Where is it then?"

"I was passing it just as it turned off 180 onto 61. Hell, ain't no trucks take 61. I thought it was damn stupid at the time. I asked the guy, I asked him where he was deadheading, but like I say, he didn't have his ears on, I guess."

"Where's 61?" Mark tried to get it all straight in his mind so he could follow the directions. Take 180 north out of Deming, look for 61.

"61's a two-laner this side of Bayard. It only goes east, but you gotta watch for it."

The trucker's voice was fading, moving out of the antenna's range. "Okay, thanks a lot. Listen, do me a favor and get on channel nine to tell the police, will you? They want this guy almost as bad as I do."

"Check, Killany. This is Gold Nugget signing off."

Fifty miles. The last sign he saw for Deming said it was fourteen miles distant. That meant 61 had to be more than thirty miles on 180 north. Not so far. He was close now and it was doing strange things to his heart. He had been driving flat out for hundreds of miles, driving like a man on the way to a fire. Or a preventable murder.

If he could just catch up with them in time. If only he could save his baby from dying.

If only time would stop and allow him to reach her before she was taken away from him forever.

Molly was swept along with the tide of Cruise's rushing madness. The stories he told were disjointed and pointless. They dropped off before reaching any conclusion. There was a story about when he was a boy and something about an incident with a lawn mower that ended before she could get the sense of whatever meaning it held for Cruise. There was another story about a fishing trip with his brothers that veered off into a different tale about going hunting for deer in the Arkansas woods when he was just twelve years old. There were stories of people he killed and robbed, nameless people he remembered only because of the places they died. Memphis. Chicago. Seattle. Jacksonville. Cincinnati. Austin. Sacramento. Little towns she'd never heard of, colorful names of places that sounded like they shouldn't exist within United States borders. Selah. Chewelsh. Brillion. St. Johnsbury. Carrizo Springs.

The people were hitchhikers and kids on the run and store clerks and travelers with car trouble and gas-station attendants and one was just a girl riding a horse along a rural back road on an Alabama summer day.

Her head whirled with the names and the people. How could she ever remember all this to tell the police if she survived the trip with Cruise? She'd never remember it all. There were too many places, too many people. Years and years of madness and dying that left her astonished and trembling with outrage. How could one man create such destruction and loss of human life? It was one long horror story that stretched the mind to its limits of understanding. Her mind rebelled at the carnage left along Cruise's trail. He might be the most dangerous man in the entire country. Had she not been frightened before, she was now petrified and speechless before his revelations.

He told her all these secrets while driving steadily through the night. After he stopped and shaved off the beard and mustache, his stories came in a flood told in a voice that chilled her to the very bone. Each new admission scored her mind with bright new pathways of fear. She feared to move, to speak, to break into his reverie and remind him she was there.

He not only looked like a different man bereft of the beard and mustache, but he sounded like a different man.

He wasn't the same Cruise that offered her Cokes and paid for her shower room in the truck stops. He wasn't the Cruise who held her in the circle of his arms in the Mexican cemetery as if she were a fragile bird with a broken wing. Ever since he had heard on the radio reports that he was being hunted, he had become more and more unstable. He was like a star flying out of orbit, disintegrating into trailing fire as it sped through space. He was a comet burning itself out.

She despaired when the stories faltered to a stop near Deming, New Mexico. He left the interstate and took a smaller highway north. She had hoped he would remain on I-10 where a patrol car might spot them. The silence unnerved her more than his admissions of murder for the next forty miles. She cleared her throat a couple of times, wishing to question him about where they were going, but she just couldn't get the words out. If he was a burning comet, his fire could burn her to cinders at any moment. She could say the wrong thing, move the wrong way, and she knew her life hung by a slender filament.

He promised to keep her, maybe to insure safe passage if he were captured, but she knew he was not operating the way a practical man would act. She couldn't trust him to save her to save himself. He was so far over the edge she could never reach him now.

When he turned off the main highway onto another road, she sat up in the seat and looked around, trying to memorize the route. Where in holy hell was he taking her?

A sign read CITY OF ROCKS STATE PARK.

Cruise turned left and downshifted to cross a cattle guard. They bumped and rumbled across the metal grid, the truck trying to lurch to the left, then to the right. He slowed even further so that they were crawling across a desert floor. About a mile away Molly could see flat-topped blocks of rock. City of Rocks? A state park? But there was no guard gate or guard, no camping facilities, no concession booths or souvenir stands. Just the desert, the standing rocks, prickley pear and barrel cacti, the twisted, thorn-infested mesquite trees.

Hideout.

Of course. He had been looking for a place to hide and lucked onto the City of Rocks. Or had he known about it before and came directly here? She didn't know. She was afraid to ask.

"Fifty miles more and you could have seen the Kneel-ing Nun."

His statement clarified the mystery for Molly. He knew this place. "Kneeling Nun?" Her voice sounded small, apologetic.

"There's a huge mesa that split into two. One piece was weathered or something and it looks like a gigantic nun kneeling. She's so big she throws a shadow over the town. But this is more private," he added. "Much better for us."

"Oh."

"See those mountains back there?" He pointed behind the rock formations standing isolated on the desert.

"Yes."

"Mount, Holt's there. And Old Baldy. You can't see much at night, but during daylight you can tell there's snow up near the summits. The Continental Divide's not too far north of us."

As they approached the City of Rocks, Molly could see that at one time the entire cluster of one-story rocks had probably been all of one piece. A vast slab of mesa sitting out here by itself. Over generations of time heat and cold contracting within the rock had caused it to splinter down straight north–south, east–west fault lines so that now the blocks stood apart. As Cruise stopped the truck and sat staring into the crevices between the rocks, Molly could see that some of the lanes were wide enough to allow entrance of a vehicle and some were too narrow. Altogether the geological formation made a sort of city, a city of rocks, the rocks like houses built along cramped streets. A maze. A dead place.

She shivered uncontrollably and locked her hands around one another. She didn't want to be here. It was the worst place he could have taken her. It was barren and lonely and there was no one here to help her. The police would never . . .

"We . . ." She had to find some spit in her mouth so she could talk. "We . . . could we . . . this is . . . uh . . ."

"What's the matter, don't you like it?"

"But it's so . . ."

"Empty?"

She nodded and licked the split in her lower lip.

"Yes," he said. "It's empty and pretty much stays that way. Not many tourists ever find their way here. That's why I like it so much. With food and water, we could stay some time before anyone ever showed up. As it is, we should be able to stay until the heat gives up. The cops will think we just disappeared into thin air."

Oh, no, Molly thought, *not here, not out here at the end of the world. I don't want to disappear with Cruise, not in this terrible place.*

Cruise pulled the truck into one of the wider streets leading into the City of Rocks. He parked it and turned off the motor. He climbed from the cab. Stood looking overhead past the tops of the rocks on either side. There were a million trillion stars, more stars than he had ever seen from any vantage point. They twinkled and blinked and shone down steady, silver and gold and icy blue and crystal pink.

He took in a desert-cool breath, feeling easier. He heard the cab door open on the other side of the truck and knew the girl was looking around. If she'd look up, let her gaze travel heavenward, she too would feel better about his chosen hideout.

He heard a rustle along the ground and turned his attention there. He saw a gila monster scurry away, pushing aside small stones and pebbles in its way. Sometimes on his visits to the City of Rocks he heard coyotes wailing out on the plains.

They'd never find him here. When he left it could be weeks before anyone found the body of his witness.

Fifty miles seemed to spin out to five hundred. He should have driven it in an hour or less, and according to his watch he had, but the hour seemed to be ten while he drove and cursed and called Molly's name in a whisper.

He almost passed Highway 61 and had to slam the brakes, skid to a complete stop halfway past the turnoff. He passed a sign that read CITY OF ROCKS STATE PARK. He continued to a small town. Sherman. Were they here? He needed to check with someone. He tried the CB, but the streets were devoid of traffic this time of night. And there were no trucks along this route.

He realized that Sherman was just a spot in the road. There were no lights on or places of business that were open this time of early morning. As he crept along at less than twenty miles an hour, he saw the glow of a cigarette in front of a closed service station. He whipped the steering wheel to his right and pulled up to a stop. He hopped from the car, left it running. He must have scared the older man as he came toward him. He saw him drop the straight-backed chair he'd been leaning against the wall to the ground with a hollow thump. He saw a six-pack of beer at the side of the chair. The man had one open in his hand and a cigarette in the other.

Mark had to hurry.

"Listen, I hate to bother you, but have you been here the last hour or two?"

"Sure, mister. What's the trouble?"

"I'm with the state police," he lied smoothly. "We're searching for a truck. It isn't pulling a trailer. It's dark blue, has a snub nose, a cabover truck. Have you seen it?"

The man shook his head and his long hair moved like a sheaf of white wheat. "Ain't nothing come by here since about midnight. I close up at eleven. I sometimes sit out here with a beer afterward. I like the peace and quiet, and those stars up there." He pointed overhead with his beer and Mark caught himself looking up too. The sight at this elevation was spectacular. He had never seen so many stars in Florida.

"I don't get too many customers through here this time of night," the man continued. He laughed as if that was supposed to be a joke on the town.

"You didn't see a truck? Any kind of semi-truck?"

"No, sir. I would have noticed. I've been sitting right here in front of the place all night. Last sale I had was a pack of Salem Lights to Jerry Salinas, and that was around closing time. He stops by after work at the hospital and gets either cigarettes or a brewski."

Mark thought it over. "No truck?" He couldn't figure that out. The station was right on 61. There were no other highways crossing 61 they might have taken.

The sign he'd passed flashed through his mind. CITY OF ROCKS STATE PARK.

"That state park back on 61," he said. "What is that anyway?"

"What is it? Well, it's just a big bunch of squared-off rocks. You can walk down through them and all. It ain't much."

"Could you drive into them? Park a semicab in there?"

The man gave it some thought. "Oh, there's one or two streets in it, well . . . they ain't *streets* really, just lanes where the rocks have split, but there's a couple you could drive a big cab into, sure."

"Thanks." Mark turned on his heel and was back inside his running car before the man could ask any questions. He turned the car around and headed back out of town.

That's the only place Molly could be. Parked in the City of Rocks. Hidden from view. He just knew it.

Once they were off the road, time fell back into a familiar pattern. In fact, it might have slowed now. The stars wheeled overhead in dazzling array. A caressing wind blew down the canyons between the rocks.

Cruise made Molly walk with him through the maze while he worked out his tension and stretched his legs. When they came to the outer edge of one of the streets, he would pause and look out at the plain. There were desert spoon plants, small yucca-type plants that Indians sometimes used for spoons. There were straggly mesquite blowing in the starlight, dry beans rattling like strings of tiny clicking bones.

"You think this is desolate?" he asked Molly.

She didn't answer. She was a most uncooperative witness, a sad little companion.

"This is paradise," he said. "There's the wind and the stars, the rocks that have been here longer than man has wandered these plains. I love it here."

Prodding her, he turned back to take another stroll down another canyon street.

He had time.

All the time he needed.

Mark turned off his headlights before he turned onto the cattle guard crossing that led to the City of Rocks. He could see the formation not far away. He didn't want to alert the killer. He pulled over onto the desert sand and shut off the ignition. He'd walk. If he was wrong about this, he'd kick himself all the way back to the car. He prayed he was right.

He sat trying to think of a weapon to use to get Molly back. He wished he had a gun. He should have asked the trucker who put in the CB at Guthrie's Truck Stop.

All he had was the tire iron in the trunk and the strength of his resolve. It would have to do.

Cruise was leading Molly down a street hardly wide enough for his shoulders. As they approached one of the intersections he heard footsteps. He stopped abruptly.

He pulled Molly to him and clamped his hand around her mouth. She struggled in his arms until he tightened his grip. "Sshh," he whispered close by her ear. "Someone's here."

The footsteps neared, halted, neared again. They paused every few feet as if to listen.

Cruise suddenly thought about Boots, his old infantry buddy in 'Nam, how he crept through the jungle so lightly so as not to alert the Cong.

Boots. *Boots.*

No, it couldn't be. Boots had not visited him in twenty years. Boots died in 'Nam, everything leaking from the stumps of his legs. He was buried shallow under leaves and forest debris.

Some of the stories Cruise told Molly were lies. Tall tales to fill the time driving over so many miles. Sometimes Cruise had told his stories to the witnesses so many times that he came to believe they were true. Sometimes, and he just now realized this truth, he couldn't distinguish between his lies and the real past. But the story of Boots was true. It was Boots who had persistently showed himself even though he had been dead, Boots who rallied him when he faltered, who woke him when he slept, who lured him ever onward to the copter pickup point. Boots who saved his ragged ass.

Molly struggled anew. He held her fast, furious that she would give him trouble now when he least needed it. One more time, one more move, and he'd break her goddamned neck right where she stood.

The footsteps neared.

The wind gave a low whistle as it eddied down the narrow rock walls.

Cruise kept still and waited for someone or something that was coming for him out of the night.

Mark found the truck. The front grille was still hot to the touch so it had not been here long.

Where was Molly? Where had the son of a bitch taken her?

The City of Rocks was an endless maze of lanes leading he knew not where. He might follow them for hours without getting close.

His training kicked in and he began to creep down the canyons like a sniper on reconnaissance. He would move forward a few cautious steps, stop, listen so hard his ears started ringing, move forward again. Stop. Listen.

They were here somewhere.

Somewhere.

Cruise thought it the worst possible time for the worms to start wriggling beneath the skin of his arms.

He jerked Molly to the side and back again. She made

a sound muffled behind his hand and he tapped her on the head with the heel of the knife. She shut up.

He jerked her back again, trying to relieve the pressure building along the veins and muscles of his forearms. He had meant to show her, ask her opinion of what he might do. He hadn't had the chance. Time had come unraveled, then the peaceful stars shining down on the City of Rocks had made him forget for a while.

But the closer the footsteps came, the more he wanted to throw the girl to the ground, and rip off his shirt, tear apart the bandages. Something had to be done and soon. He could cut off his arms they felt so inflamed. There were rolling sparks falling down his shoulders to his hands, leaving behind them burning tracks that made his muscles spasm.

He nearly cried out in agony.

The footsteps were close now, just around the corner, coming to get him. If it was Boots, by God, he'd have to kill the motherfucker, make him die a second death. He didn't care who it was. Orson. Edward. Minde. Riaro. The screaming fat man with the diamond ring. The cowboy, the woman in the Pick 'N Save, the truck driver.

Lannie.

Daddy.

Didn't care. Had to stop the creeping footsteps.

And then a man with a crew cut, bearing a tire iron before him, stepped into view.

Molly didn't know what happened. One minute Cruise was genial and trying his best not to frighten her, telling her about desert spoons and coyotes, and the next minute he had his hand around her mouth, crushing her lips against her teeth.

She fought to get free, adrenaline racing, heart pounding, thinking this was the end, but the more she tried, the harder he held her. Then she felt the blade of the knife cold against the throb of her throat and she turned to stone, she couldn't have moved had she wanted.

With her eyes wide searching back and forth for some way out, she saw him come around the corner not four feet from where Cruise held her in the vise of his arms.

Her father.

Mark came to the intersection with a stealth he thought undetectable. He did not expect to move beyond the wall and look to his right and see Molly imprisoned in the arms of the man. He almost dropped the tire iron. A weakness born of relief at seeing his daughter alive attacked his arms and legs in successive waves. The weapon wavered unsteadily in the air just above shoulder level. Her name fell from his lips. "Molly."

That's when it all went out of control. There was a flurry, the man moving faster than his vision could track, and he tried to keep Molly in view, saw her go down, flung aside, hitting the rock wall, crumpling to her knees with a cry. The man came at him holding out one arm as if he carried something in it, but Mark couldn't see anything, just a closed fist. A fist, nothing up against the tire iron, nothing to stop him from dropping the man to the ground.

He swung, strength returning from the place it had scampered, and imagined he hit the larger man, but knew a second later he was wrong, he hadn't touched him. How could that be?

How could it be that he felt the arm holding the tire iron loosen of its own accord and fall at his side like a mannequin's arm? The tire iron dropped against his knee, fell onto his right foot.

Mark looked down, then up, and the man was moving away from him down the street, turning into another intersection, disappearing from sight.

Molly appeared next to him, a daub of darkness—blood?—on her forehead. She threw herself on him, but he could not get his right arm to work, couldn't get it up to hold on to her. When she stepped back screaming, the darkness dripping from her hands now, he realized finally that he was wounded. Badly.

He reached up with his left hand and touched his right arm where he saw now a river of fluid that soaked him. Jesus God. The muscles of his upper arm were slashed to the bone. Blood pumped over the lip of the slash and covered his hand the moment he touched open flesh.

He grunted and went to his knees. "Molly . . . Molly . . ."

She was frantic, crying, making gibbering noises. Gone crazy.

"Molly! Tear up your shirt. Tie it around my arm, make a tourniquet. Quick!"

He felt light-headed. He began to sway on his knees. He said again, "Molly, hurry."

She rushed to him, tearing at the shirt she wore, ripping it from the neck across the shoulder and down the side. He hung his head wondering how he was going to get them out of the maze of rocks if he couldn't get back his strength. It left him with each pint of blood that streamed down his useless arm.

He barely remembered hearing the screech of tearing cloth, the painful clutch of her hands as she wrapped the shirt around his upper arm above the cut and began to tie it off.

He felt along the ground with his left hand for the tire iron. Goddammit, where was it? Why was everything so goddamned fuzzy and unreal? The ground was a mile away, his hand elongated as the rubber fingers felt along the rocky earth, his head spinning. He slumped into his daughter's arms as he passed out. His last thought was, *I'm going to brain that bastard for this.*

• • •

It was too much work to cut the intruder a second time. He knew he had opened his arm with one slice, and that should be enough. Let them both die out here from exposure for all he fucking cared. He was taking the truck and leaving. Right now.

He stood at the cab, feeling in his pockets for the key. Where was the fucking key?

He had the knife in one hand and that hindered the search. But the knife was bloody. His hand was drenched. His arm. One of the legs of his slacks.

Shit. Couldn't stand the blood. Needed to bathe. Needed some water. Left it in the trunk of the Chrysler.

Shit.

Where was the key to the truck? What had he done with it? He had to leave now.

Molly tied off her father's bleeding arm, caught him before he fell, and lowered him to the dirt. She put her hand to his heart and felt the beat. He could live. He needed a doctor soon, but he wouldn't die if . . . She stood up, shaking.

Where was . . . ?

The truck! If Cruise took it, she might never get help in time to save her father from death.

He couldn't take it. She wouldn't let him.

She grabbed a strip of her torn shirt and tied it around The Nubs.

She picked up the tire iron where her father had dropped it and stalked down the canyons toward where they had left the truck parked.

Daddy had done all that he knew how.

Now it was up to her.

• • •

In his agitated state, Cruise didn't remember that he had never taken the truck keys from the ignition. They dangled from the keyhole in the cab while he spent valuable time feeling his pockets, not believing the key wasn't there, and feeling the same pockets over again like a man who is being lied to by his senses.

His arms were jumping and throbbing, live wires jolted by bolts of electricity. He had to do something soon, soon. Take off his shirt, that's what he had to do, get the bandages free. Then he'd find the key and leave the bitch and the man behind.

He broke open the front of his shirt, buttons popping, some of them pinging off the metal door of the truck. He shucked out of it, and began immediately to tear at the bandages over his arms. He felt the wounds weeping great bloody tears as the last of the cloth slipped free and was thrown onto the ground around his feet.

He dropped the knife, sick of the slippery feel of it in his hand. He caught his arms with both hands, pushing, pulling at the flesh as his chest heaved up and down like an engine pushed to the limitation of its power.

Had that been Boots back there trying to ambush him?

Had he really struck Boots a killing blow and ripped open his arm?

Fuck, fuck, he hadn't wanted to do that, not to the only friend he ever had.

Molly came into the lane where the truck was parked and sneaked behind where Cruise stood tearing at himself like a madman, his back to her.

She didn't pause to reflect on what she was about to do.

There was no turning back.

She had been left no choice.

• • •

Cruise felt the blow glance off his collarbone with a sharp crack that seemed to explode his eardrum. He howled and went to his knees from the impact. Bone fragments drove into his muscle and scraped against open nerve ends. He rolled onto his back, hands up to his chest like a man having a heart attack. His scream echoed off the rock face.

He saw Molly bending. He saw her leaping onto him. She straddled his middle and in her hand glinted the knife blade. *His knife!*

He tried to turn aside as she fell forward, both hands clasped around the knife hilt. The blade slashed into the tender area between shoulder blade and arm. He threw her off and groped for the knife.

A growling that rose like a hundred wolves baying at the moon made him crouch, the found knife clutched in his hand. He turned his head, listening. It was coming across the desert from the direction of the highway.

What?

Molly had sprinted away during the scuffle. He didn't even see in which direction she went.

His attention came back to the sound coming off the desert.

What?

He got to his feet, every movement a torment as bone and muscle tore and ripped at him.

It sounded like an earthquake. Even the earth beneath his feet shook to the deep-throated rumble.

He hurried down the street to the closest exit. He had to get away, get out of the City of Rocks, make his escape before disaster was able to bring him down.

Molly wept at not killing him. She leaned against a rock wall, clinging to it with her fingernails. When the sounds came she knew what they were and her heart rejoiced.

She began to run for the nearest exit from the City of Rocks.

Mark came to, his head trembling slightly against the hard ground. He didn't know what it was, but he had to find out. He had to find Molly. He had to save her from the killer.

He had to get to his feet and make it to the nearest exit from the City of Rocks.

Cruise saw them coming for him as he ran jagged lines across the desert floor. There must have been dozens of them, could have been a hundred for all he knew. Headlights shining across the plain from the shaggy heads of monsters. They came from across the desert in a single sweep, side by side, bearing down on him, skirting the City of Rocks, closing ranks again, coming straight for him as he limped and staggered, his hand over the gaping fracture and the hole in his flesh where the knife had sunk. Miniature tornado trails of dust plumed behind the tons of metal bearing down on him. The trucks broke through mesquite trees and lumbered over ruts and hillocks of sand. They flattened cacti and came on, relentlessly, trailers banging across the land behind the cabs.

He ran as far as he could, as fast as his legs would carry him, and he knew it was not enough.

He stumbled to a stop and turned to face them. The headlights swarmed and surrounded him, forming a perfect circle. He growled deep in his throat, a cornered animal. Then they came to a standstill, engines lowering to idles, and from the cabs of the semis dropped men with mallets and baseball bats and guns and knives and lengths of pipe.

Cruise began to smile. A mob of determined men. He had always known that about them. Hoping they'd never find out, it was a fraternity he had long abused.

They'd caught him. And so it goes. He'd get off some way. They'd send him to some institution, know he was crazy. He'd make sure they knew that.

Even if they sent him to prison, he wouldn't stay long. Sooner or later he'd be out.

Fucking truckers thought they had won.

They just weren't as smart as Cruise Lavanic.

Molly came behind the trucks, racing as hard as she could. She saw her father off to her right and veered toward him. Together they hurried across hummocks and around squashed cacti and broken mesquite.

"What are they doing?" she yelled at her father over the roar of the combined engine noise.

He shook his head and hurried on. He held his bad arm to his side to keep from jarring it as he ran.

They reached the back of a trailer and moved down between two of the trucks. Cab doors stood open. They had to close one to get past it and into the magic circle of lights.

What they saw stopped them both cold. From their vantage point to his left they saw Cruise standing in the center of the men. He was naked from the waist up, bleeding from his shoulder, blood streaming down his chest. Both his arms looked notched with cuts that ran with blood. The front of his slacks were blackly wet. He was grinning like a death's-head, his freshly shaven face gleaming with sweat in the glare of the headlights.

He was bragging to the advancing men. His voice carried above the trucks' motors.

"Any of you heard of Minde? M-i-n-d-e? Lot Lizard out of Charlotte, North Carolina. She's off your hands for good. I buried her deep in the woods. What about Connie outta El Paso? Heard of her? You want names? I know names, faces.

Never forget them, never do. There was a girl called herself Cupcake, ever hear of her? Haven't in a while, have you?"

The circle grimly advanced, tightening, drawing closer around Cruise. The men gripped their bats and pipes. They took the safeties off their guns and socked clips into place with hard metallic bangs.

"Molly back there behind you. Molly, I almost did. She was one of my best ones. I kept her around too long, though, didn't I? Sweet kid, but lots of trouble, let me tell you, she was real trouble."

He couldn't stop talking, couldn't get his mouth closed for nothing. He knew he shouldn't be saying anything, that he was egging them on by what he said, but the words simply kept coming, refusing to stay unspoken. He hadn't this many witnesses in all of his life, and it was too good a chance to pass up.

"I sat up during the hours when Molly slept and watched her, fantasizing about what I was going to do to her. I had it in mind to kill her here at this special place. If you hadn't all come, if Boots hadn't . . ."

He paused and swiveled his head from one side to the other, watching the grim faces of the men surrounding him. He wasn't going to tell them *everything*.

"I'd stay awake and watch Molly," he repeated. "I thought about dismembering her, taking off her head first, and then her arms, her legs, taking my time to watch the life run out of her eyes . . ."

He kept telling them what he wanted to do to Molly and so many of the things he had done before. All about the blood and the dying, the cleansing rites and the time, way back, when he knew he wasn't going to be like the rest of the men, not like them, the ones coming to . . .

Bash in his head.

Shoot out his eyes.

Break the bones of his legs.
Murder him.

They weren't going to hand him over to the cops. He realized that hard truth with a shock that ran through his chest and down into his legs. He wobbled slightly on his feet.

And still he kept talking, telling them what he had wanted to do to Molly, all the intimate details of his fantasy of blood.

Molly stood next to her father behind the closed line of men, the hair on the back of her neck standing up as Cruise talked about what he had planned for her. The mutilation. Burying her somewhere he could come visit the way Henry Lee Lucas did with the girl he had traveled with and dismembered and left beside a roadside fence in Texas during one of his murderous sprees.

And as the hair rose on her neck, Molly felt again the humiliation Cruise had allowed to befall her. She felt again the ropes digging into her wrists and ankles. She saw clearly the way he killed the woman in the Pick 'N Save, the poor soul's eyes still begging Molly for help even in the last moments. She relived the night she ran from him across the desert toward one of the ranch houses near the Mexican border. She thought she was dying. She thought she couldn't breathe.

She thought about how many hours of her young life she had lived in fear of dying. How close she had come to death.

Her gaze lowered to the man in front of her, to his hand. He held a claw hammer, loosely gripped in his fingers. She heard Cruise's voice. She saw how the men stood there unmoving and suddenly she feared they would never move on him, they'd let him get away with all the crimes he listed for them. Before she knew it she had grabbed for the hammer and ripped it from the trucker's grasp.

She was running across the circle, coming at Cruise's

back, the hammer raised. She heard faintly her father calling her. She felt the circle tremble as if made of one body. Everyone stepped in closer, but they wouldn't stop her now, she was almost upon him, and still his words would not cease, the words kept coming to spew the filth of murder into the open. His very existence made the world a squalid and dangerous place to live, his madness made the night a time of terror for the innocent who died at his hands.

She rushed behind him and landed a blow to the back of his head, but it glanced off his ear, nearly ripping it from his skull. He turned screaming and she raised the hammer again, sound far away and muted, the sound of her father's voice calling to her, the combined roar of the men as they screamed in unison a battle cry.

The hammer claw caught him in the side and she pulled with both hands to free it. She must kill him. She must stop him for good. Forever.

His flesh gave and an incredible spout of blood pumped out from his side even though he hunched over and tried to hold it with both hands.

Then the circle of men had reached them, led on by her example, yelling like men at war, descending on the despicably evil human in their midst.

She felt someone take her around the waist and haul her backward off her feet. She dropped the hammer and kicked and fought.

Her father said into her ear, "No, Molly. No!"

The first man to reach Cruise stove in the side of his head.

Cruise didn't feel the rest. He thought—his last thought— that maybe he had made a few mistakes, but all in all it was worth it to live his life the way he chose.

• • •

Mark thought he hadn't seen anything, even in Vietnam, like the savaging the truckers gave Cruise Lavanic. He was horrified that it was his daughter who started it. When the men finished, there wasn't anything recognizable upon the ground. Just blood and bone jumbled together, it could have been a large animal worked over by desert scavengers.

When the highway patrol arrived, trailing more dust across the desert into the dawning red streaks of sun to the east, the truckers were already in their cabs, tidying up logbooks, and talking on their CBs about a good place to eat off I-10.

Everyone agreed the killer tried to fight them, that he threatened them with a knife, that he even, by God, jumped one of them and wanted to cut his throat and would have succeeded had they not all intervened.

One officer overheard by Mark said, "Lucky if we can get a fingerprint off the son of a bitch. Might not be enough left even for that. I hope to shit they got the right guy."

In the ambulance on the way to the hospital, Molly sat beside him, holding on to his good hand. He smiled up at her and she slowly smiled back. *Molly.*

Molly wasn't the same girl her father knew before she left him. In one week of separation she had lived a lifetime of experience. She could tell from the look in his eyes that it didn't matter. He was glad to have her back.

For her part, she was glad to be back.

She took a cloth offered to her by the ambulance attendant. She wiped her hands. He pointed to her face and she wiped there, smearing Cruise's blood across her cheeks so that she looked like an Indian painted for the warpath. She handed back the cloth and thanked him.

She didn't care how she looked. She was happy just to be alive and free.

Happy just to be.